I walked into the dark ~~~~ ~~~~ hesitated. That was odd. If they'd already unlocked the door, why hadn't they also turned on the light?

"Hello? Rhonda?" I called out, advancing a few steps. "Mr. McDermott? Anybody here?" I stood uncertainly halfway between the entrance and the counter until the door behind the counter opened.

Rhonda McDermott appeared, flicking on the lights. "Oh, hello, Della." She looked around, puzzled. "Where's Philip? Didn't he give you your purse yet?"

"I didn't see him. I just got—" Before I could finish, Rhonda screamed. And then she dropped behind the counter. I rushed over.

I rounded the counter and froze. Mr. McDermott was lying on the floor in a pool of blood. His face was ghostly white, his strangely dark gray eyes staring blindly and his white shirt soaked red. My pulse raced. For a second I thought I might faint.

Rhonda was kneeling next to her husband, almost as pale as he was. "Philip, look at me." She shook him. "Philip, say something." But her husband remained motionless.

Also Available from Carol Ann Martin

Looming Murder

Tapestry of Lies

A WEAVING MYSTERY

CAROL ANN MARTIN

AN OBSIDIAN MYSTERY

OBSIDIAN
Published by the Penguin Group
Penguin Group (USA) LLC, 375 Hudson Street,
New York, New York 10014

USA | Canada | UK | Ireland | Australia
New Zealand | India | South Africa | China
penguin.com
A Penguin Random House Company

First published by Obsidian, an imprint of New American Library,
a division of Penguin Group (USA) LLC

First Printing, January 2014

Copyright © Penguin Group (USA) LLC, 2014

OBSIDIAN and logo are trademarks of Penguin Group (USA) LLC.

ISBN 978-0-451-41361-1

Printed in the United States of America
10 9 8 7 6 5 4 3 2 1

To Eddie

Chapter 1

*L*ife is full of surprises. A bit over a year ago, I was a business analyst for an investment firm in Charlotte, North Carolina. I owned a great condo on Third and Tryon, drove a BMW, carried a laptop everywhere I went and wore designer clothes and skyscraper shoes. (Actually, I still wear four-inch heels.) The last thing I expected was to suddenly find myself living in Briar Hollow, a small town at the foot of the Blue Ridge Mountains, owning and operating a weaving shop. Yes, life is full of surprises.

I only wished life would surprise me now by turning my shop into a success.

Since my opening of Dream Weaver a few months ago, money had been flying out of my business account faster than it was coming in. And since I'd cashed in my Roth IRA to buy the building where I now lived (upstairs in one of two apartments) and operated my business (downstairs, in a space way too large for my little business alone), my financial safety net was almost entirely gone. Needless to say, I was not feeling very secure. Oh, what the hell? The truth is, I was scared to death.

But not scared enough, it seemed, to prevent myself from making one more impulse buy.

I studied that purchase now—an antique Irish loom I'd picked up on craigslist. The contraption was a thing of beauty—more than a hundred years old and in perfect working order. It was also a monster—eight feet wide and imposing as hell. Now that it stood in the middle of my shop, I wasn't at all certain what I would do with it. The thought of actually working that loom was overwhelming. Perhaps I would just use it for display purposes.

I took a few steps back and studied it again. It did look amazing, and it helped fill the store, which otherwise still seemed way too bare. I planted my hands on my hips and took in the entire area.

The ceiling was fourteen feet high, with schoolhouse pendant lights hanging from large wood beams. The floor was made of wide oak planks, worn and darkened from decades of footsteps and waxed to a sheen. One of the previous owners had chipped away the plaster wall, exposing the red bricks on the west side and giving the store even more character.

No wonder I'd fallen in love with the place at first sight. It was filled with architectural details that would cost a fortune to emulate. But everything here was original—the real thing—right down to the two windows of diamond-paned leaded glass that looked on to Main Street.

When my friend Jenny had suggested we separate the floor space into two distinct areas so she could open a tea shop in the back, I jumped at the offer. Having someone pay a small part of the mortgage helped. But even with Jenny's shop, the space was still too large, so I'd brought in some furniture and my woven goods. I'd scattered colorful rugs on the floor in one corner, the old armoire full of white hand towels, napkins, place mats and tablecloths in the other. Behind the counter at the entrance, a bookshelf held skeins of yarn in a rainbow of colors. I had shawls, afghans, blankets, tapestries and countless other items on tables, in shelves and on chairs. The place looked so beautiful it could have been professionally decorated. I allowed myself a self-congratulatory sigh.

The bell above the door jingled. I swung around just as Jenny breezed in, carrying a large box of assorted goodies—cakes, muffins and pies. She looked stunning, as usual, wearing black leggings with a flowing turquoise top and a Navaho squash blossom necklace. I had the tiniest moment of envy. I had always wanted to be tall and thin, but I was five-foot nothing and more curvaceous than lean. What can I say? Eating was right up there among my favorite things.

"Good morning," she said with a bright smile. She came stumbling over and plunked the large box onto my counter. "Ooh, will you look at that," she said, ogling the loom I'd just bought. "What is it?"

"What do you think it is? A loom, of course."

She gave me an exasperated smile. "Of course it's a loom. What I mean is, what in the world will you do with it? It's gigantic. You could probably weave widths of ten feet with it."

I chuckled. "Actually, that's what it's for—wide yard

goods. I saw it on craigslist, and after seeing the picture, I just had to go and take a close-up look."

She laughed. "And knowing you, you were smitten the minute you laid eyes on it."

I tilted my head. "Something like that. It was so inexpensive, I couldn't afford to pass it by." That last bit wasn't quite true. Considering my circumstances, any amount was too much.

She wandered over for a closer look. "It's not broken or anything, is it?"

I shook my head. "Not at all. The owner was hardly more than a teenager. I think it was incredibly risky for her to start a business at her age, and in the end she had to close her studio. But she was passionate about weaving. I got the feeling she would never have sold this loom if she hadn't absolutely had to."

"That's sad." And then, seeing the concern on my face, she continued. "Don't worry. You'll be successful. It's just a matter of time."

"I only hope it's during this lifetime. What do think of this loom as a display piece? Doesn't it look amazing here? I could drape tablecloths on it."

"It sure uses up a good chunk of space." Her tone told me she thought that was probably the only good thing about it.

She returned to the counter. "By the way, have you found a tenant yet for your apartment?"

Of the two apartments in my building, I used the larger for myself and was trying to rent the other. I had been posting ads on craigslist weekly since I'd taken possession, but so far, nothing. I guess not many people were looking for apartments—at least in Briar Hollow.

"Not yet."

"It shouldn't take long. It's such a pretty apartment."

I nodded. "I know, but it had better be soon. I need the money."

She picked up her box of goodies, heading to the back of the store, where a glass-beaded curtain hung between two rows of tall shelves separating her area from mine.

"How about a cup of tea?" she called over her shoulder. Her question was followed by the tinkling of glass as she parted the curtain.

"Make mine a coffee," I replied. "You should know by now I need my daily dose of caffeine." Coffee was my weakness. I'd already had a few cups of Kona before leaving my apartment and should have refrained from yet another. But I didn't smoke. I didn't gamble—except for launching a business in this terrible economy, that is. I hadn't even dated in almost a year. Coffee was my one vice. I was bloody well going to enjoy it.

A second later the smell of freshly ground coffee wafted over, and my mouth watered in anticipation. For all her outspoken preference for tea, Jenny still made a mean cup of coffee.

At that moment, the bell above the door jingled, and a stunning blonde in a bubblegum pink leather pant-suit walked in. My eyes nearly popped at the sight of the diamond earrings she wore. They were practically chandeliers. Their sparkle told me they were real. They must have cost a king's ransom. This woman had money, and if she liked my wares, I just might have a good day.

I wandered over to greet her. "Welcome to Dream Weaver. Can I help you?" I'd picked the name at the spur of the moment the day I decided to chuck my career and follow my dream.

The blonde smiled, tossing her mane of bleached hair. "I'll just look around, if you don't mind."

"Take your time." I returned to my counter, under which a box of merchandise waited to be priced and tagged. I hefted it up to the counter and opened it. Gently unfolding the silk paper, I counted the number of place mats—an even dozen—and sighed. Only twelve—I needed at least double that many. Place mats outsold all other items three to one, and I was almost out of them as it was. I was constantly pressuring my weavers to bring in more; even my friend Marnie, who was by far my best supplier, couldn't crank them out fast enough. That was in part because she also happened to be the wonderful baker who supplied all the pastries for Jenny's tea shop. I might have been tempted to put pressure on her to give up the baking so she could concentrate solely on weaving, but I couldn't do that to Jenny. She was my best friend; plus a lot of customers came for the muffins and left with a hand-woven item. Besides, a year ago, Marnie had put in a professional kitchen as an addition to her house. Now she needed the income from her baking to help pay for that expensive renovation. No, my only recourse was to find more weavers. I made a mental note to ask the students in my next advanced-weaving class. As a last resort, I could always place a wanted ad on craigslist.

I opened the drawer, pulling out the stock book and a box of my beautiful tags. One of the first things I'd invested in when I opened the shop was thick, creamy store tags with the name "Dream Weaver" embossed in gold. They looked so rich, they made every item to which they were attached seem all the more precious. I flipped open the book and entered the merchandise, all the while keeping a discreet eye on the flashy blonde.

She was examining a tablecloth and matching napkins displayed on an antique sideboard I'd brought in a few days earlier. I'd worked on that thing for weeks, sanding down the old finish before repainting it a lovely creamy white. I'd given the edges a quick sanding, and voilà, shabby-chic. That was where I now displayed all my priciest pieces. I held my breath, hoping she would bring the items to the counter. But she dropped them casually and moved on to an occasional table, where she picked up a table runner. I was tempted to point out that the table was for sale too—not only the woven items—but decided that might have seemed pushy.

After purchasing this building, I'd scored a houseful of old furniture for next to nothing, which was a good thing, because next to nothing was all I could afford. There had been more than enough pieces to furnish my apartment. And even after deciding to use the remaining pieces in the store, I still had many left over. Since then I'd been working on refinishing them to sell alongside my weaving. It was hard work—sanding and painting and buffing—but I'd already sold three pieces last week alone, making the extra effort well worth it.

I finished entering the merchandise and began tagging the pieces, still keeping a surreptitious eye on the woman. There was something oddly familiar about her, but try as I might, I couldn't imagine where I might have met her. She couldn't have been a local. Briar Hollow was tiny, and I already knew—at least by sight—everyone in town. I was also sure she wasn't someone I'd known back in Charlotte. So where could I have . . .

Bunny Boyd. The name came to me in a flash. I had seen this woman on television. She was an interior designer with her own reality-TV show. *Wow.* Bunny Boyd was in my shop! A surge of hope flashed through me. Maybe she would buy a ton of my merchandise, mention it on one of her television shows, and the plug would turn my business into a huge success. *Hey, a girl can always dream.*

She moved away from the occasional table and stopped at a rocking chair, picking up a handwoven afghan. She examined it for a moment, and then, noticing a tablecloth on the gateleg table a few steps away, she dropped the throw as if it were a rag. She snatched the delicate cloth, fingering it for a second and then discarded that too. She wandered on from one display to the next, turning her nose up at everything she saw.

But as I decided that—just my luck—she was heading for the door without buying so much as a napkin, she stopped before the antique loom and circled it, wearing a puzzled expression, much as Jenny had just a few minutes earlier.

"This is for weaving yard goods, isn't it?" she called over to me. "That's what weavers use to make woven fabric by the yard, right? Do you use it?"

I left the counter and joined her. "Yes, it is. I'm surprised you know that. I haven't used it yet—I just got it—but that's the reason I bought it." Now, that was stretching the truth, but—hey—if Bunny Boyd was looking for handwoven fabric, far be it from me to not seize the opportunity. "You're Bunny Boyd, aren't you?"

She smiled.

"I'm Della Wright, the owner."

She nodded. "Nice to meet you. I've been looking for handwoven fabric heavy enough for draperies and upholstery. Would you be able to produce that?"

My hope surged. "Of course I can. But it would be expensive."

She chuckled, as if I'd just said something amusing. "If I like it, the price won't matter. I have an important client, and I'm redoing his entire house— twelve thousand square feet." *Twelve thousand square feet? How much yardage will she need?* "I'll need at least fifty yards of material," she added as if she'd read my thoughts.

At least fifty yards? That was an insane amount of yardage—months and months of work. It was the best news I'd heard in a long time. I was almost giddy with excitement.

Bunny returned to the display table and picked up a hand towel, bringing it over. "This is the pattern I want." She pointed to the fine chevron. "But I want it much larger, at least two inches."

I studied the cloth. "That wouldn't be a problem. I do that sort of thing all the time."

"As for color, I'm looking for something discreet. I like simple and elegant."

Clearly not when it came to her hair and makeup, but all I said was, "That sounds lovely."

She snapped her fingers as an idea came to her. "My client, Bernard Whitby, is throwing a small party to-morrow. He sent out hundreds of invitations. Everyone in town is welcome."

She calls that a small party?

"Did you get one?"

I shook my head. "No. But if it was just addressed to 'occupant,' I might have thrown it away without a glance."

At that moment, Jenny came forward with my cup of coffee. "Sorry. I didn't mean to interrupt. Can I get you something?" she asked Bunny.

"Jenny, I'd like you to meet Bunny Boyd."

Bunny gave her a patronizing smile and then contin-ued. "The party is tomorrow at five o'clock—cocktails. I'll introduce you to my client and walk you through the house. You'll see what I've already done, and I'll explain my plans for the rest of the house. You'll understand exactly what I'm looking for." She paused. "You'll come, won't you?"

I hesitated. "Are you sure your client won't mind?"

She waved my concern away. "Don't be silly. He'll be thrilled. The more the merrier. He has an announcement to make and wants as many people as he can get." Seeing me still hesitate, she turned to Jenny. "If you or any of your friends didn't get an invitation, please bring them along too. I mean it."

A party did sound like fun. I hadn't been to one since moving here from Charlotte months ago. And if it increased my chances of landing this contract—"All right, I will."

"Wonderful." She moved over to my counter, pulled out a business card, and on the underside, wrote the address. She handed it to me. "After you've seen the place, if you're interested, you can make me some samples, and we'll take it from there."

"I'm sure I will be."

She nodded. "See you tomorrow." And just as quickly as she'd walked in, she was gone, leaving me in a daze. This was almost too good to be true. It was the answer to all my prayers.

Jenny handed me my cup of coffee "You know who Bunny Boyd is, don't you? She has her own decorating show—one of the most popular ones on television. You should have turned her down."

I turned to her, dumbfounded. "I don't understand. Why should I turn her down?"

"Believe me. She's trouble."

Jenny was possibly the nicest person I'd ever met. I had never, ever, heard her say a mean thing about anyone, which was why I was so surprised. "What in the world makes you say that?"

"If you saw her aura, as I just did, you'd know that all that smiling sweetness is just a veneer." Ah . . . her *aura*. Whenever Jenny mentioned people's *auras*, or her *feelings* about them, I had to hold back from rolling my eyes. She continued. "Underneath, she's hard and calculating. Mark my words. If you do business with her, you'll regret it."

Even though I knew Jenny was convinced everything she'd just said was irrefutably true, I didn't believe in auras and tea leaves and tarot. But I had to choose my words carefully or risk offending her.

"What if you're wrong? You once told me that auras can sometimes be misread." Her frown melted, and I continued. "Can you imagine what that contract would mean to me? It would make the difference between barely eking out a living, and my business thriving."

She sighed. "You've already agreed to go to the party, so I suppose you have to. But make sure you think twice about signing any contract with that woman."

"Fair enough." And then, being curious, I asked, "By the way, did you get an invitation to that party?"

"No, but I'm like you. Anything that comes unaddressed, I simply chuck out."

"What about her TV show? I've seen promos for it, but I've never actually watched. Have you seen any of them?"

She nodded. "I have to hand it to her; the woman is talented. You should see the rooms she does. She can turn the ugliest places into showcases." She grew quiet for a moment. "She's sweet as sugar when she wants something, but I've seen her get hard as nails when things don't go her way."

I was tempted to point out that the networks were known for editing reality shows until the characters seemed totally different from the way they really were—which begged the question, where was the reality in reality shows?

Jenny planted a hand on her hip and sighed. "I wish you'd seen her aura, like I did."

As I said, Jenny was the nicest person in the world, but she was also a bit flaky—believing in crystals and runes and palm reading. On the other hand, that was what made her Jenny. It was also the reason she'd originally named her shop Tea and Destiny, where she not only served tea and coffee and all sorts of delicious pastries, but she also told fortunes. This service she sold solely as entertainment, but her clients swore by her predictions. As for me, I was of the opinion that all Jenny really had was an ability to read people—nothing magical about it. If she was right about Bunny being difficult, so what? Believe me. During ten years as a business analyst, I'd seen more than my share of difficult clients. They didn't scare me.

Jenny was staring at me. "Something tells me you've already made up your mind."

This proved my point. All she really did was read people.

At the sound of a bell in the back, she hurried away, calling over her shoulder, "That's the oven. Your muffin is ready. Don't let your coffee get cold." She paused at the beaded curtains and turned. "You should know by now, I'm always right about my feelings. I hope I won't have to say I told you so."

Chapter 2

I finished tagging and putting away the new stock
and moved on to sorting through my supply of linen
yarns. If Bunny Boyd wanted to see samples, I would
be ready. The bell above the door tinkled. I looked up
to see Winston, my friend Matthew's French bulldog,
come trotting in. Winnie, as I had nicknamed him, was
thirty pounds of hard muscles in a compact body. His
eyes held a perpetually puzzled look. And even though
his squashed face and pointy teeth gave him a fero-
cious appearance, an intruder was in more danger of
being licked to death than bitten. Behind him, Matthew
appeared for no more than a second. He propped open
the door with a brick and disappeared again—probably
going back to his car to get something.

"Winnie, what are you doing here?" I hurried to my
counter and fished through my catchall drawer for a
liver treat. Winston's butt hit the ground with a thud.
He looked at me with pleading eyes. I threw him the
treat, and he gobbled it up faster than I could say
"woof." "Good boy."

"Are you spoiling my dog again?" From the doorway, Matthew came stumbling in under the weight of a large beribboned box. "No wonder he prefers your company to mine."

Matthew was a heartthrob—at least to me he was. He was not movie star handsome, but he was tall, with dark hair and dark eyes that turned more golden than brown whenever he smiled. And when he did, my knees turned to jelly.

I grinned. "All that proves is he has good taste."

A second later my friend Marnie Potter came waddling in. Marnie was a middle-aged redhead with a propensity for wearing clothes that were way too tight for her weight or age. As if to prove this, today her outfit was a pair of zebra-striped leggings coordinated with a leopard-print three-quarter-sleeve jacket. The woman sure liked her animal prints. Her lids were painted with heavy black eyeliner and electric-blue eye shadow. I stifled a chuckle.

She smiled brightly. "Surprise." Her double chin wobbled.

Matthew lugged the box to the counter and, with a grunt, hefted it on top. "I ordered this weeks ago," he said, breathing heavily. "I was hoping to get it here in time for your official opening, but it arrived only this morning."

I'd thrown a small party for the few local friends I'd made, most of them weavers who placed their goods on consignment in my shop—hardly what anybody would call an official opening.

I came around the counter. "You got me a present?"

"Of course I did. You didn't really think I'd let a special occasion like that go by without a housewarming gift, did you?"

I grinned. "Are you sure this isn't in celebration of my moving out?" When I'd first moved to Charlotte, he and I had switched homes. I had moved into his house, opening my shop in his two front rooms. Meanwhile, he had moved into my condo in Charlotte, and somehow I had lulled myself into believing the arrangement could go on like that indefinitely. After all, Matthew was a professor of criminology, teaching at the University of Charlotte. Why in the world would he choose to move back to Briar Hollow and a two-hour daily commute when he could live in my condo, ten minutes from his work?

Then, out of the blue, Matthew had suddenly landed a book deal—his lifelong dream—and had chosen to move back to Briar Hollow, where he could write in peace and quiet.

He laughed. "I admit, it is good to get my living and dining rooms back, but it was nice having you around." I felt myself blush.

Matthew and I had known each other all our lives. His mother and mine had been roommates at college and were like sisters. In fact, our families had spent holidays together for as long as I could remember. During all those years, I had never felt anything for him but friendship—maybe because of my mother's constant efforts to match us up. Then suddenly, during last year's holiday visit, I found myself fantasizing about running my fingers through his hair.

When he moved back into his house, we found ourselves sharing the same home for a few weeks. It wasn't long before I realized I had to find a place of my own. Living in close quarters with someone who doesn't share your feelings is a tenuous situation at best.

Jenny, of course, professed to know otherwise. She had a *feeling*, she said, that if I'd only give him time, Matthew would come around. He'd realize he was just as in love with me as I was with him. It sounded so much like something my mother would say that I couldn't help wondering if she was bribing my friend to have a talk with me. I wouldn't put it past her.

Jenny came hurrying from the back, carrying a tray of coffee cups. "Hi, Matthew. Hi, Marnie. I heard you come in and brought you some coffee, and, Della, your muffin." She set the tray at the other end of the counter. She looked at the box, then at me. "A gift. Wow. What are you waiting for? Open it."

I tore open the flaps of the box, pulling out handfuls of shredded paper until the entire area around my counter was littered with paper. I pushed aside a few more rumpled sheets and gasped. "You got me a cash register?"

"And not just any cash register," Marnie said. "It's a *candy* cash register."

Matthew lifted it out. I pulled the cardboard box from under it, and he carefully set it back down.

"It's magnificent." My fingers trailed the engraved silver top, touched the ivory keys carefully. "I love it."

Jenny systematically picked up the shredded paper, throwing it back into the box. "It's exactly what your counter was crying out for."

Matthew grinned. "When you mentioned that you could just imagine an antique nickel-plated register in your shop, I knew I had to find one for you."

My throat tightened. He had gone to all that trouble—for me. Surely that meant he had *some* feelings for me? I was so afraid he might read the emotions on my face that I dared not look him in the eye.

I cleared my throat. "That's so generous of you, Matthew. I don't know what to say. Thank you."

"Oh, for God's sake, kiss the man, won't you?" Marnie exclaimed with a hint of exasperation.

I leaned over and gave him a chaste peck on the cheek. Over his shoulder, I spotted Marnie rolling her eyes.

"I have a gift too," she said. "But this one is for Jenny."

"For me?" she said, looking stunned.

Marnie gave her a teasing smile. "Don't tell me you didn't know? Didn't you read your tea leaves this morning? Some soothsayer you are." And with that, she marched out of the shop. Matthew hurried to catch up. A few minutes later he reappeared, pushing a dolly carrying something tall and wide. Whatever it was, it was covered with a cloth, on top of which was a big pink polka-dot bow.

"I know what it is," I exclaimed.

Marnie wagged a pudgy finger at me. "Don't you dare spoil her surprise."

I had been to Marnie's house only once, but it was an experience I was not apt to forget. Her living room was right out of a comedy. It was a mishmash of oddi-

ties and memorabilia, all crammed together in the most
whimsical way. She had a red sofa shaped like a giant
pair of lips. Her lamps were Hawaiian hula dancers.
One of the most interesting pieces in the room had been
an antique fortune-telling machine. It was in perfect
working order, right down to the gypsy gazing into a
crystal ball. I had *ooh*ed and *ahh*ed over it and inno-
cently commented that Jenny would go nuts over
something like that. But I never expected that she
would give it to her. Those machines were rare and
worth a fortune.

Marnie followed Matthew back into the store. "I
know just where it should go." She hurried ahead,
leading the way through the beaded curtains.

Matthew grunted with the effort. "Winston, get out
of the way." Winston galloped away from the dolly's
wheels in the nick of time. I grabbed Jenny's arm and
we trailed along.

Coffee, Tea and Destiny was a small but charming
shop. It held half a dozen luncheon tables, each covered with a simple white cotton tablecloth and a lovely
woven runner—my shop-warming gift to her. Every
table had a three-tiered pastry dish, begging to be filled
with an assortment of tiny cucumber or watercress
sandwiches and Marnie's wonderful scones. Along the
back wall was a long counter with an array of tempting
pastries on display. Behind it was a bookshelf filled
with coffee-making and tea-making paraphernalia: tea-
pots, fancy cups and saucers, boxes of fine imported
teas, and for the coffee lovers, there were mocha and
espresso machines and bags of rich coffees.

"What are you staring at, Winnie?" Jenny whispered. His nose was pressed against the glass counter, behind which sat a row of muffins.

She hurried around the counter and sneaked him a peanut-butter cookie. Winston gulped it down and then stared at her with large wounded eyes, no doubt hoping for another treat—the bum.

Marnie pointed to the far corner. "There. That's the perfect spot for it."

Matthew rolled the dolly in place, leaned it forward and very carefully wiggled the large piece off.

Jenny came closer, placing a tentative hand on the cloth covering. "What is it?"

"Well," Marnie snapped, "you won't know unless you take off the wrapping. Or do you want to divine it?" Marnie Potter was most certainly an eccentric—and at times a curmudgeon—but underneath her gruff exterior beat the heart of a pushover. It was my theory that her harsh attitude was no more than self-protection—a veil to keep people from taking advantage of her generous nature.

Jenny pulled at the bow, which dropped to the floor. She tugged at the tablecloth, which instantly followed. She slapped a hand to her mouth. "Oh! It's gorgeous." She circled the machine. "I remember seeing one of these at a penny arcade when I was a kid. You're giving it to me? I can't take it. It's too much."

"Don't be silly," Marnie replied, sounding almost curt. "If we added up all the times you read my cards without charge over the years, I'd probably owe you two of these. Besides, I don't have room for it in my place anymore."

This was a blatant lie. The more cluttered her home, the better she loved it.

Jenny whooped and threw her arms around her. "Thank you so, so much. I love it. I absolutely love it."

"Glad you do," Marnie said, sounding embarrassed. She disentangled Jenny's arms from her neck. "Now, if you don't mind, I'll go enjoy that coffee you got me before it gets completely cold." She marched out front to my shop. We followed.

She picked up her cup and took a sip. And then she said curtly, "So, what's new?"

"I have news," I said. "We're all invited to a cocktail party tomorrow night—five to seven. Afterward, you can all come to my place and I'll make dinner."

Marnie scowled. "You? Cook? What do you want to do, kill us?"

Jenny laughed. "Come on. She's not that bad. I've had perfectly good frozen pizza at her place."

"Ha-ha, very funny. For your information, I make excellent pasta."

Matthew winked. "As long as the sauce comes out of a jar."

"Tell you what," Jenny said. "We'll be happy to accept your invitation, as long as you let me do the cooking."

I shrugged. "Fine. If that's the way you want it. I was just trying to be—"

"Poison us," Marnie said. "I'm with Jenny on this one. I'll be happy to come, but she has to cook."

"Tell us more about the party," Matthew said, offering a welcome change of subject.

I told them about Bunny Boyd's short visit. "Didn't any of you get an invitation?"

"I think I did," Matthew said. "I guess I forgot about it. I'm not much of a party type."

"I did too," Marnie said. "But I threw it away. I can't even remember where it's being held."

I shuffled through my drawer for Bunny's card and read the address. "She said Bernard Whitby was throwing the party."

"The Whitby place?" Marnie repeated, surprised. "Are you sure?"

"Della's right," Matthew said, reading the address. "It is the Whitby place."

I looked from one to the other. "What's the Whitby place, and why is everyone behaving as if it's a big deal?"

"Because it *is* a big deal," Matthew answered. "Bernard Whitby is one of the richest men in North Carolina—"

Marnie corrected him. "One of the richest men in the *country*."

"His family goes back generations," Matthew added. "They made a fortune in cotton. When slavery was abolished, they sold off most of their land parcel by parcel, but kept the house. I think it was recently designated a historical property. Then the family invested their money, first in coal and in railroads, getting out just in time. They then invested in electricity. During the twentieth century, the Whitby men became interested in politics. Bernard Whitby's grandfather was the first. He became governor of North Carolina in the fifties, and then some years later, Bernard Whitby's father followed in his father's footsteps. That was sometime during the seventies or eighties, if I remember right."

"That family sure has a gift for making money," Marnie said. "Everything they invest in seems to turn to gold. They're as rich as Croesus. I wish I knew what he's investing in these days. I'd copy all his moves." Scowling, she added, "Not that I have any money to invest."

Matthew looked puzzled. "What I'd like to know is why he's inviting so many people to this party. He's practically been a hermit his entire life. Suddenly he becomes gregarious?"

"He wasn't being a hermit. He was being a snob," Marnie said with a smirk. "He always had time for the ladies."

I shrugged. "It seems he has an announcement to make."

Marnie put down her cup. "If he's inviting all the townsfolk, it means that bitch Rhonda McDermott and her creepy husband will be there." She harrumphed. "You go if you want to, but there's no way I am setting foot in that place."

"Aw, come on, Marnie. Don't be like that," Matthew said. "I wasn't planning to, but if Jenny and Della are game, I say we should all go and have a good time. If the McDermotts happen to be there, just ignore them." Matthew was clearly unaware of the feud between Marnie and the McDermotts. Rhonda and her husband,

Philip, owned the Coffee Break up the street. A while ago, after investing her life savings in a Ponzi scheme and being desperate for income, Marnie had approached the McDermotts with an offer to supply their shop with her homemade baked goods.

The couple had originally expressed interest and asked for samples, and then more samples, and even more samples. They *ooh*ed and *aah*ed over every recipe, insisting that they needed the list of ingredients to answer customers' questions. Marnie had spent days baking, convinced she had found the answer to her money problem. Finally, after weeks of putting her off, they turned her down.

She was heartbroken. She'd been so certain they would use her services. They had certainly led her to believe they would. Then, a few weeks later, she was devastated to find out that the Coffee Break had suddenly added a number of new items to their menu— every one of which was a blatant copy of a recipe she'd baked for them.

Whatever hurt and disappointment she had felt was instantly wiped out and replaced with fury. As far as Marnie was concerned, the McDermotts' action was tantamount to declaring war. But there wasn't much she could do about getting vengeance.

But things changed. The moment Jenny announced that she would be opening Tea and Destiny, Marnie insisted on doing all the baking. "I won't rest until I've steered every last one of their customers to you." Marnie had also convinced Jenny to add "Coffee" to her shop name. "There are more coffee drinkers in this town than tea drinkers," she'd insisted. Jenny agreed and the shop became "Coffee, Tea and Destiny," and judging from the rate at which business was growing, Marnie's point had been a good one.

"So who wants to come to the party?" I asked. "Come on. It'll be fun."

Jenny nodded enthusiastically. "I'll ask Ed to join us. We can all go together." Ed, otherwise known as Dr. Green, was Jenny's boyfriend.

Marnie grumbled, "If I come within a foot of McDermott, I swear I'll slap that smug look off his face."

"Matthew's right. You should come," I began, but before I could continue, she stormed out, the door banging shut behind her.

The room became quiet for a few seconds, until Matthew glanced at his watch. "I have a favor to ask you, Della. Would you mind keeping Winston overnight? I have to drive into Charlotte, and I won't make it back until sometime tomorrow afternoon."

I bent down to scratch the back of Winston's neck. "Sure I will. Don't rush. You can pick him up when you come over for dinner after the party." Winnie looked up at me with soulful eyes. "You and I are buddies, right?" He arched his back in gratitude. I looked up at Matthew. "Why don't you drop him off for a few hours every morning? Poor thing must be lonely alone with you all day. While you write, you wouldn't notice if he was scratching at the door with his legs crossed." I bent down. "You want to stay with me, don't you, Winnie? You don't want to be lonely, do you?"

"I suspect you might be right about that. I get so wrapped up in my work, I totally forget about him. You wouldn't mind?"

"Of course not. Why would I?"

"In that case, why not? You're going to stay with Della, Winston." Winston looked up at him, perplexed.

I cleared my throat. "Why are you driving all the way to Charlotte?" I asked, hoping the answer would not be "another woman."

"I have to meet with my editor and go over a few of the chapters I sent in. They want the book to sound less technical so they can market it to a wider public."

Jenny nodded. "That makes sense. Criminology is a hot subject these days."

"How do they suggest you make it less technical?" I said.

He shrugged, looking unconvinced. "They want me to include anecdotes, examples of how different techniques have been successful in catching criminals."

I didn't know much about criminology or even about writing, but it seemed like a good idea. "I can see how that would work. I love that kind of book."

He and Jenny broke into laughter. "That, my dear," Matthew said, still chuckling, "is because you have a thing for chasing crooks."

Over the past year I had stumbled upon two crimes, which I had solved for the police. To my surprise, this had brought me a bit of local notoriety. Since then, whatever crime happened to be in the headlines, friends and neighbors made a point of asking my opinion.

"Hold on a second," I said defensively. "It's not like I go looking for them."

"How can you say that? The minute you hear of a crime, you're off investigating," Matthew said. "You missed your calling. You should have been a snoop. Oh, wait. You are a snoop."

My calling was for weaving—I had no doubt of that—but admittedly, I did have a thing for snooping. But when that happened, it was invariably because I was trying to help someone I cared about. Before I could defend myself, he pulled up his sleeve, glancing at his watch.

"I'd better get going or I'll be late. Why don't I pick you both up around five tomorrow? We can all go in the same car." He gave Winston a pat on the head, me and Jenny equal pecks on the cheek and then took off with a "See you tomorrow."

At least this time he hadn't called me "kiddo," a habit that drove me crazy. Every time he did, it drove home the point that he saw me as no more than a buddy or a pal.

I snapped out of my morose thoughts to find Jenny watching me. "What?"

She smiled. "I wish you'd flirt with him instead of behaving the way you do. No wonder he doesn't ask you out. But the party might be your chance, so dress sexy and, for heaven's sake, be nice to the man."

"I thought I *was* being nice to him. Don't you think so, Winston?" He looked up at me, his expression mocking. "Thanks a lot, Winnie. You can forget about getting any more treats from me."

He covered his face with his paws, doing a wonderful imitation of sorrow—what a ham.

Jenny laughed. "Anytime you're hungry, big boy, come and see me." She threw me a teasing look and headed to the back.

The day flew by with a steady stream of customers. Most of them were clients of Jenny's, but a few paused at my displays on their way in or out. In some cases those pauses translated into sales, and those customers left swinging a bag from my shop in their hands.

Jenny sneaked over during one of the lulls. "How's Winnie doing?"

I glanced at the dog snoring behind my counter. "I swear that dog sleeps all the time. He wakes up only when there's food."

To prove my point, at the word "food," Winston's ears perked up and he jumped to his feet, instantly alert. "Go back to sleep, Winnie," I said. He glanced at me with a wounded look and then dropped onto his cushion. A second later, he was snoring again.

"Guess what," I told Jenny. "I had a couple of your clients stop by. I must have had four or five extra sales that way."

"That's great. I know some of my new customers came in after being attracted by your displays." She smiled. "Isn't that what I predicted?"

When Jenny had first approached me with the idea of renting a part of my shop space, her sales pitch had been that sharing the space would help increase our sales. "It seems to be working. I'm already seeing a slow but steady increase in my business. If it continues to improve this way, perhaps it won't be long before I have a little left over after covering my overhead."

She gave me a confident smile. "Your shop will do great. I just know it. The weaving classes you advertised for October will bring some new students. And I bet your ads will attract new suppliers and clients too."

I crossed my fingers. "That's what I'm counting on."

Jenny returned to her shop to tidy up before closing, and I prepared my deposit for the day. Running a craft shop was sometimes frustrating. Apart from making beautiful display windows, advertising in the local media and offering classes, there wasn't much I could do to attract new clients. There were days when all I seemed to do was watch the door, hoping for customers to show up. Today I felt reenergized. If I was lucky enough to pick up that weaving contract from Bunny Boyd, it would bring in enough income to keep my business financially healthy for a long time. I closed my sales book, tallied the daily sales and placed the cash in a night deposit bag.

"Come, Winnie," I called, picking up his leash. "Want to go for a walk?"

He instantly hopped off the mat and galloped over. I clipped on his leash, called out, "See you tomorrow," to Jenny in the back, and we took off. Soon we were strolling along Main Street on our way to the bank. Or rather, I was struggling and Winnie was pulling with all his might.

"Will you please slow down, Winnie? I'm wearing heels, in case you haven't noticed."

He threw me a backward glance that told me he didn't feel the least bit sorry for me. If anything, he marched on even faster, the brat.

It was late afternoon—almost dinnertime. The street was quiet. The sun was descending behind the mountain, painting the sky with strokes of pink and gold. At times like this, I knew that moving to Briar Hollow had been the best decision I had ever made. Rich or not, I was happy here.

The next morning, I opened my shop hoping for another day of brisk business. I was not disappointed. Within two hours of opening, I was already out of place mats, and when yet another customer requested some, I had to pull out a set from the window display. But from lunchtime on, business slowed, and from two o'clock on, not a single soul crossed the threshold.

Jenny came forward, pulling off her apron. "Wouldn't you know it? I've made three fresh pots of coffee, every one of which I had to throw out. Not a single person has come in all afternoon."

"You shouldn't make coffee ahead of time. Why don't you wait until a customer comes in before making a fresh pot?"

She grimaced. "Maybe you're right. But I'm always so worried when I have to make customers wait. What if word got out that the service here is slow? With the McDermotts just down the street, it would be just as easy for customers to go there."

"I think you're doing much better than you give yourself credit for. Marnie's baking is more delicious

than anything they serve—even with their stolen recipes. Marnie bakes heart into her food. If anybody
should worry, it's them, not you."

"Thank God for Marnie," she agreed. She stepped
over to the window and glanced out. "It's dead out
there. There's not a soul on the street." She looked at
her watch. "I might as well go home and get ready for
the party. Why don't you lock up and do the same?"

I was weaving samples, large tweed patterns made
of thick linen thread. Maybe it was optimistic on my
part, but I was hoping to have my samples ready to
show just as soon as Bunny gave me the word. I wanted
to impress her.

"You go," I said, throwing the shuttle through the
shed a few more times. "I won't be far behind."

"You don't mind being here by yourself?"

"I'm not alone. Winston is with me." At the mention
of his name, he popped his head up from the mat I'd
moved to the foot of my loom. "You'd protect me if I
were in danger, wouldn't you?" He looked at me as if I
had clearly lost my mind.

Jenny returned to the back. I heard some clicking of
glassware and dishware. A few moments later she returned, throwing a lovely handwoven wrap around
her shoulders. "I'll be at your place by five fifteen, in
time for Matthew to pick us up," she said, and the door
closed behind her.

I continued throwing the shuttle and walking the
pedals, but the silence lent a spooky feel to the shop. I
kept darting worried glances around until, twenty minutes later, I couldn't wait to get out of there. I marched

over to the door and peeked out. Up and down the street as far as I could see, the shops showed CLOSED signs in their windows. Was I the only business left open? I flipped my own window sign to CLOSED.

Winnie and I did the day's bank deposit and then headed upstairs to my apartment. Just opening the door gave me a lift.

My new home was as different from my condo in Charlotte as antique is to modern. In the city, I'd prided myself on my Zen-like decor. Everything there had been smooth lines and sharp angles. In Briar Hollow, I had shed my old preferences and replaced them with a desire for everything cozy and comfy. I now lived in an old apartment built during the 1940s. I had replaced all my modern furnishings with the collectibles Matthew had helped me refinish.

My living room was beautiful. It had inlaid hard-wood floors and a working fireplace with an antique mahogany mantel. I'd slipcovered a sofa, added an armchair and a few coffee tables, and the room was complete. For the dining room, I'd picked a small, round white table, and Matthew and I had painted four cane-back chairs to match. As a finishing touch, I'd hung a light fixture with toile cabbage roses above the table—very French country.

Of all the rooms, the kitchen was my favorite. The first time I'd walked in and seen the old Chambers gas stove, I thought I had died and gone to heaven. And then I'd noticed the farm sink with a drain board, the high cabinets that reached all the way to the ten-foot ceiling, and the black Formica countertops finished with stainless-steel edging. I couldn't have wished for a more perfect decor.

When the real estate agent suggested gutting the place and renovating with laminate floors and stainless-steel appliances, I'd been outraged. In hindsight, I probably bought the building as much to save it from destruction as for the long-term investment.

I filled a water bowl for Winnie, picked up his doggy bed and carried it to my bedroom, where I dropped it in the corner.

"There you go, big boy. Make yourself right at home."

He threw me a grateful look, climbed onto his cushion and promptly closed his eyes. A few seconds later, he was already asleep—lucky dog.

The phone rang, and I picked it up.

"What are you doing home at this time of day?" my mother asked, sounding worried. "Is everything all right? I called the shop and got no answer. You didn't close your shop, did you?"

"No, Mom. Sorry to disappoint you, but I'm still in business. There's a big party tonight and half the town is going. It was a slow day, so I decided to close early and get ready."

There was a sigh at the other end of the line. "I still can't believe that you left a wonderful career as a business analyst to become a weaver." This was a familiar refrain. I steeled myself for a long diatribe, but thankfully she changed the subject—to her next favorite one. "But I suppose in this case there is a silver lining. You and Matthew live so close to each other now. Is he going to the party with you?"

"Don't get too excited. A bunch of us are going together. It's not a date."

"Still, wear something nice—a dress. How about that beautiful blue dress, the short one? It shows off your legs so nicely."

"I'll wear a dress. I don't often get a chance to dress up out here."

"And wear some makeup too—not just a touch of mascara and lipstick."

"I always wear makeup. You know that."

"And flirt with him, for God's sake."

"I'm hanging up now, Mom. Love you. Good-bye." I put down the receiver and looked at Winston. "How would you deal with a mother like that?" He groaned. "You got that right."

Just a few days ago, my mother had reminded me that I was in my midthirties and that if I wasn't going to listen to my own biological clock, then I should at least remember hers. That she was in her late sixties and wanted grandchildren. Was it just mine, or do all mothers drive their daughters crazy?

Winston stared back with one eye closed. "You're the only one who isn't trying to get Matthew and me together." He blinked and dropped his head onto his front paws.

I opened my closet and riffled through in search of the perfect outfit. I wanted to look sexy for Matthew, yet not too obviously so. This was a small town. In these parts, wearing anything other than jeans was considered dressing up. I pulled out the blue dress my mother had mentioned and noticed a small stain. *Damn*. Hopefully, it would come out with some spot remover. But no time for that now. I returned to my closet. I continued searching until I came across my red jersey dress. It was my favorite because it made me look tall and thin, a real feat, considering my height. I held it in front of me and turned to Winnie, who was snoring softly.

"What do you think, Winnie? Will Matthew think I look sexy in this dress?" He opened one bleary eye and stared at me, unconvinced. "Come on, Winnie. Help me here." I hung the dress back up and pulled out another. This one was navy and rather plain, with a turtleneck and long sleeves. "How about this one?"

This time, he raised his head and barked.

"Oh, so you think I'll look better with every inch of my body covered up. I think you're trying to sabotage my efforts here, big boy. That's it, isn't it? You don't want Matthew to fall in love with me." I returned the navy dress to the closet and picked up the red one again. "So there. That's what I think of your advice." Winnie gave a low, disapproving growl, but I stepped into the red dress nonetheless.

At five o'clock I was ready. My mother would approve. I had paid extra attention to my hair and makeup, and I looked great. My dark brown hair fell in lustrous waves onto my shoulders, and my eyes looked deep and sultry under smoky makeup. As I transferred my wallet and lipstick to a small evening bag, the doorbell rang. I hurried to the intercom.

It was Jenny. I buzzed her up, and a moment later she breezed in, carrying a pastry box and looking like a vision of beauty. This was the first time I'd seen her wear something other than her eternal black yoga pants. Instead she wore a short green gauzy shift with gold hoop earrings and bangle bracelets. On her feet, she wore high strappy sandals, which made her nearly six feet tall. Her hair, which she'd recently lightened with streaks of honey blond, fell in cascading curls to midback.

"Wow, you look incredible," I said, selfishly hoping she didn't outshine me too much. I made a mental note to not stand anywhere near her at the party.

"I clean up good." She grinned. "And you," she said, circling me. "You look gorgeous. Matthew will be putty in your hands." I only wished. "Oh, and before I forget, here's a flourless chocolate cake that Marnie dropped off for dessert tonight."

I sneaked a peek inside the cardboard box. "Yum. It looks delicious." I closed the box and carried it to the kitchen. "It's too bad she's not coming."

"Actually, she is coming," Jenny said, following me. "She was too embarrassed by her behavior yesterday to come with us, so she's hitching a ride with her neighbors. But if we ask nicely, I'm sure she'll join us for dinner."

At that moment the doorbell rang again and I hurried back to the foyer. "It's me," Matthew called up from the street.

"We'll be right down," I replied. I gave Winnie a dog biscuit and looked around for my bag, locating it on my sideboard. I grabbed it and we hurried down.

Matthew was leaning against the hood of a late-seventies forest green Jaguar. He looked drop-dead sexy in a dark suit—so handsome that my heart skipped a beat. He stared at me and his eyes lit up. He let out a low, appreciative whistle. "Wow. You look hot."

"Thanks. Is that a new car?" I asked, hoping he wouldn't notice the blush that was creeping over my face. "What did you do with the other one?" Matthew was a car buff, his hobby, restoring old classics.

He grinned. "Sold it for a nice profit and bought this one. I'm almost finished restoring it. What do you think?" He held the back door open for Jenny.

She slipped in. "It's gorgeous."

I studied the car. It looked perfect to me, but knowing him, he was probably shopping for some rare part, like nickel-plated hubcaps or an antique hand-carved steering wheel. Once, when I'd mentioned to my mother how Matthew spends hours taking care of his old cars, she'd stated that it was a well-known fact that any man who took good care of old cars was sure to treat a woman like a queen. Trust my mother to turn any mention of his name into an opportunity to promote him.

Matthew closed the door and opened the front passenger one for me. "I think maybe I should make a point of taking you ladies out once in a while. It's nice to see you all dressed up."

"Tell you what," Jenny said as Matthew climbed into the driver's seat. "You can take Della out. I don't think Ed would like it very much if I went out with another man."

My mouth grew dry. I searched for something to say, anything that might come across as flirtatious, and came up with a blank. Here was Jenny, doing her best to get Matthew and me together, and what was I doing to help? Nothing. No wonder he never asked me out.

I cleared my throat. "Speaking of Ed, why isn't the good doctor coming to the party?"

"He's on call at the hospital tonight," she said, looking disappointed.

The car roared to life, and we took off.

I'd been living in Briar Hollow for about eight months now, and the sight of the Blue Ridge Mountains in the distance still left me in awe. I barely had time to register this thought when, a moment later, we turned onto a country road and they were behind us. We drove on in silence for some time, through cotton fields and cow pastures, until a beautiful white house appeared in the distance. The two-story structure was fronted by eight large columns. There were rows of windows dressed with black shutters—very formal and elegant. As we drew nearer, cars lined the road closer and closer together until they were bumper to bumper.

"Bunny wasn't kidding when she said the whole town was coming," I said.

Jenny chuckled. "I'm beginning to think we should have taken a cab. There isn't a parking spot anywhere within a mile of the place."

The Jaguar slowed to a crawl, and we craned our necks for an opening.

At last, Matthew said, "Why don't I drop you ladies

off at the door and then I'll come back and find a spot?"
He threw me a teasing smile. "I don't think you could
make it more than a few feet on those stilts you're
wearing."

"Ha-ha, very funny." Since I'd sprained an ankle a
couple of months ago, I'd had to endure nonstop teasing about the height of the heels I wore.

When his smiling eyes met mine again, they had
turned from dark brown to a light golden shade. My
heart skipped a beat.

"Good grief," Jenny said from the backseat. "Will
you look at this place? It's as big as a hotel. And it's all
lit up like a Christmas tree."

"And look at that drive," I said. It was a circular
drive around a large fountain with a trio of sculpted
fish jumping out of a seashell, streams of water cascading out of their mouths. My attention was drawn to the
massive front door, above which was a gold-leafed ea-
gle. "I don't know about you two, but I'm impressed."

Jenny chuckled. "Yes, but can you imagine having to
clean a place like this? They'd need cooks and maids
and butlers."

"They probably have them," I said, awed at the
thought of such a grand lifestyle. Noticing the neat
rows of flowers edging the drive, I added, "And gar-
deners too."

"I'm glad I don't have to pay for all that," Matthew
said. "But I doubt Whitby has more than a couple of
people caring for his property. I'm sure most of the
rooms are kept closed off, so the space he actually uses

is probably closer to that of a normal house. Nobody lives those kinds of fancy lives anymore."

We pulled up in front of the entrance, and a young man in a navy uniform—jacket and a matching cap—came rushing over.

He opened Matthew's door. "Good evening, sir. I'll park the car for you, if you don't mind." We stepped out of the car. Matthew handed him the keys in exchange for a ticket, and the attendant hopped in.

As soon as he drove off, Jenny turned to me. "Wow—a parking valet. This is fancier than anything I've ever seen. Let's go in. I can't wait to see the inside."

Matthew took my arm and helped me up the steps. No sooner had he pressed the doorbell than the door opened.

"Good evening," a butler greeted us. "Please come in." His tone was so officious, I almost expected him to add, "Said the spider to the fly."

Chapter 3

We stepped into a large foyer crowded with guests. Women were dressed in everything from jeans to sequined dresses, most of them milling around an aristocratic-looking middle-aged man. Somebody must have said something funny at that moment because he laughed out loud, his deep voice carrying over the sounds of the crowd. *Whitby*, I guessed.

I looked around, awed. Under my feet were inlaid alder floors, buffed to a glow. Above, the ceiling was more than two stories high—at least thirty feet—and in its center hung a magnificent chandelier on a silk-covered chain. Hundreds of crystals sparkled, lending dazzling opulence to the room. On either side of the foyer, richly carved staircases curved up to a mezzanine that wrapped around the foyer below. This wasn't a house. It was a mansion. Why in the world would anybody want to redecorate this magnificent home? It was perfect just as it was.

Suddenly, a woman in a black dress and white apron appeared, proffering flutes of bubbly liquid. "Would you like a glass of champagne, ma'am?"

I set my purse down on a nearby table and took one. "Thank you."

Somebody called my name, and looking up toward the opposite end of the mezzanine, I spotted a sexy blonde wearing a tight blue dress with a deep décolleté. It was Bunny Boyd, and she was waving at me. She turned to the group of people she was with and said something. And then she hurried down the stairs and through the crowd, beckoning me over.

I turned to Matthew and Jenny, smiling apologetically. She shrugged, as if saying, "You do whatever you want, but you know what I think."

"Go," he said. "We'll catch up later." I wove through the crowd toward Bunny.

"I'm so happy you made it," she shouted above the din. "I told Bernie about you. Come. I'll show you around." We made our way to the left staircase.

She paused at the first step. "I really want you to see the second floor. It's almost finished. I haven't started the third floor yet."

I followed her up to a tall carved door. She opened it, saying, "This is the master bedroom. It needs only a few more details, so it'll give you a good idea of the style I chose for Bernie's house."

I stifled a chuckle. She sure liked to drop Bernie's name a lot.

I stepped into a room almost as large as my entire apartment. The windows were dressed in sumptuous cream dupioni silk, the same fabric that covered the padded headboard of the king-sized bed. The walls were robin's-egg blue—one of my favorite colors—and underfoot was the most beautiful rug I had ever seen. It was an Oriental motif in shades of blue, taupe and cream. *Silk*, I thought, noticing the sheen of the pile. The rug was immense, stretching over the entire room. On the wall opposite the bed was a cream marble fireplace protected by a brass peacock screen. In front of it were two canvas-covered armchairs. Even without upholstery, they were magnificent. I had never seen such a luxurious room. I remembered to keep my mouth closed.

Bunny pointed to the chairs. "I need handwoven linen to cover those and two footstools I'm having made to match." She pointed to the bed. "I'll also need a few yards of the same fabric to make throw pillows."

"This is a beautiful room," I said. "I know exactly what you're looking for."

She nodded. "I knew you would." I followed her to the next room. "This is one of four guest bedrooms on this floor," she said. "There are twelve bedrooms altogether, two more on the third floor and another five in the next wing."

Did I hear right? Twelve bedrooms? Holy crap!

The walls were covered with hand-painted Oriental paper, depicting a mountain view with pagodas, gardens and birds. The furnishings, carved and gilt covered, looked as impressive as anything I'd seen in museums.

"Everything here is original to the house," she continued. "The only thing I'm doing in this room is having new draperies and bedcovers made. I'm looking for handwoven silk, the kind used in imperial kimonos. I'll have to order it from Japan."

"That will look stunning," I said, relieved that she wasn't expecting me to produce that fabric. It could take an experienced silk weaver more than a year to make even one such kimono. I couldn't imagine how long it would take to produce enough fabric to make curtains and a bedspread. She'd probably have to hire an army of weavers to complete the job. Suddenly, the contract dangling before my eyes was becoming a bit daunting. I remembered Jenny's comment about how tough Bunny could be with suppliers and then shook my distress away and concentrated on the positive. A contract like this would put me on the map.

The next room was a wood-paneled study. Bunny stepped in and crossed her arms. "I've got my work cut out for me in here." She pointed to the moose head above the fieldstone fireplace. "Look at that ugly thing." I silently agreed with her about that. She scowled. "Who wants dead animals in their homes nowadays? But Bernie won't think of letting me get rid of it. Seems his grandfather shot the damned thing."

I looked around, admiring the heavy wood desk and the leather armchairs. Behind the desk the wall was lined in barrister's bookcases, each filled with leatherbound volumes. On the opposite wall was a long display cabinet containing an extensive collection of guns. There must have been two dozen guns. I stared, surprised. I could never understand people's desire to collect weapons.

At that moment, Bunny pointed to the windows. "This room alone will need about fifty yards of hand-woven linen," she said, averting my attention from the guns. We finished the tour of the second floor and returned to the foyer, where the crowd seemed to have doubled during the short time I'd been upstairs.

"Good grief. The entire village of Briar Hollow must be here," I said.

Bunny put a hand to her ear. "What did you say?"

I repeated, this time more loudly.

"Yes, and I must have given a tour to each and every one of them, and to all of Belmont too," she said, naming a nearby town. "Bernie sent out invitations to everyone. I'd say we had a good turnout, wouldn't you? Any more people and we wouldn't be able to turn around in here."

We made our way through the throngs of partiers with an "excuse me" here and there, until I found myself facing the elegant silver-haired man I'd noticed earlier.

"Della Wright," Bunny said, smiling up at the man. "I'd like you to meet Bernard Whitby. Della is the weaver I was telling you about. She and I have just reached an agreement for her to produce all the hand-woven fabric I need to finish your lovely home."

We had reached no such agreement, but my spirit soared with hope. Did this mean the contract was as good as mine? I noticed that Bunny and Mr. Whitby had locked eyes, and the way she was staring at her client suggested that Bunny had more than just a professional interest in the wealthy man. I wondered if that feeling was mutual.

"Nice to meet you, Mr. Whitby. You have a magnificent home."

"Thank you," he said, wrapping an arm around her. "And Bunny here is helping me make it even lovelier." He gave her shoulders a squeeze.

At that moment I felt a tug at my sleeve. I excused myself and turned to find Marnie, dressed in a purple satin dress that clashed loudly with her carrot hair. On anybody else it would have looked ludicrous. But on Marnie, somehow it looked appropriate.

"You came. I'm so glad."

"Have you seen Jenny anywhere?" she asked, her eyes flashing around the room.

"We came in together. She's here somewhere. You're coming over for dinner later, aren't you? I insist."

"Well, since you put it that way . . ." Her thought went unfinished and she waved at someone. "There she is, with Matthew."

I had just caught sight of them when, next to me, Mr. Whitby muttered, "What the hell?" I glanced at him. His jaw had tightened. His mouth was a straight line. I followed his gaze to a couple standing by the grand piano across the room.

Marnie leaned in and whispered, "That's Jeffrey and Julia Anderson. He's the mayor of Belmont." Judging from Mr. Whitby's reaction, he didn't like them much. I guessed that the general invitations he had sent out were not meant for some people. Behind the mayor and his wife I noticed another couple, the McDermotts.

Marnie froze. "I knew I shouldn't have come."

At that moment, they happened to look in our direction, and Mr. McDermott blanched. Next to him, Mrs. McDermott blushed a furious red. She reached to the occasional table nearby and snatched her bag. Then, grabbing hold of her husband's arm, she half pulled, half pushed him all the way to the front door. Just before it closed behind them, he glanced back toward us with a look of relief.

I chuckled. "I guess they were more afraid of running into you than you were of running into them."

Marnie's scowl melted into a cocky grin. "As well they should be."

"Hey, Marnie, Della." Jenny was tapping me on the shoulder. "I want you to meet a friend of mine." Standing next to her was a beautiful blonde I had noticed around town a few times but had never officially met. She was tall and thin, with flawless skin and wide blue eyes. The blue was so dark it was almost aquamarine. *She could be a model*, I thought. Jenny continued. "Della, this is Emma Blanchard. Emma and I used to work together at Frannie's."

We shook hands. "Nice to meet you, Emma," I said. Behind the girl, a dark-haired man wearing a sullen expression took hold of her arm possessively.

She turned to him. "Ricky, you remember Jenny, don't you?"

Ricky gave Jenny a grudging smile and tugged at Emma, saying loudly enough for everyone to hear, "Come on, baby. Let's blow this joint. There's nobody here under thirty"—as if thirty were a dirty number.

"Hi," Marnie said, ignoring the boyfriend. "Have you been by to see Jenny's shop?"

The girl smiled apologetically. "I haven't. I heard you were supplying all the goodies. Knowing myself, I'll probably gain ten pounds just walking in." She patted her flat stomach. "I need to stay away from sweets."

Marnie bobbed her eyebrows in obvious disagreement.

"Are you still hoping to get into modeling?" Jenny asked.

She threw her boyfriend a nervous look, but his attention had moved on to the maid offering him a glass of wine. "I am," she said in a low voice. "I'm still working at Fran's, saving my money to go to New York. That's where all the big modeling agencies are. Right now I'm working on putting together a professional portfolio."

"How's that coming along?" asked Jenny.

Emma glanced worriedly at Ricky again. He had moved a few feet away and was gesturing for her to follow. "Good," she answered. "I've already got more than half the pictures I need. I think I'll be ready in another few weeks." She nodded to Ricky, who had downed his drink and set it back on the tray. "I'd better go," she said. "See you later."

A voice next to me interrupted. "Would anybody care for a glass of champagne?" The maid was standing next to me with a fresh tray of fluted glasses.

"I don't mind if I do," Marnie said, accepting a glass. I looked around, not remembering where I had put mine down.

"I think I will too," I said, and Jenny also took one.

From a distance a bell rang, and the room quieted.

The crowd turned to face the left staircase, where Bernard Whitby now stood on the third step, as if on a podium. Below him were photographers. The crowd pressed closer. Whitby waited.

This was a press conference, I realized. A light flashed, and at the same moment I noticed Matthew standing near Whitby. He saw me looking at him and waved. I smiled back.

Gradually, the buzz of conversation quieted. When all eyes were on him, Bernard Whitby cleared his throat. "I'm sure many of you are wondering why I invited you all here tonight." Murmurs went up in the crowd. Whitby raised his hand, smiling, and they quieted. "The reason, my friends, is that, following in the tradition of my father and of his father before him, I hope to become governor of this wonderful state of ours, and I'm looking to all of you, my friends, my neighbors, for your support." A smattering of applause rose.

Marnie leaned in, whispering in my ear, "That's Bunny Boyd, isn't it?" She was pointing at Bunny, standing a few away from Bernard Whitby. She was staring up at him with undisguised adoration.

I nodded.

Marnie continued. "She sure carries her heart on her sleeve, don't you think?"

I nodded again. "I hope she knows what she's getting into. Politicians aren't always the most trustworthy sort."

Marnie harrumphed. "Especially this one. He's a dyed through and through bachelor. He's dated almost every woman in the state. Maybe he thinks he needs a wife now. If he's running for state election, it might be easier to get the votes with a woman by his side."

"And Bunny is a TV star," I said. "She has a lot of visibility. That can't hurt."

Marnie nodded. "Although, I expect he'll want her to dress a bit more subdued—less like Bettie Page and more like Betty Ford."

I laughed.

Whitby's speech was winding down. "I want you all to have fun, enjoy, and remember, a vote for Whitby is a vote for a prosperous North Carolina." Applause broke out, and Bunny, who had been standing a few feet away, moved closer. She posed sideways, smiling at the camera. Lights flashed and the applause wound down.

Whitby raised his hands. "Thank you. Thank you very much." He stepped down.

I noticed Matthew approach Whitby as if to ask him a question, but at that moment the butler stepped in between them and whispered something in the man's ear. From where I was standing, it looked as if Matthew were trying to eavesdrop on their conversation.

Looking worried, Whitby turned toward the butler and said something. The butler spoke again, at which point Whitby turned to those around him and seemed to apologize. And then he followed his butler up the stairs and down the hall toward the study.

"I wonder what that was all about," Marnie said.

"Whatever it was, it wasn't good," Jenny replied. "I have a feeling something bad is about to happen."

Soon, Whitby reappeared, hurrying down the stairs with a pacifying smile. "Everything's fine," I heard him say. "Nothing to worry about. Just a false alarm." But behind his confident smile, I sensed nervousness.

I scanned the room for Matthew and spotted him moving toward us through the crowd.

"Let's go," Jenny said as soon as he reached us. "We have to get out of here." Without giving us a chance to argue, she rushed to the entrance. I looked around for my purse and spotted it on an occasional table a few feet away.

"Come with us," I said to Marnie.

We stepped outside, and Matthew handed his ticket to the parking attendant. "Right away, sir," the young man said and jogged away.

"Why are we leaving so soon?" Marnie said. "I never get to go anywhere. For once I was having a good time."

Jenny looked worried. "I can't explain it. I just know we have to get out of here. Something bad is going to happen. I can feel it."

"Something bad like what?" Marnie asked, looking wistfully through the open door into the room we'd just left.

"Jenny might be right," Matthew said.

He was agreeing with Jenny about a bad *feeling* she had. I was skeptical about Jenny's *feelings*, to put it mildly, but Matthew was an out-and-out disbeliever. What the heck was going on? Noticing the confusion in my eyes, he said, "I'll explain later."

Soon, the attendant returned with the Jaguar. He

stepped out, handed the key to Matthew and we piled in.

"Okay, so what's going on?" I said, buckling my seat belt. "What makes you think something bad is going to happen?" The question was for Matthew as much as for Jenny.

He waited until we were halfway down the drive. "You know, at the end, when the butler whispered something in Whitby's ear?"

"Yes," Marnie and I answered simultaneously.

"I was standing right there. I overheard him tell Whitby that one of his guns was missing." I was still mulling over the meaning of this when Matthew continued. "As far as I'm concerned, whenever a gun goes missing, it spells trouble, especially in a large crowd. I don't want to be anywhere around if anybody starts shooting."

I thought he was making a big deal out of nothing. Maybe the gun had just been misplaced.

He glanced at me. "I hope you're not too disappointed, getting whisked out of there before you could start investigating."

"I would never do such a thing," I said, maybe a touch defensively.

He gave me a look of patent disbelief. "Yeah, right."

Although I would never have admitted it, I did have a niggling desire to turn around and go back. "Did Whitby happen to mention what kind of a gun was missing?"

He grinned. "Aha! I knew it. You're already investigating. You can't help yourself."

In the backseat, Jenny burst out laughing. "You might as well admit it, Della. Matthew knows you too well."

"It's not that I want to get involved," I argued, my voice rising. "It's just that I happened to be in Whitby's study no more than half an hour ago. I saw his gun collection. He has an entire wall of cabinets full of guns. He's got rifles, pistols, handguns. Some of them looked really old. Others looked modern—not that I know anything about guns."

Matthew took his gaze off the road for a second and glanced at me. "Did you happen to notice if any of the spaces was empty? That could help determine when the gun was taken. If all the guns were there when you were in the room, then it had to have been stolen between the time you visited and the time the butler found it missing. Only somebody at the party could have taken it."

I tried to picture the racks, but all I could remember was rows of guns stored according to size. "I couldn't swear to it, but I think all the guns were there when I was in the room. I bet it will turn up. And even if somebody did steal it, how would they ever find out who? There must have been two hundred people at the party."

"What I'd like to know," Matthew said, "is what kind of gun was stolen. Was it a valuable gun? If it was, then it was probably taken for its intrinsic value."

"What other reason would anybody risk stealing an old gun for?" Marnie asked.

The car was silent as we all mulled that over.

"I suppose," I said, chuckling, "that if somebody was planning the perfect murder, then stealing a gun during a party would be a great idea. It would be nearly impossible to trace the weapon back to the killer."

Jenny did not find my comment funny. "Don't joke. I have a really bad feeling about this."

I glanced at Matthew. He looked as worried as Jenny.

Chapter 4

I fumbled through my pocket for my house keys and stepped back to let everyone in.

"Marnie, you've never seen my place. Come. I'll show you around." I walked through the foyer. "I fell in love with its charm. Don't you just love the oak floors?"

She nodded approvingly at every detail I pointed out. "I can see why you would like this place. But personally, I prefer a place with a bit more character." I almost laughed out loud. Her house had so much character, it would have looked perfect in a circus. "But to each her own," she concluded, making a beeline for the kitchen, where Jenny was dropping a fistful of fettuccini into a pot of boiling water. Winston watched in rapt attention.

"Winnie, get away from there. That's people food." He slouched away with a look screaming of being abused. "You started dinner," I said to Jenny. "Thank you."

"Oh, it's nothing." She laughed. "I boiled the water."

Matthew laughed. "That's about all Della knows how to do."

"Thanks a lot," I said.

I filled Winston's water bowl and poured some kibble into his food bowl. He lunged for it the second I set it down. "Just like a man," I said. "Not even a thank-you, you ingrate."

"What is that supposed to mean?" Matthew asked, chuckling.

"If the shoe fits, wear it," Jenny teased.

"I haven't lived in Briar Hollow for long, but having my friends around makes it feel like home," I said. "It's nice having you all here. I should invite you over more often."

"It's nice being here," Matthew replied, and something in his voice made me look up at him. He was staring back at me with an expression I couldn't quite read. I felt heat rise to my face and quickly turned away. I grabbed an apron from the hook behind the kitchen door and tied it behind my neck.

"It's true I'm not the best of cooks," I said to Jenny. "My mother is still trying to get me to take lessons." I opened the refrigerator and retrieved the container of ready-made Alfredo sauce I'd bought. "But as long as I know how to cook pasta, that's all I need to know."

I threw a discreet look at Matthew. He was no longer looking at me. He was at the kitchen table, struggling with the cork from a bottle of red wine. At last he pulled it out with a soft pop. "Who wants a glass of zinfandel?"

I pointed to the cabinet at the left of the sink. "The glasses are in there." While Jenny set the glasses on the counter and Matthew filled them, I busied myself setting plates and cutlery.

"What beautiful dishes," Jenny said, picking up one of the plates I'd just put down and admiring it.

"You've seen those before, haven't you?" I asked. "They were part of Mrs. McLeay's estate." That was the houseful of furnishings I'd bought for a bargain.

"They're beautiful, especially on this gorgeous linen tablecloth."

"That set was part of the estate too. And so was this set of bone-handled cutlery. I still can't believe all the wonderful treasures Mrs. McLeay kept hidden in those cupboards."

Matthew picked up one of the knives. "I hope you have some sharper knives than this. It won't cut anything harder than butter." He set it back down.

"That might be because it *is* a butter knife," I said.

He shrugged. "What do I know about table knives? The only ones I know well are weapons."

Jenny shuddered. "Oh, God, will you please stop talking about weapons? Guns, knives, next you'll be talking about hatchets and meat cleavers." Even Marnie joined in the laughter.

Soon we were sitting around the dining room table, sipping wine and enjoying our dinner. Across from me, Marnie was batting her lashes madly—sending me a message to flirt. I chanced a look at Matthew. He was twirling pasta on his fork. I racked my brains for something flirtatious to say and came up blank. I gave Marnie a furious look. I hoped she got the message and stopped pushing.

Jenny reached for the bread basket. "What did you

think of Whitby's house?" she said as she buttered her roll. "Isn't it spectacular?"

"I'll say," Marnie said, between bites of pasta.

I glanced up, relieved that she'd introduced a casual subject. "It's so gorgeous I don't quite know why Whitby hired a decorator."

Marnie smiled knowingly. "I suspect the lady may have pushed her way into Whitby's life. It looked to me like this designer has designs on more than just the house."

"I noticed that too," I said. "But after seeing the rooms she worked on, I have to admit, she knows what she's doing."

Jenny looked up from her plate. "In more ways than one, I'm sure."

Marnie glanced at her. "I wonder if she's after the man or his money."

Jenny shrugged. "You said yourself that he probably dated all the women in the state. He doesn't have to flash his money. He's handsome enough. I'm sure he can get a woman with his charm alone."

I put my fork down. "Jenny warned me that Bunny is trouble. She thinks I should turn down the contract if she offers it."

Marnie's eyes grew wide. "She did? You'd be crazy not to take her advice. When Jenny has a feeling, I, for one, take her seriously. As far as I know, she's never been wrong."

I put on my most serious face. "I'd be more inclined to take her advice if I didn't need the business so much."

The house phone rang. I excused myself and hurried to the extension in the kitchen. Winston plodded along, hoping for a treat. I opened the doggy cookie jar and threw him a dog biscuit. He dove in the air and caught it. I picked up the phone.

"Is this Della Wright?" asked a voice I didn't recognize.

"Yes, it is."

"Hello, Della. This is Rhonda McDermott. I'm sorry to disturb you, but I think you and I left with each other's bags this evening. I got home a little while ago, and when I went into my bag, I discovered somebody else's wallet inside. I checked the driver's license and it's yours. I'm sorry about the inconvenience. Your bag looks so much like mine, it was an easy mistake to make. The only difference is yours has a silver clasp instead of a gold one. Still, it was silly of me not to check before leaving."

I remembered how abruptly the McDermotts had left. "Well, if you're right, then I made the same mistake."

"Would you mind taking a look at the bag you have?"

"Hold on. I'll be right back." I walked through the dining room under the curious glances of my friends. I explained. "Rhonda McDermott and I seem to have left with each other's purses."

Marnie muttered something indistinct. I picked up the purse from the foyer console where I'd left it and looked inside. Sure enough, instead of my familiar black leather wallet, there was a brown suede one. I hurried back to the telephone. "Hello, Mrs. McDermott? You're right. I do have your bag. I'm just sitting down to dinner, but if you like, I can drop it off later this evening."

"Actually, I'd rather you stopped by tomorrow morning, if you don't mind. Maybe just before we open—say, seven forty-five or so?"

We agreed on the time and I returned to the table, where the mere mention of the McDermotts' name had put Marnie in a bad mood.

"And do you know," she was saying, "that they copied every single one of my recipes, right down to my burnt-caramel muffins, which are my own personal creation? They even copied my pies and my cakes."

Jenny smiled soothingly. "But none of them taste anywhere as good as yours."

Marnie leaned back in her chair, pushing her plate away. "I wish I could be sure of that."

"If it will make you feel better," I said, "I have to drop by their shop tomorrow morning. While I'm there, I'll pick up an assortment of their pastries and we can have a taste test."

Marnie frowned worriedly. "But she knows you and Jenny work right next to each other—in the same space, for heaven's sake. Won't she figure out what you're doing?"

I shrugged. "What is she going to do? Take her bag and kick me out? I already know who the winner will be. Your baked goods will outshine theirs, hands down. And then you'll be able to stop worrying about those people once and for all."

"The only way I'll stop worrying about them is if they went bankrupt."

Jenny looked shocked. "Marnie! You should never wish harm on others. It brings bad karma."

Marnie looked only slightly embarrassed. "Okay then, if they moved out of town." She crossed her arms. "I don't know why they had to be such creeps. I don't give a damn that they turned me down. What I can't forgive is the way they tricked me into giving them all my baking secrets."

"Baking secrets are a dime a dozen," Jenny said. "The real secret is the love the baker puts into their work. And that's what you do. You put all your love into it."

Matthew turned to me. "Have you found a tenant for your apartment yet?" It was an obvious attempt at changing the subject. To my relief, it worked. When I said that, no, in fact, I had gotten only a handful of inquiries, Marnie suggested she create tear-off ads and put them up on all the local stores' bulletin boards.

I frowned. "I hadn't thought of it, but it sounds like a good idea. You wouldn't mind?"

"Where were you advertising?" she asked.

"Craigslist."

"That's good, but a lot of older folks around here aren't computer savvy. However they all read bulletin boards. I'll put one up at Mercantile's and another at the church." She named half a dozen other places. "This way, you'll be reaching more people."

Jenny looked around. "Who wants a piece of Marnie's flourless chocolate cake?"

There were yeses all around. Matthew pushed away from the table. "I'll clear the dishes."

"And I'll serve the dessert," Jenny added.

Over coffee and dessert everyone agreed that this was the best chocolate cake they had ever eaten. This seemed to pacify Marnie a bit, and by the time the party broke up, she was her usual charmingly gruff self.

"Okay," she said, as she was leaving. "Anybody in favor of me running them out of town with my baking?"

"Be my guest," Jenny said. "I'd be ever so grateful."

They continued chatting on their way down the stairs.

"Bye, everyone. See you tomorrow," I said.

A chorus of thank-yous and good-byes replied.

"Bye, Winnie." He didn't even look back. I closed the door and headed for bed.

The next morning was the third Tuesday in September, still a long time away from it being officially winter, but the day brought a chilly wind, a hint of the season ahead. I buttoned myself up in a red wool jacket and wrapped a long white silk scarf around my neck. I looked a bit dressed up by Briar Hollow standards, but my wardrobe was full of clothes from my days of living in Charlotte. I wasn't about to chuck them out.

Across the street from the Coffee Break, I stopped by a newspaper vending machine and picked up a copy of the *Belmont Daily*. I glanced at the headline, and just as I'd expected, there, in big bold typeface, the headlines screamed, LOCAL MAN ENTERS STATE ELECTIONS. Underneath the caption was a picture of Bernard Whitby standing on the third step of his staircase and smiling to the camera. I remembered that Bunny Boyd had sidled up to him, but all that remained of her in the picture was her right elbow and a wisp of her hair. The woman had been cropped out. *She wouldn't be pleased about that*, I thought, stifling a chuckle.

I folded the paper under my arm and hurried across the street to the McDermotts' shop. I hated to be late. It wasn't eight o'clock yet, but no more than a minute or two away. Mrs. McDermott had made a point of wanting me to drop by before the shop opened. I glanced at their window. It looked on to a seating area—the ubiquitous leather armchairs and dark wood coffee table. It looked nice and modern but no different from every other coffee shop in the country—except for Coffee, Tea and Destiny, I thought.

When Jenny and I had first agreed to share the shop, I'd given her one of the two large windows that looked on to Main Street. I had decorated mine with an armoire full of skeins of colorful yards, a small loom from which hung tea towels and place mats, and a large wicker basket filled with an assortment of rolled-up rugs in a fanlike arrangement. It was so attractive that people often popped in just to compliment me on my display.

A few feet away, Jenny's window was furnished with a small shabby-chic tea table and two antique wing chairs slipcovered in a large pink, cabbage-rose chintz. On the table was a crystal ball, a teapot and teacups. Neither of our windows would attract the testosterone set, I had concluded upon studying them, but that hardly seemed to matter. Most of my clients were women. Only rarely did men walk in, and when they did, they usually hurried out, much the way they do when they accidentally find themselves strolling through the lingerie department of a store. As for Jenny, she had wisely pointed out that, since most of the career people worked out of town, it left mainly stay-at-home mothers in town during the day. It was good business to go after the female clientele. She must have been right because her business was flourishing.

I walked into the dark interior of the Coffee Break and hesitated. That was odd. If they'd already unlocked the door, why hadn't they also turned on the light?

"Hello? Rhonda?" I called out, advancing a few steps. "Mr. McDermott? Anybody here?" I stood uncertainly halfway between the entrance and the counter until the door behind the counter opened.

Rhonda McDermott appeared, flicking on the lights. "Oh, hello, Della." She looked around, puzzled. "Where's Philip? Didn't he give you your purse yet?"

"I didn't see him. I just got—" Before I could finish, Rhonda screamed. And then she dropped behind the counter. I rushed over.

I rounded the counter and froze. Mr. McDermott was lying on the floor in a pool of blood. His face was ghostly white, his strangely dark gray eyes staring blindly and his white shirt soaked red. My pulse raced. For a second I thought I might faint.

Rhonda was kneeling next to her husband, almost as pale as he was. "Philip, look at me." She shook him. "Philip, say something." But her husband remained motionless.

I stood frozen for a moment, horrified at the scene before me. The poor woman was beside herself. My eyes took in the details. The blood had come from at least one wound in the man's chest—a knife, a gun? I didn't know. I glanced around but saw no weapons. Nor were there any spent cartridges. If Mr. McDermott had just come in to open the store, that would mean the attack had happened a short time ago, maybe only minutes before I walked in. Yet I hadn't heard any gunshots. A few feet away from the body, a bundle of soiled bar towels littered the floor. I knew better than to touch them. They were now part of the crime scene.

I crouched and felt the man's wrist, not really expecting a pulse. Nobody could survive the loss of so much blood. He was still warm, almost normal. I told myself he might still be alive, though, looking at the amount of blood, I had my doubts.

Mrs. McDermott looked across her husband's body at me, tears quivering on her lashes.

I cleared my throat. "I think we should call an ambulance—and the police," I added.

The ambulance arrived in minutes, which felt more like hours. During the wait, Rhonda had tried to check her husband's pulse. This had resulted only in spreading more of the victim's blood all over the crime scene and also his wife, who was now almost as bloody as he was. The attendants, two young burly men, burst into the shop.

"Where is the patient?" asked the first one.

"Over here." I popped my head out from behind the counter.

They raced over, dropping into crouches and immediately checking the victim's vital signs.

"Sorry, ma'am. You'll have to get out of our way," the fair-haired attendant said, opening an emergency kit.

"Come with me," I said to Rhonda. "We have to give them room to work." Wrapping an arm around her shoulders, I guided her to one of the tables and onto a chair.

"Who could have done that?" she asked, looking dazed. "Who could have wanted to hurt my Philip?"

I had no answer for her.

Seconds later, a police car screeched to a halt in front of the door, siren still blaring. The officers came running in only to stop short at the sight of the ambulance personnel still working on McDermott.

"Pulse?"

"Negative."

"Respiration?"

"Nil." With every pronouncement, their voices grew more ominous.

I suddenly became aware of the crowd that had gathered at the window. A dozen or so people were peering through the glass, staring at Rhonda and me. The poor woman had enough on her mind without having to contend with curiosity seekers.

I leaned toward her. "Can I get you something? A glass of water? A cup of coffee, maybe?"

"Coffee, yes, that's a good idea," she said, and then she surprised me by jumping to her feet. "I'll make it." She scurried off toward the coffee counter from the opposite side. Soon she reappeared carrying a pot of coffee and a stack of paper cups. "I made coffee for everyone," she announced with a shaky voice. She was holding on to her self-control by a very thin line.

The older of the two policemen, a heavy, balding man with beagle eyes, came toward us. Rhonda looked up at him, her eyes filled with hope.

"I'm sorry, ma'am. There was nothing they could do. He's gone."

She let out an anguished wail and ran toward her husband's body. The other officer stepped in front of her, blocking her way.

"Sorry, ma'am. You can't go there."

"But he's my husband," she cried, trying to get around him. "He needs me."

"There's nothing you can do for him now," he said firmly. Behind him, the attendants were putting away their medical equipment. He turned to them. "I think this lady needs help." They dropped what they were doing and gently guided her away.

"Don't touch the body," the same officer said to nobody in particular, which was odd, considering that whatever part of the crime scene Rhonda had not already contaminated, the emergency attendants had destroyed.

I stood nearby uncertainly. "Is it all right if I leave now?"

"Not right away," the officer said, and I sat back down.

The older policeman, who had made a phone call as soon as the victim was declared dead, hung up. "The coroner is on his way."

The coroner in Briar Hollow was Dr. Cook, a general practitioner, not a medical examiner of the type we're now used to seeing on TV. I'd been shocked when Matthew first told me that coroners were appointed in many small towns, and they were not necessarily professionally trained. He'd even heard of cases where the local coroner had no more training than a weekend seminar, and according to him, knew less about medicine than a butcher.

Mrs. McDermott was now crying openly. She shouldn't be with strangers at a time like this. I wondered if she had friends or family I could call.

Before I could ask, the beagle-eyed policeman joined me at the table. "Sorry to make you wait," he said, pulling out a chair. "I hope you don't mind answering a few questions."

"Not at all."

He handed me his card—Officer Bailey—and flipped open a small notebook. "Just for the record, your name is?"

"Della. Della Wright. I own a shop—Dream Weaver—up the street."

He nodded and jotted down a few words. "Can you tell me what happened?"

I swallowed hard, still shaky from the sight of Mr. McDermott's deathly pallor and of so much blood. "I was at Bernard Whitby's party last night," I said, and explained about the purse mix-up. "I didn't even notice until she phoned me at home. We agreed that I'd stop by this morning to exchange them." Officer Bailey was taking copious notes. "The door was unlocked when I got here, so I walked in. I thought it a bit strange that the lights were off, but I didn't attach much importance to it. I called out a few times, and that's when Mrs. McDermott came in and stumbled on her husband's body. I called nine-one-one right away."

"At what time was that?"

"It must have been a minute or two before eight."

He jotted down a few more words and continued. "So you didn't witness the victim being shot?"

That answered one question. McDermott had been shot and not stabbed. I shook my head.

"Did you happen to see anybody come out of the store?"

Again, I shook my head.

"What about on the street? Was anybody walking away from the store?"

I thought back, trying to picture the street as I'd made my way over. "There was someone walking away, but I wasn't paying attention. I couldn't even tell you if it was a woman or a man."

"How far away was this person?"

I thought quickly. "Roughly a block and a half, maybe two."

He nodded and seemed pensive for a few minutes. "Do you know of anyone holding a grudge against Mr. or Mrs. McDermott?"

Marnie Potter, I thought, and my mouth dried. But all I said was, "No, nobody that I know of."

The questioning didn't last more than ten or fifteen minutes, but by the time it was over, I was drained.

"I'll call you if I think of anything else," I said and hurried out, avoiding eye contact with anyone in the gathered crowd. I was in no mood to talk to anyone. I hoofed it over to the shop, where Winston greeted me with his usual overexuberance. I wasn't even in the mood for a doggy kiss.

"I was beginning to wonder if you were going to show up today," Jenny said. "Matthew just dropped Winston off." She stared at me, tilting her head sideways. "Are you all right? You look as if you just saw a ghost."

"Close enough," I said, collapsing into a chair. "Mr. McDermott is dead—murdered."

She blanched. "Oh, my God. That's terrible. Ever since I got up this morning, I had a feeling something bad was going to happen. Didn't I tell you? And you never believe me." She studied me again, her eyes softening. "Let me get you some coffee, and then you can tell me what happened."

"Thanks. I could use a cup right about now."

She stepped toward the back, and Winston wandered over to me. He rested his head on my knees, staring at me with big, doleful eyes.

"Oh, Winnie," I said, throwing my arms around him. "It was terrible."

He whimpered sympathetically, and I pulled myself to my feet. "Okay, come." He followed me to the counter, from under which I pulled out his cushion. "Here, Winnie, sleep."

I opened the drawer to put away my purse and stopped. "Oh, shit." Of all the stupid mistakes. I still had Rhonda McDermott's purse. We'd never exchanged them. I was about to drop it in the drawer when it slipped out of my hands, its contents scattering all over the floor. I bent down to pick them up.

A moment later, Jenny was back with a steaming cup of coffee and a warm cranberry-lemon muffin. She frowned. "What are you doing?"

I was slipping credit cards back into the purse. "I dropped it; just putting everything back." I paused to look at a wallet-sized photo of her husband. It brought a fresh wave of sadness.

She gasped. "Why are you looking through her stuff?" From the expression on her face, I might as well have been stealing her money.

"Don't worry. It's just a picture of Mr. McDermott. See?" I showed her. "I promise not to take her social security number or any of her credit cards." Seeing the disapproval in her eyes, I chuckled. "Oh, all right. Here, I'm putting it a—" I stopped. "Hold on. What's this?" I was looking at a small piece of paper that had been folded into the size of a card and slipped into the protective window meant for a driver's license. The only reason a person might store away a paper that way was to hide it. Being the nosy person that I am, I unfolded it.

Curiosity got the better of Jenny too. She came closer, trying to read it over my shoulder. "What is it?"

"It's a name and phone number." I showed her.

She moved closer, squinting. "Emma Blanchard," she read. "Why would Rhonda McDermott have Emma Blanchard's phone number?" she said, puzzled.

"Why wouldn't she?"

"For one thing, Rhonda can't stand the girl."

"How would you know that?"

"Whenever she shopped at Frannie's, she would let anybody *but* Emma wait on her. There was one time Rhonda said something that sent Emma running to the storage room in tears. She wouldn't come back out until she was sure Rhonda had left. When I asked her what happened, all she said was that Mrs. McDermott was a certifiable bitch." She looked thoughtful for a moment. "Hmm, Emma has been getting crank calls lately. I have a feeling I know who was making them."

"You think it was Mrs. McDermott?"

"I wouldn't be one bit surprised." She pointed to my cup. "Want some cream?"

"Yes, please." I copied Emma's name and number onto the back of one of my business cards and stuffed it into my pocket. And then I refolded the paper and slipped it back inside the wallet just as I'd found it. As I sipped, I wondered what could have happened between Emma and Rhonda. People didn't usually go around hating others unless something happened to make them feel that way. Hmm. How could I find out what had started this animosity?

"Jenny, how would you like to come shopping at Frannie's with me? I think I need a new pair of pants."

"What?" She looked at me as if I'd just sprouted a second head. "I don't understand. You always said the styles she carries are not for you." A light went on her eyes, and she wagged a finger at me. "You want to question Emma, don't you?"

"Yes," I admitted. "But don't ask me why, because I'm not even sure myself."

Word must have gotten out about McDermott's murder and that I had been at the coffee shop when his body was found, because suddenly my shop was crawling with customers.

"I heard there was a lot of blood," one woman whispered over a display of tablecloths and runners. "Do you know if he was shot or stabbed?"

"I was so overcome with shock," I answered, "that I didn't even notice."

Normally I would have been thrilled to see my shop so full of people, but I knew these were gossipmongers, not shoppers. But that didn't have to mean I wouldn't try my best to turn them into buyers.

"Poor Mrs. McDermott. I can't imagine how she must have felt. Did she completely break down?"

I pretended not to hear. Pointing to the item in her hands, I said, "Isn't that is a beautiful table runner? Do you read *Home & Design* magazine?"

"Sometimes," she said, disappointed that I was changing the subject.

"Did you see last month's issue? They featured a gorgeous dining room where the designer used table runners like this one instead of individual place mats. I thought it was such an original idea." Seeing that I wasn't divulging any juicy details, the other gossipers slowly drifted out.

A few minutes later, I was adding up the woman's bill. As she walked out, I looked up to see Emma walking in. *Well, what do you know?* I wouldn't have to go shopping at Frannie's after all.

It's one thing for a girl to look gorgeous all made-up and in dim lighting, but even in bright daylight and—except for a bit of black mascara—without a trace of makeup, this girl was magnificent. She wore tight jeans that showed off her long, perfect legs. Her hair was thick and golden, falling halfway down her back. I almost expected her to shake it out in slow motion, the way models do in a shampoo commercial. She was flawless.

"Hi, Emma. Welcome to Dream Weaver. What can I do for you?"

She hesitated, looking around warily. She came closer. "Is Jenny here?" she asked.

"She's in the back. Did you want to say hello? She's got a shop full of customers right now."

She shook her head, relief washing over her features. "You're the lady who caught that murderer a couple of months ago, right?" Before I opened my mouth, she continued. "I need to talk to you alone." I waited, guessing that whatever it was, it probably had to do with Mr. McDermott's death. She leaned in and whispered, "You didn't happen to see any photos while you were there, did you?"

"There?" I said, frowning. "You mean at the Coffee Break?" I couldn't imagine what she was talking about. Some shops, I knew, had photos of famous customers displayed on their walls, but there was nothing like that at the McDermotts' shop. "No. What kind of photographs are you talking about?"

She blushed and then cleared her throat. "It's just that Mr. McDermott took pictures of me . . . for my portfolio," she added in an even lower voice. "And, well, some of them I wouldn't want anybody else to see."

The image of Emma striking a calendar pose flashed through my mind. "Were these nude shots, by any chance?"

She nodded, blushing deeper. "I should never have agreed, but Mr. McDermott was so convincing. He said that if I wanted to break into the New York market, I would need nude shots for my portfolios."

I was pretty certain this was not true—on the part of McDermott, not Emma. I suddenly remembered what Jenny had told me about Rhonda hating Emma. "Is that why his wife doesn't like you?"

Emma's eyebrows jumped up. "No, thank God. If she'd known, she probably would have killed me. Did you see the way she dragged him out of the party when she spotted me last night?"

I pictured the way Rhonda had blushed and the

hateful look she'd launched in our direction. At the time I'd thought it was meant for Marnie, but as I remembered, Emma had been standing right behind us. So she was the person Rhonda had been looking at. *Interesting.* "I noticed," I said sympathetically. She seemed so nice; it was difficult to imagine anybody hating her.

The girl's eyes widened. "She really hates me. Do you know what she called me? A whore—just because I phoned her husband at home one time. All I wanted was to find out when I could pick up my new pictures. Any girl who so much as glanced at her husband was a whore in her books. It's a wonder that shop of theirs ever made a profit. With the way she treated the female clients, I can understand why so many of them prefer coming to Jenny's shop." And then, looking worried, she added, "Believe me; I never, ever had sex with him."

I was surprised that Emma was sharing all this with me. "I never imagined you did." At least I was pretty sure she hadn't. On the other hand, I knew that young girls sometimes did desperate things to become fashion models.

"She was crazy," Emma continued earnestly. "She even called me at home and left me the bitchiest message. I wish I'd kept it, but I was afraid Ricky might hear it." Her voice lowered. "He doesn't know about the nude shots. He'd kill me if he ever found out." And then, as if realizing what she'd just said, she blanched. "Oh, I don't mean that he . . . He would never."

"We all say things we don't mean literally," I said, as

I tucked that little bit of information into my mind.
Well, well, what do you know? I already had a suspect.

"One time I stopped by the shop for coffee and Mr.
McDermott was behind the counter. All I did was say
hi and give him my order and Mrs. McDermott had a
fit. She was screaming that if she ever caught him
talking to me again, he was as good as dead. Everybody in the shop overheard. It was so embarrassing."

My suspicious mind reared up. Mrs. McDermott
sounded as if she was obsessively jealous. Another interesting tidbit, one that conjured up an entirely new
possibility.

I wanted to hear more about the McDermotts. "How
odd," I said. "Why would she be so jealous?"

She shrugged. "Maybe because he *was* having an affair, only not with me. I had an appointment to meet
him at his studio one night, and when I showed up
about half an hour early, he was in his darkroom with
the door partly open. I didn't see much, but I saw
enough to know he was with another woman and that
his hands were all over her. I got out of there before he
saw me."

Within minutes, I had gone from no suspects to three
suspects—Ricky, Rhonda and McDermott's mistress.
"Did you happen to see who the woman was?"

"No," she said, sounding disappointed. "I wish I
had. I would have been more than happy to tell the
bitch who her husband was really screwing."

"Maybe you should tell the police what you know."

"Oh, no." Her mouth twitched. "I could never do

that. I don't want anyone to find out about . . . you know."

By "anyone," I figured she meant Ricky. Otherwise, why would she be telling me?

Emma hesitated. "He rented an apartment in Belmont. He wanted to keep it a secret, which I thought was really weird." She scowled. "He said he couldn't have it in Briar Hollow without half the town knowing about it."

"That does sound strange. Why would he have wanted to keep it a secret?"

"I suspect it was because of his wife."

I supposed that made *some* sense, I thought.

"Della . . ." She started hesitantly, and I knew she was about to reveal the real point of her visit. "I was wondering if you would mind . . . I mean, could you do me a favor?"

"What kind of favor?"

She continued. "I don't dare go back there myself, but if I give you the key . . ." Long pause. "Do you think—I mean, would you mind—maybe you could go and look for those pictures of me? Now that I think about it, I'm sure they're there. He would never have brought them to his house."

My mind raced. Go to the studio and steal those pictures? "Me? Why me?"

"I thought, since you solved that case a few months ago, maybe . . ." She let her words drift away, looking so hopeful.

The girl seemed so sweet and innocent, hardly more

than a child. My heart went out to her. And the truth is, I was intrigued. If McDermott was keeping that studio a secret, I wondered what he was hiding. Surely it was more than a few nude pictures. "I'll see what I can do," I found myself saying, even though I knew I could never steal those pictures. Even if they were hers, as she claimed, it would be viewed as tampering with evidence. I didn't want to get into that kind of trouble.

"I'll write down the address for you," she said, relief washing over her face. Looking around furtively one last time, she scribbled it on the back of one of my business cards. Then she pulled a key from her pocket. "He gave me my own key to the place." *I bet he did*, I thought, getting angrier at the deceased. I hated when men took advantage of young girls. *Pervert!* If the man made a habit of taking advantage of girls, there could be a lot of people angry at him.

Emma handed me the white metal key. And a moment later she was gone.

She had no sooner left than the doorbell chimed and Officer Bailey walked in carrying my purse. "Mrs. McDermott asked me to bring this to you," he said, handing it over. "And if you don't mind fetching hers, I'll take it back to her."

"Of course." I bent down behind my counter and retrieved the woman's purse. "Here you go." I clicked open my own bag and gave it a cursory inspection.

"Everything there?" he asked.

I nodded, closing it. "I'm sure it is." I paused. "How is she doing?"

"As well as can be expected," he answered, which told me nothing at all.

"Is she in the hospital?"

He shook his head. "No, the attendants gave her a shot to calm her, and she's sleeping."

He looked around to make certain we were alone. "I forgot to ask you a couple of things. On your way to the coffee shop this morning, did you happen to notice any cars on the street?"

"There were cars," I said. "Just normal morning traffic, but I couldn't even tell you how many or what colors, let alone the makes or models. I am not much of a car person."

I was tempted to ask whether the police were considering Mrs. McDermott as a suspect but changed my mind. The poor woman had just been through a terrible shock. The last thing she needed was to become a suspect in her husband's murder. There would be time enough for that if evidence pointed in her direction. I suddenly snapped back to find Officer Bailey looking at me strangely. "Miss Wright? I was asking you a question."

"I'm sorry," I said apologetically. "I can't seem to get the image of Mr. McDermott out of my mind."

"I was asking you about the owner of Coffee, Tea and Destiny. Do you know of any feud between her and the McDermotts?"

Chapter 5

Jenny and I were in my apartment when the telephone rang. I knew even before looking at the call display that it was my mother. "Hi, Mom."

I could hear the worry in her voice. "My God, Della. I just found out there was a murder in Briar Hollow and that you found the body."

"How could you possibly have found that out?"

"June told me. She happened to call Matthew, and he had just heard about it."

Trust Matthew's mother to call my mother the minute she heard anything. Those two were thick as thieves. "Actually, I didn't find the body. I just happened to be there when the victim's wife found it," I said. "Is that what you were calling about? Because if it is, there's nothing to tell. Or were you calling to find out about last night's party?"

That was all I needed to say to steer her off the subject. Her voice brightened. "How did it go? Did you dress up for Matthew? Has he asked you on a date yet?" I covered the speaker with my hand, mouthing,

"My mother," to Jenny. She smiled and nodded knowingly.

"No, Mom, he hasn't. I keep telling you he's not interested in me that way."

"That's not what June says." June and my mother were coconspirators in a plan to match us up. My mother continued. "She thinks he's secretly in love with you."

"Well, if he is, he sure hides it well."

"If only you'd give him a chance. I still think you shouldn't have moved out of his house."

I interrupted. "Jenny's here, Mom. I can't talk."

"Oh, she is? Jenny is such a nice girl. Say hi to her for me."

"I will. Bye, Mom. Love you." I quickly put down the receiver before she started on another tangent.

"She's still trying to match you up with Matthew, is she?"

I nodded. "Her and everybody else I know."

Jenny laughed. "I know she drives you crazy, but I still think she's great."

"You do, do you? Well then, how would you like to adopt her? She can be your mother for a while. I won't even charge you a borrowing fee."

She waved my offer away, laughing. "Where's that glass of wine you promised me?"

I went to the kitchen and got the half-full bottle from last night and was pouring her a glass when I mentioned Officer Bailey dropping by.

"What did he want to know?" She sat.

"He asked if you and the McDermotts had any disputes," I said, rolling my eyes. "Can you imagine?" The minute I saw the color drain from her face, I wanted to take my words back.

"Oh, my God, they think *I* killed him?" She fell against the back of her chair.

"Of course they don't think you killed him. That was just one question among many. None of the other questions had anything to do with you. You, of all people, should know how the police work." Until her divorce a year ago, Jenny had been married to the local chief of police, a marriage that had lasted ten years. "You've spent years hearing stories about police procedures and investigations."

"I have a really bad feeling about this. They're going to try to pin this on me. I just know it."

"Oh, for heaven's sake, now you're just being silly. They've barely started their investigation. You know as well as I do that everyone is a suspect at the beginning. Chances are they asked somebody else the same question about me. It'll take them a while, but they'll eventually get it right and catch the killer." I paused, wondering what I could talk about that would take her mind off her worries. "Guess who stopped by today." At her blank look, I said, "Emma."

A spark of interest lit her eyes. "She did? Why didn't she come to the back and say hi?"

"She wanted to speak to me privately." I hesitated.

"I promise to not tell a soul." Seeing me still uncertain, she continued. "If I'd been here, Emma would have told me too. She always confided in me."

I did want Jenny's opinion, I thought. "Maybe you're

right." I glossed over the conversation. "I feel sorry for the girl. That man took advantage of her. She seems very embarrassed by the whole thing."

"Nude photos—poor girl." She shook her head. "I can't say I'm surprised. Emma is so bent on a career in modeling she'd listen to any Tom, Dick or Harry for advice. I'm just relieved McDermott didn't do worse."

I shrugged. "We don't know that he didn't." I was quiet for a moment. "How much do you know about Emma's boyfriend?"

She glanced at me, frowning. "Not much. He works as a mechanic at Al's Garage down the street. According to Emma, he has a bit of a temper. Why do you ask?"

"At the party, he seemed irritated when she was talking to us. I got the impression that he's the possessive type. You know him better than I do. How do you think he might react if he found out about McDermott getting Emma to pose nude for him? Do you think he could lose control of his temper over something like that?"

Jenny played that over in her mind. "I have no idea. All I can say is that I got the same impression you did, that he's possessive and controlling. But could he kill someone? I wouldn't even want to hazard a guess."

"You're right. It was a stupid question." We were quiet for a few minutes, sipping our wine companionably. I tried to get my mind on something other than the murder and gave up.

"Did you know Mrs. McDermott suspected her husband of having an affair with Emma?" I repeated Emma's story, adding what she'd told me about catching him in the darkroom with another woman. "As it turns out, Mrs. McDermott was right about her husband having an affair. Only she was wrong about which woman."

"Well, that explains the way she treated Emma in the store."

"Do you have any idea who his mistress might have been?"

"How would I know? He was no more than a passing acquaintance." She shook her head slowly. "The McDermotts are about fifteen years older than I am. Imagine a man that age still being unable to keep it in his pants. Shameful."

"You think they're in their late forties, early fifties?"

She nodded. "They must be. My aunt—my mother's younger sister—went to school with them, and she's forty-nine."

I took a long breath. "The way I see it, I've already got three suspects: Ricky, Mrs. McDermott and the woman McDermott was having an affair with. I just wish I knew who she was."

She threw me an amused glance. "Playing detective already, are you?"

"No, not at all. I just feel so awful for poor Mrs. McDermott."

"*Poor* Mrs. McDermott, yet you consider her one of the suspects."

She had a point. "I don't really. Still, there is something about her that just seems off—obsessively jealous."

"I say everybody has a bit of ESP. Maybe you should listen to your gut feelings."

I almost laughed.

She frowned, looking pensive. "Whose idea was it that you stop by the coffee shop before they opened this morning, yours or Rhonda's?"

"Rhonda's. Why?"

"Well," she said, tilting her head, "if Rhonda was already planning to kill her husband, she might have been setting you up as her alibi. You were there when she found the body. You can confirm how upset she was, that she tried to resuscitate him. That sort of thing."

"I hadn't thought of that." I remembered something. "Hmm, I *was* surprised she insisted I come by at precisely eight forty-five this morning, rather than last night." Another idea came to me. "She was at the party last night. I wonder if she happened to take a tour of Whitby's house too."

Jenny's eyes flashed with sudden understanding. "You think she might have stolen Whitby's gun."

"All I'm doing right now is looking at possible scenarios." Without saying another word, I pushed back my chair and went to the kitchen, returning with the house phone in hand. I punched in a number.

"Who are you calling?"

"Matthew."

A second later, his deep voice answered. "It's me," I

said. "I hear you told your mother about McDermott's murder."

"Uh-oh. I take it your mother called," he replied.

"Is the pope Catholic?" I replied with all the sarcasm I could muster. "I wish you wouldn't say anything to your mother that you think I might not want mine to know." And then, feeling slightly bad for my sharp tone, I added, "Am I interrupting your writing?"

"No. I was just about to take Winston for a walk."

"Oh, good. Mind if I take a few minutes of your time?"

He chuckled. "What difference will it make what I say? You'll just go ahead anyhow."

"Ha-ha, very funny." I waited a beat, wondering if I should be circumspect and then decided against it. He'd see right through me anyway. "Did you speak to anyone at the station?"

Matthew was a local celebrity—at least to the local police department. As soon as he moved to Briar Hollow, the local police department had learned of his background as a criminologist at Quantico. It didn't matter that he had left that career almost a decade earlier, they still asked for his help at every opportunity.

He hesitated. "I stopped by and had a talk with the officer in charge—Officer Bailey."

"Bailey's in charge? He's the one who questioned me. Did he tell you anything? What did he want to know?"

"How about you invite me for a glass of wine and then I can tell you everything in person."

My heart went into a sudden happy dance. "Come on over," I said, and hung up.

Jenny put her glass down. "Matthew's on his way? What are you standing there for? Go put on some fresh makeup."

I shook my head in mock frustration. "You and my mother—I swear." I hurried to the washroom nonetheless and pulled out my makeup bag. I freshened up as well as two minutes allowed and stepped back out. "What do you think?"

"Go put on that sexy red sweater of yours," she ordered. "You know—the one with the V neck."

I raced back to the bedroom and returned just in time to answer the buzzer. "Hi, Matthew. Come on up."

I opened the door as Matthew came up the steps, a bottle of Chablis in his hands and Winston trotting along.

"My contribution to the party," he said, taking off his leather jacket. Underneath he wore a camel-colored sweater, almost the same golden shade as his eyes. He smiled down at me. "You look good," he said. I mouthed a silent "thank you" to Jenny.

She winked back and then looked down at the dog. "Hey there, Winnie, It's nice to see you. Want a treat?" Winston went into an immediate break dance. "Come with me," she said, leading the way into the kitchen.

Matthew handed me the bottle and headed for the living room. I hurried to the kitchen, returning with a glass of wine. "Here you go."

"Thank you." He took a sip and set it on the coffee

table. He gave me a serious look. "So, Detective Wright, what would you like to ask me?" I could think of a lot of things I would have liked to ask: Why didn't he think I was sexy? What did I have to do to seduce him? I pushed those thoughts out of my mind.

"I want to hear everything the police told you. How was McDermott killed? Did they find a weapon? Do they have a suspect?"

He leaned back against the cushions and put his feet up on the coffee table. He stopped and pointed at his feet. "Er, do you mind?"

"Go right ahead. If you scratch it, you can just help me repaint it."

He made himself comfortable. "So far they don't know much other than McDermott was shot at close range—because of the stippling."

I knew that stippling was the pattern left by powder burn.

He continued. "Dr. Cook thinks he was killed no more than half an hour before Mrs. McDermott found the body, and that time matches her version of the events. She says her husband went downstairs to get the shop ready to open, same as he did every morning. When he didn't return, she didn't think anything of it. It wasn't until she heard you calling that she came downstairs and found his body."

I nodded. "That sounds plausible."

He shook his head from side to side. "Having said that, we all know that determining the time of death by measuring body temperature is not an exact science unless it's done in a laboratory and with specialized equipment, something Dr. Cook does not have."

"But I touched McDermott's wrist when I was there." I shrugged. "He didn't seem cold to me at all. In fact, I thought he couldn't have been more than a degree or two lower than normal."

Jenny returned, Winston trotting at her heel. She sat and he curled up at her feet. "I'm glad you're here," she said. "Della told me that Officer Bailey came by the shop to question Della about me. What does that mean? Do you think they suspect me?"

Matthew laughed. "I wouldn't worry about it if I were you. This is just the first day of the investigation."

I bobbed my eyebrows at her. "Isn't that exactly what I said? Believe me. You have nothing to worry about."

She seemed only slightly relieved. "I'll feel better when they catch the killer."

Matthew nodded. "I understand. But keep in mind that during the early days following a murder, it's common for people to come forward with all kinds of tips. Even knowing that most of them will turn out to be false, the police still have to follow up on every one of them."

"Do you mean somebody gave them a tip about *me*?" Jenny sounded horrified. "Who? And what did they say?"

I was as surprised by this news as she was. I searched Matthew face.

He hesitated. "It seems you were seen walking away

from their coffee shop a few minutes before eight o'clock this morning." He took a sip of wine, studying her over the rim of his glass. "Did you go by their shop this morning?"

"I did not!" she retorted, incensed. "I can't believe you would even ask me something like that."

"I didn't ask you if you killed him," he said calmly. "I asked if you stopped by the coffee shop."

"Of course I didn't. If I had, I would have been the first one to tell the police. That would narrow down the time of death."

"Speaking of which," I said. "Are the police relying solely on Dr. Cook's report? Or are they sending the body to a proper medical examiner? I'm not saying that Dr. Cook isn't competent, but he has made a couple of mistakes." A while ago Dr. Cook had declared a local death an accident, and a few months later that same death was proved to be a murder.

"Yes. In this case we know it was murder. The prosecutor will need a full examiner's report before making an arrest. The body is already on its way to the county medical examiner."

"Was Dr. Cook able to tell what kind of a gun was used?"

"I haven't heard. Why do you ask?"

"I wonder if the murder weapon might have been Whitby's missing gun."

Matthew nodded at me, much the way a professor might look at a star pupil. "The same thought occurred to me too. But we won't know that until we find out the type of gun that was stolen and get the report from the ME."

Jenny interrupted, her brow creased with worry. "I'm sorry, but I can't get it out of my mind. Somebody gave a false tip about me. I want to know who told that story and why they would lie about something like that."

"I doubt it was a lie," I said. "I think it's more likely that they mistook somebody else for you—just a case of mistaken identity." I looked at Matthew, hoping he'd agree with my comment.

"You know I can't tell you who made that call. But Della is right. The police are considering the same theory."

This seemed to calm her. The lines on her forehead softened and she smiled weakly. "You had me really scared for a minute."

"Tell me something, Matthew," I said. "Could this person have called in that tip to take suspicion away from herself?"

"She might have," said Matthew, confirming what I really wanted to know, that the caller was a woman. Interesting. I wondered if the person who called the tip line could have mistaken Emma for Jenny. I pictured her and Jenny standing side by side. Both were tall. Both were thin. And with the blond streaks Jenny had recently gotten, her hair was more blond than brown.

"One more thing," I said. "Did anybody hear the shots?"

He shook his head. "Not a soul. If they had, we'd know the exact time McDermott was killed. Turns out the shots were muffled."

I gasped. "The killer used a silencer?" That conjured up images of gangland killings, Mafia or organized crime.

"In a matter of speaking," he said. "The police found a bunch of bar towels nearby. They were full of holes and gunshot residue. Apparently, the killer wrapped them around the gun. This not only muffled the shot, but it also protected him from residue."

"That doesn't tell us much. Anybody who watches TV could have known to do that."

I glanced at Jenny. She was sitting on the edge of her seat, just itching to say something. She gave me a pleading look. I wasn't sure what she was trying to say, but I suspected she wanted me to tell Matthew about McDermott's photo studio. I gave her a small head shake. She sighed and shrugged, as if to say, "your call."

It wasn't that I was planning to keep it from him. I would definitely tell him, just not right now. The minute I did, he'd be obligated to tell the police. I wanted to help poor Emma, so much so, in fact, that now I was even considering snatching those nude photos of her if they were there. She'd made a valid point. They were hers, after all.

This thought led to me to another question. How probable was it that the police already knew about the existence of this studio? McDermott had kept the place a secret from his wife, so they wouldn't have learned about it from her. As for Emma, she had every reason to keep the information to herself. There was always the possibility that somebody else had already informed the cops. But not likely. If I wanted to search the place, I'd have to do it tonight. Tomorrow would already be too late.

Call me crazy, but suddenly I was eager to get going. If McDermott kept his studio a secret from his wife, he was hiding something. I had no idea what I might find, other than Emma's photos. *I must be spending too much time with Jenny,* I thought, because I had a strong *feeling* there had to be more in that studio than a few embarrassing photos. The question was, what had McDermott really been hiding?

Chapter 6

At last the bottle was empty, the last drop of wine in every glass drunk. I dared hope Jenny and Matthew would now leave so I could set my plan into motion. I jumped to my feet and picked up the glasses.

"I'll take these back to the kitchen," I said.

"Not so fast," Jenny said. "How about we open another bottle? My treat. I'll replace it tomorrow."

I hesitated. "I'm sorry, guys. I hope you don't mind if I make this an early evening. Maybe it's the shock of finding the body, but I'm wiped. I can hardly keep my eyes open." I yawned deeply as proof.

Jenny stared at me, puzzled.

"That's okay," Matthew said, jumping to his feet. "It's totally normal under the circumstances. I should have thought of it myself." He turned to Jenny. "I don't know about you, but I'm getting a bit hungry. Want to join me for a bite at Bottoms Up?" He looked at me. "You too, Della."

"Maybe another time," I said, yawning again. "I'm going straight to bed."

Jenny threw me an incredulous look. *I* was turning

down an invitation from *Matthew*. No wonder she was confused. To my delight, Matthew looked disappointed. Maybe I should make a point of turning down his invitations once in a while. He might appreciate me more than when I always accept.

"I'll call Ed," Jenny said. "If he finishes early, he might be able to join us." She punched her boyfriend's number into her cell phone, and a few seconds later she hung up, grinning from ear to ear. "He agreed to meet us. He'll be there in fifteen or twenty minutes. Are you sure you don't want to come, Della?"

"How about I take a rain check on that?" To Matthew, I said, "You can leave Winston with me if you like. That way you don't have to detour by your place. You can pick him up tomorrow afternoon, same as usual."

"Good idea." Matthew patted Winston's head. "See you tomorrow, buddy." I walked them to the door, faking a few more yawns and squashing my guilt for deceiving my friends. Poor Emma. She needed somebody to help her. The second the door closed behind them, I sprang into action.

"Let's go, Winston." He followed me to my bedroom, where he plopped onto the cushion I kept in the corner for him. I tore into a pair of black jeans, grabbed a black turtleneck, and rummaged through the bottom of my closet until I located my running shoes. I knew I'd bought those for a reason. After I pulled my hair back into a ponytail, it occurred to me that I was now dressed as a cat burglar. Great. If anybody spotted me going in, they'd think I was up to no good, which I was—sort of. I hesitated, as the full impact of what I was about to do hit me. Nobody would see me. I'd make sure of it. I hurried to the kitchen and grabbed a flashlight from my catchall drawer.

There is nothing like doing something you know is wrong to make you paranoid. At the bottom of the stairs, I stopped. What if Matthew had guessed my little ploy and was now lying in wait? I stuck my head outside, glancing both ways—no sign of him. I took off, sprinting around the building to the lane where I parked my Jeep. I had no sooner hopped in than I stopped again. What if somebody in Belmont noticed my Jeep? It was candy-apple red, not exactly an inconspicuous color. Supposing the cops suspected me of trespassing, what excuse could I have for being in Belmont? On the other hand, taking a cab would be more dangerous. A driver could later recognize me and testify against me. I had to use my car or not go at all. And since that was out of the question, I turned on the motor and drove out.

Everything would turn out fine, I told myself over and over. And it might have been, except that by the time I was halfway there, my steering wheel suddenly began to vibrate. It wasn't much more than a slight tremor at first, but the faster I drove, the worse it got, and it didn't disappear until I slowed to less than thirty miles an hour. I pulled to the side of the road and checked my tires—no flats. I hopped back in and settled for a speed somewhere between shaking like crazy and perfectly smooth. I checked the speedometer again—forty miles an hour. *Crap!* I'd be lucky if I didn't get a ticket for driving too slow.

I entered the Belmont city limits and cruised along until I spotted the place. It was a typical old-fashioned commercial building not unlike my own, with a business on the first floor and residential apartments above. I slowed as I drove by, then turned and went by again. At the street level was a camera shop—*how appropriate*. I looked upstairs, making certain all the lights were out. They were. *So far, so good.*

I drove on, turning left at the first corner and then right. I pulled to a stop on a quiet residential street, where my Jeep would hopefully go unnoticed among half a dozen other parked cars. I hopped out and forced myself to walk slowly. I hoped that to any passersby I looked like just another person out for an evening stroll.

In front of the building, I glanced up and down the street quickly—no police vehicles anywhere. As for witnesses, the only people I could see were a block or two down the street, nowhere close enough to later be able to identify me.

I slipped the key into the lock and almost fell on my face as the door swung open on its own. Why would the door be unlocked? Was there already someone up there? I slipped inside, my heart thudding hard against my ribs, and listened. Nothing. I took a steadying breath and tiptoed up the stairs slowly, all my senses on high alert. If I heard as much as fly go by, I would be out of there. I reached the landing and stopped again, trying to get my bearings. I was already inside the studio, I realized. That meant it took up the entire upper floor of the building. I could make out a shape—the outline of a chair.

Suddenly, the dark shadow moved. It wasn't a chair at all, but a person in a crouch. He thudded into me hard, and I went sprawling to the floor. I leaped back up, looking about frantically. Footsteps were racing down the stairs. The intruder was already on his way out. A second later, the downstairs door slammed shut. A reverberating silence followed.

My pulse slowed until I felt pretty sure that I might not die of a heart attack after all. But I had to get out of here fast. Whoever had run out could come back any minute. I groped my way toward the stairs and was halfway down when I stopped. Whoever that was, he was long gone. I had probably scared him as much as he had me. *He*? Why had I automatically thought it was a man? And then I noticed the smell of aftershave, a detail my subconscious had obviously picked up before I'd become aware of it.

Other than the fact that this person was a man, I knew nothing. What had he been after? Was he looking for photos? Or did he want something else? I stood still and thought. There was no way I was going to leave without at least taking a quick look around. I climbed back up.

I felt my way along the wall until I reached the windows. They were covered in thick feltlike fabric—blackout drapes. I made sure they were tightly closed, and when I was certain that none of the outside light shone through, I turned on my flashlight and swung the beam around.

The studio was the size of a bachelor apartment. Against one wall was a roll of white background paper stretching from floor to ceiling. Photo lights were everywhere—spotlights, umbrella lights and floodlights. There were power packs and camera stands, and the floor was a jungle of cables. McDermott must have spent a fortune on his hobby. How did he explain to his wife where all that money was going? Could she really have been oblivious to it? I found that hard to believe.

Along the opposite wall was a plush reclining chair, which conjured up images of nude models posing seductively. I looked around for cameras or photos, but there were none that I could see. How strange, so much lighting equipment and not a single camera or photo, not even a file cabinet where they might have been stored. *Probably in the darkroom.* I spotted two doors along the far wall and I tried the first. I shone my light around the floor and caught a dozen or so silverfish running around the base of a toilet. *Yuck.* This bathroom needed a good scrubbing. I shut the door, disgusted, and tried the next one. I swept the beam of light around. It was a small galley-type kitchen. On one counter were two plastic containers filled with liquid. Developing solutions. Above stretched a clothesline from which hung a dozen or so photos. I stepped closer. Each was a picture of Emma in various stages of undress, Emma posing, pouty and sultry, reclining on the chaise I'd noticed. I focused the beam of light on one of the pictures. It was seductive, yet innocent. For all her curves and the maturity of her body, Emma had a childlike innocence about her. Her expression was sweet, trying to look sexy and not quite succeeding. Nobody could have called those pictures pornographic. Still, I could understand her not wanting them to get around, especially in a small town, where the morals were more rigid. I was about to grab them when I stopped. I had somehow lulled myself into believing I could take them, but now that I was faced with it, I was hesitating. Before making up my mind one way or another, there was something I wanted to do.

I moved on to a stack of photos at the far end of the counter. *I should have brought gloves.* I glanced around for something to use and tore a paper napkin off a roll, using it to riffle through the photos. There were dozens of different girls, and judging by the makeup and hairstyles, some were as old as twenty years or more. I paused at one picture of a young brunette with a rather large nose and full lips. She reminded me of someone. But who, I couldn't say. I flipped through the next few pictures, none of which were of the brunette.

I continued through the stack, pausing at another picture. This one was different, not a nude shot at all, but that of a couple sitting close to each other and gazing into each other's eyes. And then I recognized the woman—*oh my*—Mrs. Anderson, the mayor's wife. I'd had only a quick glimpse of her at the party, but there was no question that this was her. And the man with her was none other than Mr. Whitby, who was running for governor. I flipped through a few more shots, all of which were of Mrs. Anderson and Whitby. *What do you know? The mayor's wife was involved with Bernard Whitby.*

I studied the pictures some more and, judging by her hair and makeup, concluded that the shot was at least ten years old, maybe older. That explained it. The Andersons were probably not even married at the time. Suddenly, I heard something. It was just a slight creak, but it told me that somebody else was in the studio. I dropped the stack of pictures, slipped the paper napkin into my pocket and ran out so fast that whoever was there couldn't have seen more than a blur. That's if the lights were on—which they were not.

Chapter 7

I drove out of Belmont like a bat out of hell, or rather, like a bat in a martini shaker, and didn't slow down until I was halfway back to Briar Hollow. Only then did I take the pressure off the gas pedal, slowing down to thirty. I prayed I wouldn't be pulled over by the cops.

Who had come into the studio? Was it the same man who had knocked me down? Or was it someone new? The only thing I was certain of was that whoever it was had no more business in there than I did. Otherwise they would have turned on the light.

As I got closer to Briar Hollow my thoughts moved on to the pictures I'd seen. The mayor's wife and Bernard Whitby—I still couldn't believe it. It made me wonder if the person who had crashed into me had been sent to destroy those pictures. Damn! I suddenly realized that in my panic, I'd forgotten all about Emma's pictures.

What was I supposed to do now? There was no way I was going back. Another thing occurred to me. The police should be told about that studio. Should I call them with an anonymous tip? Or say nothing and hope somebody else did?

By the time I reached the town limits of Briar Hollow I had decided to leave it all up to Matthew, and I headed for Bottoms Up, where he, Ed and Jenny had gone. I needed to calm down, and time with my friends would be perfect. With any luck, they'd still be there.

Bottoms Up was Briar Hollows's foremost restaurant. Their menu used to offer everything from Thai to Chinese to French to Japanese and Italian, most of which was barely edible. But they had recently hired a new cook and changed their menu to good, old-fashioned home cooking. And their desserts were to die for.

I walked in and stood still while my eyes adjusted. Before me was a bar that ran the length of the entire far wall. On one side of the cavernous room was a pool table, which was surrounded—as always—with a rowdy group of men. On the other side was the main dining area. That was where I headed, my eyes darting around for my friends. I discovered them sitting at a table near the window, Matthew on one side of the table and Jenny and Ed on the other.

"Della, what are you doing here?" Jenny asked when she spotted me.

"I couldn't sleep, so decided to join you. Am I too late for dessert?"

Matthew hopped to his feet, pulling out a chair for me. "Are you sure you only want dessert? If you're hungry, order something. We'll keep you company until you're finished."

"I would love to stay, but my shift is starting in an hour," Ed said apologetically.

"Don't worry. I really only want a piece of cherry pie and ice cream." I smiled at Jenny and winked. "I'm happy your boyfriend gets an evening off once in a while."

He looked at Jenny, smiling. "She's the only person who can pull me away from my ER."

"Did you hear that? '*My* ER' he says. He really believes he's the only doctor capable of saving lives. When he's not there, the entire system falls apart."

"Trust me, it does," he said, grinning.

Matthew raised a hand and waved, catching the waiter's attention. He turned back to me. "Cherry pie? Each time we come here, that's what you order. Have you ever had anything else from this menu?"

"A couple of times. They make great fried chicken and biscuits. But I like their pie. What can I say? I'm a girl of simple tastes. When I like something, I like it for life."

"Does that go for love too?" he asked with a teasing glint in his eyes.

I felt myself blush, but answered casually. "When I fall in love, it will be for life."

"Whoever he is, he'll be a lucky guy." He leaned back and studied me over the rim of his wineglass.

I looked at Jenny, but she shrugged, smiling casually. Had she said something to him? If she had, I would so kill her.

"So what have I missed?" I asked, suddenly in a rush to change the subject. "Anything interesting?"

"You missed an amazing pot roast," she said, looking toward the waiter a few tables away. "Thank goodness they got that new chef."

The waiter, a big burly guy with curly red hair, ambled over. "Hey there, Della. What can I do you for? I have a great pot roast on special tonight. I also have fried liver with bacon and onions and chicken cordon blue."

"I'll have the usual."

"Cherry pie and ice cream," he said, jotting it down. "And a cup of coffee. It'll be ready in two minutes." He took off.

Matthew slid out of his seat. "I'll be right back," he said and headed for the washrooms.

As soon as he was out of earshot, I leaned in to Jenny and whispered so Ed would not hear. "What did you say to him?"

"What are you talking about? I didn't say anything."

"Then why was he making those comments about me falling in love?"

She raised her brows. "How would I know? Ask him, not me."

"What are you two gossiping about?" Ed asked.

Jenny turned to him and gave him a smile. "Just girl talk. Della wants to know how to get a man to ask her out."

Ed laughed. "Easy. Get him to talk about himself, bat your eyes and listen in rapt attention. That should do it." He grinned. "Is there anybody in particular you're hoping to attract?"

I prayed this conversation would end before Matthew's return. I forced a teasing smile. "I was asking because I was wondering what trick Jenny used to catch you."

He looked at Jenny adoringly. "Ah, well, that's different. She didn't have to do a thing. It was love at first sight."

Jenny gave him a peck on the cheek. "Isn't he the best?"

Matthew came strolling back just as the waiter returned with my order. "Here you go. Enjoy." He set the plate before me and took off.

I was halfway through my pie when Jenny and Ed excused themselves and left. Matthew waited until they had walked out and then turned to me. "Now, tell me the truth. What were you really up to tonight?"

I gave him my most guileless look. "I have no idea what you're talking about."

"Don't play innocent with me, Della Wright. Did you really think I'd fall for your whole 'I'm so tired' routine? You never go to bed early. And you never turn down an invitation to dinner. And you never, ever wear flats, and here you are, not two hours later, dressed like a cat burglar and wearing running shoes." He crossed his arms. "Out with it."

I scrambled for a way to tell him without sending him into an apoplectic fit. Since I'd moved to Briar Hollow, I'd gone clue hunting a few times, and I had gotten hell from Matthew for it. As a criminologist, he was a stickler for the law. One time he'd been horrified to learn that I'd, as he put it, "tampered with evidence."

Granted, that was exactly what I had done. But, as I'd pointed out, I was only trying to get at the truth. And I had succeeded. Remembering that episode, I was almost grateful I hadn't taken Emma's pictures after all. I just hoped she wouldn't be too disappointed.

He glared at me. "Are you going to sit there and shovel pie into your mouth all evening, or are you going to give me an answer?"

I rolled my eyes. "First of all, I am not shoveling. I am eating. And second, I was about to tell you. I was just deciding *how* I should tell you."

"How about you start from the beginning?"

So, for the second time that day, I recounted Emma's visit and her request that I stop by McDermott's photo studio.

Matthew choked on his coffee. When he recovered, he glared at me. "Please tell me you didn't go."

At that moment, the waiter returned and refilled our cups, during which time Matthew struggled to remain calm. Meanwhile, I was seriously considering lying. The waiter left and Matthew said, "At least tell me you didn't steal any of the pictures."

I threw him a reassuring smile. "Steal a picture? Me? How can you even ask? I left everything exactly as it was." I took a bite of pie, wondering if I should tell him about the man who'd sent me sprawling. And about the second intruder—or third, if I counted myself as one. "But I think somebody else might have."

"Might have what?"

"Might have stolen some pictures." He looked at me

suspiciously, and I explained. "Somebody else was in there when I walked in. He ran by me so fast he knocked me down."

"Della!" he said, gasping. "You could have gotten hurt, killed even. What if that was the murderer?" He was looking at me with such concern. And then he continued. "Forget what I said earlier. Any man who falls in love with you should get his head examined. You, my dear, are nothing but trouble."

I covered my dismay with a laugh.

"Did you happen to see his face?"

I shook my head. "I smelled his aftershave. I might recognize it if I came across it again." I told him the rest of the story.

"Another person! You're lucky you're still alive." He gave his head a shake. "Are you absolutely sure neither of those people saw you?" He scowled at me. "If either of them was the killer and they think you might be able to identify them, you could be in serious danger. Witnesses have a way of turning up dead." Seeing the fear in my eyes, he softened his tone. "Della, I'm not trying to give you a hard time. I just want you to be careful. You can't go around taking chances the way you do. One of these days you'll find yourself in jail—or worse, dead."

I nodded. "You're right, of course."

"Promise me you'll never do anything stupid like that again?" he asked. And then before I answered, he continued. "Forget it. Even if you gave me your word, you'd only break it."

I have him my most earnest look. "I promise to be more careful in the future."

He sighed, obviously not believing me. "All right. Now give me the address of the studio—and the key."

"Under one condition."

He gave me a hard look. "What's the condition?"

"I don't want the police to know I gave you the information."

He crossed his arms and leaned against the back of his chair. "You know I can't do that."

"Why not? The police have confidential informants all the time."

"I'm not the police."

"You can argue that since you help them on cases, you having a private informant is to their own benefit."

His glare melted into a mocking grin, and I knew I'd just won my argument. He threw some money on the table and rose. "Ready to go?"

I nodded, and a minute later we parted in the parking lot, but not before he gave me another piece of advice, this one, to make sure my door was locked tonight. I went home, shaken up by his warning. What if someone *had* recognized me? I'd been so worried about being stopped by the police that it had never occurred to me to be afraid of anyone else.

I got home, filled Winston's water bowl, patted him on the head and climbed into bed, wishing Matthew would have decided to protect me in person rather than with a piece of advice.

I was half asleep when I realized I had completely forgotten about the Anderson-Whitby photos.

Chapter 8

The next morning when I stepped into my store, I was surprised to find the message light on my answering machine blinking.

"Come, Winston." He lumbered over to his cushion behind the counter, and I pushed the playback button.

I had not one, but two messages, both from Bunny. "Hi, Della, I'm sorry to call you after hours. I'm hoping you'll get this message tonight. If you do, please call me back." I took down the phone number and moved on to the next message. "Hi again, Della. I don't know what time you open in the morning, but I just want you to know that I need to see some samples of the hand-woven fabric for the master bedroom chairs as soon as possible. Tomorrow, if possible."

Bunny had left the message last night. "Tomorrow" meant today. I erased the messages and picked up the phone. This time it was my turn to get her voice mail.

"Hi, Bunny. I just got your messages. I started working on those samples yesterday, and I should have two, maybe three, ready to show you by the end of the day." I hung up and hurried over to my loom. The sample I'd started sat half finished. I settled before the loom and picked up where I'd left off. Before long, I was walking the pedals rhythmically while throwing the shuttle from hand to hand.

The bell above the door tinkled. I looked up to see Jenny walking in wearing a glowing smile.

"Hey, aren't you the busy bee?" she said.

"You sure look like a happy lady," I said. "I thought the good doctor had a night shift, but looking at you now, I suspect that might have been a fib."

Jenny blushed and hurried through to the back, ignoring my comment. Instead, she called, "How about a cup of tea?"

I chuckled to myself. It had become a daily routine. She offered tea. I requested coffee. "I'll have the usual, thanks."

"Coming right up."

The phone rang. I put down my shuttle and picked it up. As I half expected, the call was from Emma. "Hi, Della. I'm just wondering if you had a chance to—you know—drop by the studio."

"I did go. But I'm afraid it was a waste of a trip. I did see your pictures. But somebody else came in while I was there. I just ran out and I'm afraid the pictures stayed behind."

There was a groan at the other end of the line. "Oh, God, Della. You could have gotten hurt. I'm so sorry I asked you to do that. It was really stupid of me."

"Don't worry about it. I'm here now and that's all that counts. If it's any consolation to you, I thought the pictures were lovely—not at all something to be ashamed of."

"Thank you for saying that. It's just . . ." There was a long pause, and I knew she was thinking about Ricky. "Do you have any idea who was there?"

"I have no idea. I never saw his face."

Her voice quavered. "It couldn't have been Ricky, could it?"

"You would know that better than me. Do you think he might have known about the studio?"

"I told him a photographer was taking pictures of me, but not about me posing nude." She was quiet for a long time. "It had to be somebody else. He would never do something like that."

"Emma, I need to ask you something," I said. "Yesterday, did you happen to walk by the Coffee Break around eight o'clock in the morning?"

"I didn't walk *by* it," she said. "I was on my way to Al's Garage to drop off Ricky's lunch, same as I do every morning. Ever since that scene Mrs. McDermott made, I won't even go past the shop without crossing the street."

"So what you're telling me is that you did walk by, but on the other side of the street."

"Yes," she said hesitantly. "Why do you ask?"

"No reason," I said, and turned the subject back to her photos. "Emma, my fear is that Ricky will find out about those pictures."

"I know," she said in a tone steeped in worry.

"Please let me know if there's anything I can do," I said. "I worry about you."

"That's sweet," she said. "But Ricky wouldn't hurt me." I wasn't convinced.

After we hung up, I got back to work, mulling over

what I knew of the murder as I wove. By the time Jenny returned with a hot cup of coffee, I was no closer to figuring out who was the most likely killer.

"Thanks." I put down my shuttle and took the cup. "Tell me something. What do you know about the Andersons?"

"The Andersons?" she repeated blankly.

"The mayor of Belmont and his wife."

"Oh, them." She shrugged. "I don't know much about them, except what everybody in town knows—that he'll be announcing his own candidacy for the gubernatorial elections, which is why I was surprised to see them at Bernard Whitby's party." She studied me. "Why do you ask?"

"I wasn't exactly honest with you last night when I said I was going to bed early."

She laughed. "I knew that. You would never turn down a date with Matthew unless you had something important to do."

"That wasn't a date."

"Well, what else would you call it? I was there with Ed, and you would have been there with Matthew." She studied me. "Sometimes I wonder if you really do want Matthew to fall in love with you. For every step he takes toward you, you take three giant steps back."

"I do no such thing." She gave me the eyebrow. "Well, I did have something important to do, and it couldn't be put off."

She planted a hand on her hip and gave me the eyebrow. "Like what? Or is it something I don't want to know?"

I told her.

"You broke in?" She stared at me with her mouth open. "That was dangerous. You could have gotten yourself killed."

"I didn't *break* in. I had a key, which I didn't even need in the end. Besides, nothing happened. But guess what. Not only were there nude pictures of half a dozen different models, but there were also pictures of Mrs. Anderson having dinner with Bernard Whitby. They didn't look recent, but it made me wonder how long she and her husband have been married."

"At least twenty-five years. They had an anniversary party a while back. It was covered by the *Belmont Daily*."

I gasped.

"What?"

"Call me crazy, but the case just took on an entirely new angle." She looked at me, puzzled. "A political angle—and I have two new suspects." I was talking to myself, trying my suspicions out loud. "I have no idea whether Mrs. Anderson and Bernard Whitby are still involved—probably not, but regardless, if news of her having an affair got out, I imagine it could be quite a disaster for her husband. Some people might kill to avoid that kind of scandal, especially if there was a danger of it harming their political career."

"You're crazy. You know that, don't you?"

"You can call me crazy all you want, but somebody killed McDermott. And whoever it was had a motive." I stopped. There was another possible new suspect I hadn't thought of. As much as a politician might kill to avoid a scandal, a political adversary might kill to start it.

I flashed back to the present when the bell above the door tinkled. It was one of Jenny's regular customers.

"Good morning, Mrs. Drummond," she greeted the woman, then escorted her customer to the back, throwing me a backward glance. She still thought I was nuts, which was fine by me. I thought she was nuts often enough too. I gave Winston a liver treat and returned to my weaving.

I now had five suspects, six if I counted Bernard Whitby. There were Emma, Ricky, Rhonda McDermott, the woman Philip McDermott was having an affair with, and Mr. and Mrs. Anderson. As for Whitby, I couldn't see why he would even care about those old pictures. He was a bachelor. If anybody found out he'd had an affair with Anderson's wife, so what? It wouldn't hurt his reputation. But it might well hurt Mrs. Anderson's, and he wouldn't mind that one bit, now, would he? So make that seven suspects.

The first thing I wanted to do was find out more about Emma's boyfriend. But how? I was throwing the shuttle back and forth when it suddenly hit me. Emma had mentioned that Ricky worked as a car mechanic at Al's Garage up the street, and my car needed fixing. What better way to strike up a conversation? I glanced at my watch. It was only twenty past eight, and my shop wouldn't be officially open until ten. I usually spent the first two hours of my day taking inventory, fixing displays and weaving. I'd gotten into the habit of coming in early because, even though Jenny was no more than ten yards away, I didn't feel comfortable leaving my shop without supervision with her clients walking through.

As if in answer to my problem, the doorbell rang and Marnie came in, carrying boxes of pastry.

"Marnie, can you do me a favor?"

"Sure, sugar pie. What would you like?"

She was in a good mood this morning. Great. "Can you keep an eye on things for a few minutes while I take my Jeep to the garage?"

"No problem. Just let me drop these off to Jenny." She made her way over to her shop. A few minutes later she was back, waving me off with a, "Take your time, sweetie. I won't charge much."

I stifled a laugh. Knowing Marnie, she would use this as an opportunity to wheedle a part-time job out of me—as if she didn't already have enough to do with her weaving for me and baking for Jenny.

I hurried out back to my Jeep and drove off. Minutes later I drove into Al's Garage, pulling up in front of an empty bay. A fat mechanic in grease-covered overalls ambled over, wrench in hand—Al.

"Yeah," he said.

"Ricky works here, doesn't he?"

"Yeah," he said again—a man of few words.

"If you don't mind, since I already know him, I'd like to deal with him."

He shrugged and walked away, hollering, "Ricky." The young man popped his head out from under a car hood. "Some dame for you," Al said. Ricky came forth, looking suspicious.

"Hi, Ricky. I'm Della Wright. Emma introduced us at the party the other night." He nodded imperceptibly. "I hear you're a good car mechanic."

He moved closer, relaxing somewhat. "You got some problem with your car?"

"It vibrates when I drive any faster than thirty miles an hour."

He nodded. "Sounds like it needs a wheel balancing, but I'll check it out, make sure it ain't nothing worse." He opened his hand for the car key, and I gave it to him. "You'll have to come by the office to fill out the form."

I followed him into a small and filthy room with a Formica counter covered with cigarette burns. In what was the waiting area was a row of torn vinyl-covered chairs. On a coffee table was a stack of old *Playboy* magazines. I suppressed a shudder and took the pen he offered me, wondering what kind of germs I might be getting.

"Fill in everything at the top," he said. "Name, address, phone number, credit card information. And I can do the rest."

I jotted down the required information and handed the form back. "So you're Emma's boyfriend," I said, for lack of a better way to start the conversation.

He nodded, saying nothing, and started filling in the spaces at the bottom of the form.

"How long have you two been together?"

He glanced up from the form. "A couple of years. Why do you care?"

I shrugged. "I just think you're a lucky guy. She's so beautiful. Has she ever thought of taking up modeling?"

He put the pen down, placed his hands on the counter and glared at me. "Don't you go putting any stupid ideas in her head. Emma is perfectly happy right here in Briar Hollow, with me. It's hard enough to keep her out of trouble here. I'd never be able to protect her in the city."

"What do you mean?" I asked. He looked at me blankly. "What kind of trouble can a girl possibly get into in a small town like Briar Hollow?"

He scowled, and for a moment I thought he was going to ignore my question. "Some damn photographer got her all excited about taking pictures." And then, as if he knew he'd already said too much, he tightened his lips and finished filling out the form. "I'll call you just as soon as I've looked at it and let you know what's wrong and how much it'll cost to fix."

There were many more questions I would have liked to ask, but something about Ricky frightened me. I could just imagine him holding a gun to a man. I could even picture him pulling the trigger.

I thanked him and got the heck out of there.

I walked back to the store, grappling with what Ricky had just said. He knew Emma wanted to model. He knew a photographer had taken pictures of her. And he said he protected her. How exactly did he do this? By killing the photographer? Or by breaking into his studio to grab Emma's pictures? Those were certainly possibilities, but I wasn't even certain he knew the photographer was McDermott. Emma might not have told him his identity. On the other hand, I wouldn't put it past him—possessive as he was—to have secretly followed her. I somehow suspected he was the intruder who had rammed into me last night. If I was correct, that probably meant I had interrupted him before he found her pictures. I stopped. I had completely forgotten about the aftershave. I should have noticed whether Ricky smelled of aftershave or men's cologne. On the other hand, the smell of oil and gasoline from the garage had been so strong, I probably couldn't have smelled it if I tried. I walked on.

I pushed open the door to the sound of the tinkling bell. From behind the desk, Marnie looked up, grinning. "Welcome to Dream Weaver," she said. "Can I help you with anything?"

I played along. "Thanks, but I just want to look around."

Marnie chuckled. "Gee, thanks. That's the same reply I got since you left."

"At least that means some people came in." I walked over to the counter, peeling off my sweater.

"Yes," she said, excitedly. "Mrs. Anderson, the mayor of Belmont's wife, came in and made a purchase. She was disappointed you weren't here, but I sold her that extra-long tablecloth that was in the window display."

"You did?" That was one of the most expensive items I had in the store. "For full price?"

Marnie beamed. "For full price—look." She proudly showed me the sales slip. "So, what do you say? Can I come and work for you a few mornings a week?"

"How do you propose to do that and still find the time to continue baking for Jenny and weaving for the shop?"

"I can do it, no problem," she said eagerly. "At my age, not only do I have to deal with hot flashes, but now I also have insomnia. So I stay up most of the night anyhow—baking and weaving. I have plenty of time on my hands."

"In that case, how about you weave me more place mats?"

She tilted her head. "Actually, I just noticed you're almost out of them again. You really sell out of those fast."

"Told you." Seeing how hopeful she looked, I continued. "I can't afford to pay a regular employee, but whenever I need to do some errands, I promise I'll call you to come in. And the minute I need regular help, you'll be the first person I ask."

She slumped and then snapped back up. "I have an idea. Why don't I come in a few mornings a week without you having to pay me? I'll just sit and weave. Don't you think it would be interesting for customers to see weaving actually being done?"

"It would," I said slowly. "But why would you want to come in without getting paid?"

"Why? Because I'm lonely, that's why," she said. "I like baking and weaving, but those are things I can only do indoors. Sometimes I go days without seeing a soul. At least if I do some of my weaving here, I'll be seeing people and having conversations."

I'd had no idea she felt that way. Still, I wasn't totally surprised. Marnie could be very pleasant when she wanted to be, but she was known to be irritable at times. That might explain why she didn't have a very busy social life. "Of course. If it'll make you happy, I have no problem with you being here—as long as you behave."

"If you mean you want me to smile at customers instead of barking at them, I promise."

"In that case, we'll get along just great."

Marnie got her purse from behind the counter, blew me a kiss and headed for the door. "I'll go get my portable looms and yarns, and I'll start working on more place mats right away. See you soon." She walked out with a bounce to her step. To my surprise, an hour later she was back.

"You wouldn't happen to have a fan around here, would you?" she asked, looking flustered.

"Eh, I gave my fans to Matthew when I moved out. I didn't think I'd need any until next summer." I noticed how flushed she was, a fine mist of moisture on her forehead.

"Darn menopause. I get hot flashes no matter what the temperature."

"Tell you what. If you mind the store, I'll just run out and pick up a fan or two at Mercantile's. I noticed they had them on sale—getting rid of them in the off-season," I said. "I might as well get them now rather than wait till next summer when they'll be full price."

"If you wouldn't mind," she said, fanning herself with her hands.

Mercantile's was the local general store, founded almost a hundred years ago. In all that time, it had hardly changed. It still sold tractor wheels, overalls and tools at one end of the store, kitchen pots and pans and enamelware at the other and fresh farm eggs and jars of homemade jams and jellies from behind the counter.

It was a miracle the store had survived these modern times. On the other hand, perhaps people enjoyed strolling through and purchasing items that looked as if they belonged in another century.

I was debating between models of fans when I sensed somebody nearby. I looked over to see Mrs. Anderson standing by and watching me.

I nodded a hello, and she moved closer. The woman was beautiful. She was in her midforties, with soft makeup and red hair coiffed in a simple bob.

Her eyes flickered nervously left and right. She whispered, "I understand that you helped the police solve a murder recently."

"I don't know that the police would agree with that statement," I said. "I think they saw me as more of a hindrance than a help."

She glanced around once again, and it struck me that she looked more afraid than nervous. She said, "I wonder if you would take on a little job for me. I'll pay you very generously."

Something told me she wasn't talking about a weaving project. "What kind of a job are you talking about?"

She glanced over her shoulder once more, and in a low voice she told me, "Somebody has taken some compromising photos of me—photos that could cause my husband a lot of embarrassment and potentially even his political career."

Oh, my God! It had finally happened. Somebody wanted to hire me as a private detective. I didn't know whether to laugh or cry.

"Mrs. Anderson, I think you'd be much better off hiring a professional to do something like that. I'm a weaver."

She shook her head. "No. Don't you see? I can't do that. I can't trust an investigator. But you, as a woman, I know I could trust."

Why she would trust me more than an investigator, I had no idea. "Mrs. Anderson, honestly, I would love to help you, but I can't. It would be illegal."

She looked almost panicked. "You don't even know what I want you to do."

"What is it?"

"This person was blackmailing me," she whispered.

I gasped out loud. "Blackmail?"

"Not so loud," she said, and then she closed her eyes in shame and nodded. "But now the blackmailer is dead, and that means as soon as the police find those pictures, everybody will know about them. I really need to get them back before they're found. I don't want my husband to find out." She looked so miserable that my heart went out to her.

I suddenly understood what she meant about "trusting me as a woman." I sympathized. I really felt sorry for her. But these were emotions I couldn't afford. There was a killer loose in town, and I wasn't about to allow my sentiments to stand in the way of discovering the truth. I kept my voice low. "I suppose you're talking about Mr. McDermott?"

She nodded slightly, her eyes holding mine. "I had nothing to do with his death. You must believe me."

"Mrs. Anderson, if those photos were in his studio, it's already too late. The police already know. They are probably there as we speak."

She blanched. "I see." She raised her head, threw her shoulders back and plastered on a smile. "I assume you will be discreet about my request?"

I answered circumspectly. "If I'm questioned, I won't lie."

"Fair enough," she said, and walked out with her head high.

There goes a lady with a secret, I thought, realizing that since her husband didn't know, that took him off my suspects' list, but it also put her right at the top.

A store employee walked over, wearing a jovial smile. "Those are fifty percent off at the moment."

Fifteen minutes later, I walked out carrying a large box.

I got back to the shop just as a group of women was stepping out of Jenny's shop and into mine.

"Jeanine, come and see this," one of them called out to another. She was holding out a place mat. "Aren't these wonderful?"

Her friend went over and picked up another. "I love them. They would look wonderful on my dinner table." Before they left, between the two of them, they cleaned me out of place mats again.

Marnie walked over. "Good thing I'll be making more," she said, looking at the fan I was pulling out of the box.

"Where would you like it? Near your loom?"

"You can leave it behind the counter," she said. "The flashes seem to have gone for now."

Great, I thought. *I could have waited for my car to be fixed rather than lugging that heavy thing all the way here.*

The store became quiet again. Marnie returned to her loom, and I returned to mine and finished the second sample. When Bunny Boyd walked in a short time later, Marnie had just run back for a cup of coffee. I was clipping the third sample off my loom.

"Nice," Bunny said, inspecting them. "But these weren't made on your wide-width loom. How can I be certain the fabric will look the same if it's made on a different machine?"

"The heddles are the same distance apart as on my wide loom, so as long as the fabric is produced with the same yarn and the same tension, the results will be identical."

She nodded, still studying the samples. "You don't mind if I take these with me, do you?"

"Not at all."

She thanked me and folded them into her bag.

Before leaving, she paused, and glancing toward the back, she said, "Does the owner of the coffee shop— Jenny, right?—does she have anything to do with the McDermotts?"

"No," I said, surprised. "Why?"

"Oh, no reason really. It's just that I thought I saw her coming out of the coffee shop just before Mr. McDermott's body was found."

So Bunny Boyd had been the informant. I covered my surprise with a smile. "Actually, I suspect the person you saw was Emma Blanchard. She walks that way every morning, on her way to Al's Garage, where her boyfriend works."

"Really?" Bunny said. She shrugged. "Well, I suppose I was wrong." She threw me a wide smile. "I'll show these to Bernie and see if he likes them as much as I do."

If she could ask me questions, I didn't see why I shouldn't have some for her. "Did Mr. Whitby find out what happened to his missing gun?" I asked.

"You know about that?"

"A friend of mine was standing next to him when his butler told him. He overheard."

"Bernie is very upset over it. That gun is a valuable antique, from before the first world war, I think."

"It was a collector's piece? It didn't actually work?"

"Oh, it was functional, all right. Bernie took it out once a year just to test it. He does that with all his guns. They're worth much more when they're in working order."

That made sense. I adopted a pensive look. "I wonder who could have taken it. Do you know when he last saw it?"

"It was there just before the party. Whoever stole it had to break the lock to get it." She scowled. "Some people have no respect. Those showcases are valuable. Everything in that house is valuable. Do you have any idea how difficult it is to find good antique restorers?"

"If the gun was there when the party started, then it had to have been taken by one of the guests. Do you remember everyone who toured the house with you?"

"Are you kidding? I think every second person in the place took the tour. Everybody wanted to see the mansion. Bernie usually never allows anyone to the second floor, so this was a rare opportunity to visit a historical mansion." Suddenly she narrowed her eyes, looking at me with suspicion. "You're asking an awful lot of questions. Why would you want to know all that?"

I shrugged. "I'm sorry. My friends keep telling me to mind my own business, but I can't seem to curb my curiosity." And then I threw out one more hook. "I sure hope that poor Mr. McDermott wasn't killed with Mr. Whitby's gun."

Bunny's mouth tightened. "Let me tell you, nobody needs to sympathize with McDermott. That man was a creep. He got what he deserved." And with that, she turned and marched out of the store.

Well, well. Bunny Boyd didn't like the victim either. I stared at the door for a long time as a new possibility took form. Of all the people at the party, Bunny would have had the most opportunity to steal that gun. I couldn't help but wonder whether she only disliked the victim, or if her emotions went deeper than that. The next question was, did Bunny Boyd have a reason to want him dead? I found myself adding her to my growing list of suspects. Although it occurred to me that if she were guilty of killing Mc-

Dermott, she would probably not be this open about not liking him.

I picked up the phone and punched in Matthew's number. "What are you doing?" I asked when he picked up.

"Okay, out with it," he replied, a hint of mischief in his voice.

"What are you talking about?" I asked.

"I can think of one only reason why you would be calling me. What do you want to know?"

I chuckled. "I don't call only when I want something from you."

"Okay, so what—pray tell—is the reason for your call?"

"Actually," I said, now laughing out loud, "I do want something—information."

"I knew it."

"Have you told the police about McDermott's studio?"

He grew serious. "I went directly to the station after leaving the restaurant last night. They sent officers to search the place right away. I went along with them. And don't worry. I kept you out of it."

I breathed a silent sigh of relief. "Did they find anything?"

"You mean other than his collection of nude models? Nothing that I know of."

"Have they identified all the women in the pictures yet?"

"Ah, that's what this is all about. You're playing detective again, aren't you?"

"Not at all," I said, slightly incensed. "If you want to know, somebody just tried to hire me to do some detecting and I turned her down." The minute the words were out, I wanted to take them back. *Stupid, stupid, stupid.* Now he'd insist on me telling him everything.

Matthew was silent, which only made me feel worse because that meant I was in really deep trouble. At last he said, very quietly, "Della, don't you think you should tell me about this person? You said you wanted to be my informant. So please, tell me."

"Oh . . . er . . . sorry. I'll have to call you back. A customer just walked in." I hung up fast. I needed some time to think. The phone rang. *Matthew calling back,* I thought. I picked up.

"Mrs. Wright? Ricky here. About your Jeep, the problem is just what I figured. Your wheels need balancing." He quoted me a price, which I accepted, and he promised that I could pick up my Jeep in the morning. I thanked him and hung up.

By closing time, I was wondering how come Matthew hadn't called back. When I looked up, there he was at the door, looking very determined.

"Hey, Winnie," I said, "there's your daddy come to pick you up."

"We need to talk," Matthew said.

I was instantly filled with guilt. It wasn't as if I'd promised Mrs. Anderson that I would keep her request a secret, I reminded myself. But I had implied as much.

"Della?" He stared at me, hard.

What the heck. I had to tell him sometime. It might

as well be now. I threw him a smile. "How about you offer me a drink? I'll tell you all about it."

It was a beautiful, warm September day and the walk back to his place was pleasant—even though I knew what was waiting. Winston stopped and sniffed at every bush and every puddle along the way.

Matthew chuckled. "What is it, boy? Did some sexy little girl bulldog walk by? Is that what you smell?"

Winston threw him a dirty look, as if saying, "Mind your own business," and marched off in a huff.

I decided it would be a lot easier if I came clean without him having to pull every bit of information out of me. "It was Mrs. Anderson," I blurted without prompting.

Matthew swung his gaze to me. "Mrs. Anderson . . . as in the mayor's wife?"

I nodded. "One and the same."

His eyes had suddenly grown wide. "I think we'd better wait till we're inside to talk about this," he said, his pace picking up. A few minutes later, we reached his house.

Being a guest in Matthew's house—a house where I'd lived for nearly six months—felt odd. I had moved out only a month and a half ago. The decision had been an easy, albeit painful one. As much as I might have loved to continue sharing Matthew's home, it had proved impossible. During the short time we lived together, I was constantly censoring my words, controlling my behavior, always afraid of inadvertently revealing feelings he didn't reciprocate and in the process losing his friendship. I simply could not risk that.

He watched me. "I'm sure you hate how the house looks now."

The first change I'd made when I moved in was to cart all of his stuff upstairs to make room for my shop and weaving studio. Now it was all back where it belonged, including his ugly green recliner.

"Actually, it looks pretty good. That's new," I said, pointing at a leather sofa and matching armchair.

"You did such a great job with the place—the paint job and refinishing the hardwood floors. I decided some of my stuff wasn't nice enough anymore. So you don't hate it?"

I wasn't crazy about his brown leather furniture—*any* brown leather furniture for that matter—but he didn't need to know that. I pointed to the green chair. "I still think you should get rid of that monstrosity."

"Don't worry. You and Jenny gave me enough flack about it that I ordered a new one. It should be here in a couple of weeks." He headed for the kitchen, where he pulled a bottle of wine from the fridge and poured me a glass.

"Just to loosen your tongue," he said with smiling eyes.

My heart skipped a beat. "Thanks. Aren't you having some?"

He returned to the fridge and pulled out a Heineken. "I'd rather have a beer." He pulled off the cap and raised his bottle to me. "To my special informant." He took a swig and put his bottle down. Pulling back a chair, he dropped into it. "So, what did Mrs. Anderson want exactly?"

I plopped myself onto the leather sofa. "You won't believe this."

"Try me," he said.

And so I did. I repeated, as far as I could remember, everything she'd said, adding how nervous she'd looked, as if she thought she might be followed. "She said McDermott was blackmailing her, and now she's afraid if the pictures come out, it might cost her husband his political career."

"Holy shit," he said when I finished. "Blackmail and politics."

"Amazing, isn't it?"

He was thoughtful for a moment. "Well, Mrs. Anderson would have been disappointed. There were plenty of pictures, but none of her. Wherever he was keeping them, it wasn't at his studio."

I gasped. "You mean . . . the police didn't find any pictures of her?"

He shook his head. "None."

"But that's impossible."

He looked at me, frowning. "What are you talking about?"

"I saw them myself. They were there—in the dark-room. I went through the pile so fast, I looked at only a fraction of the pictures there, but there were at least half a dozen of hers there. She and Whitby were the only people other than Emma that I recognized."

"You're joking."

"I swear it's the truth."

"That means—"

"Somebody stole those pictures," I said, completing his thought.

We were both quiet as we digested this for a few minutes.

"Maybe the person who knocked me down went back and got them," I suggested.

He nodded. "But if that's what happened, whoever he was wasn't hired by Mrs. Anderson. She thought the pictures were still there."

"So who—"

"Mr. Anderson?"

I shook my head. "She was adamant about not wanting him to know."

He crinkled his forehead. "Whitby?"

"I thought about that, but Whitby is a bachelor. Even if those pictures came out, it wouldn't hurt his reputation. The only person who would suffer is Mrs. Anderson."

We discussed possibilities until one glass of wine turned into two and then into dinner. Matthew was no chef, but he was still a better cook than I was. He grilled a couple of steaks on the barbecue and served them with a tossed salad. Over our meal, we reviewed what we knew.

"So far we have eight suspects."

He frowned. "How do you figure that?"

I counted on my fingers. "Emma—" I paused. "Although I can't believe that girl is capable of murder."

"At this point we have to look at every possibility."

"And the girl did want those pictures back," I said.

He continued. "There's Ricky, Rhonda McDermott, and as you pointed out, Bunny. She did give a false tip about Jenny."

"Oh, I found out the explanation for that." I told him about my conversation with Emma. "She's the one Bunny saw and mistook for Jenny."

"I hate to point this out to you, but that now gives Emma not only a motive but also an opportunity. And then there's Mrs. Anderson and Mr. Anderson. And before you tell me that he didn't even know about the pictures, remember, we have only his wife's word on that. And Bernard Whitby makes seven. How do you get to eight?"

"There's also the woman McDermott was having the affair with. And for that matter, any woman who posed nude for him could have killed him."

He nodded. "Good point. The blackmail angle does explain one thing."

"What's that?"

"That photography hobby of his wasn't cheap. I couldn't quite figure out how he got the money to pay for the studio and all the equipment without his wife finding out."

"I wondered the same thing. I guess that could explain how he financed it." I crossed my arms and pondered a new idea. "How about this? If McDermott was blackmailing one person, he was probably blackmailing others. Did you see all the photos in his studio?"

Matthew leaned into the back of his chair. "The police allowed me to look at them. There were so many, I couldn't begin to go through them all. Some went back years, decades even."

"How can we get our hands on all of them? I'd like to try to identify the women."

"Forget that idea," he said. "There is no way the police will let those shots out of their hands. Besides, I don't want you more involved than you already are."

I'd pushed too hard, I realized, and now he wanted to end the subject. Sure enough, he glanced at his watch. "I don't mean to rush you, but I still have some writing to do."

I hopped off my chair. "Oh, of course. You're not rushing me. It's time I left anyhow."

He walked me to the door. Before stepping out, I turned and looked up at him. "I bet the police wouldn't mind some help in identifying those women."

He let out an exasperated sigh. "If they do, you're the last person they'd go to. You hardly know anyone in Briar Hollow, let alone in Belmont."

I nodded. "True, but you do."

"What are you suggesting?"

"Maybe you could offer to help. Why don't you ask them to make photocopies of the pictures? That way we can take our time and study them carefully. After all, seeing that I'm your personal informant, I think it only fair that you help me a little bit in return."

"You want me to get copies of all the pictures they found in his studio?" He looked so handsome looking down at me, I lost my train of thought.

"I—er—" I stood there, stammering.

He rolled his eyes. "You never give up, do you?"

I gave him a teasing smile. "Isn't that what you love best about me?"

He looked down at me, his dark eyes softening. "What I love best about you—" He stopped and took my chin between his thumb and forefinger. His gaze lingered until I was sure he was going to kiss me. But then he said, "Is not your detective work, nor your cooking for that matter." He chuckled, dropping his hand. And the moment was gone.

"See you tomorrow, kiddo," he said, and he opened the door for me.

Shit, shit, shit. I walked home, wondering why I could feel such electricity for a man who appeared to feel nothing in return.

Chapter 9

I'd had two glasses of wine and a steak dinner. Now I craved something sweet. In search of a sugar high to drown my misery, I made a short detour to the grocery store to pick up some ice cream.

I had my head in the freezer, going over the selection—French vanilla, strawberry cheesecake, double chocolate. Vanilla would be perfect with drizzles of hot chocolate syrup and mounds of walnuts. I was already salivating. I snatched the container and was heading for the till when I heard a familiar voice. I looked back.

It was Bunny Boyd, talking into her cell phone. "I can't believe we're having this conversation again. If you don't get that exact sofa before the next taping, you'll be out of a job. I have two words for you: Find it!" She threw her phone into her bag and then noticed me. "Oh, Della, hi," she said, not looking the least embarrassed.

I smiled. "Fancy meeting you in a grocery store. You're so fashionably thin, I didn't think you ate."

She laughed, preening at the compliment. "Oh, I eat,

all right." She glanced down into her basket. It was filled with fruit and vegetables and yogurt and cottage cheese.

I bobbed my eyebrows. "You call that eating?"

"I'm walking back—better to keep the bags light."

"Where are you staying?"

"At the Longview," she said, naming an upscale bed-and-breakfast right across the street from the Coffee Break. She continued. "I bought it years ago. It doesn't make a lot of money, but at least it pays for itself and it gives me a place to stay whenever I want to come back."

I was confused. "What do you mean—come back?"

"I grew up here. Didn't you know that? I was born and raised in Briar Hollow. I'm a regular small-town girl."

"I would never have guessed. You're so sophisticated. I was sure you came from Manhattan and went to college at some big-league university. Do you still have family here?"

"Unfortunately no. My father died when I was very young, and my mother passed away three years ago. I never had any siblings. I left when I was eighteen, couldn't wait to get out of here. Ironic, isn't it? Now that I'm away, I can't wait to come back."

I nodded. "Things that are unimportant when we are young take on new dimensions as we get older."

"True," she said in a strangled voice. I looked into her eyes and was surprised to find them watering. Was she crying? Maybe it was just her contact lenses irritating her. Yes, that must be it. Bunny Boyd did not strike me as a sentimental woman.

She blinked a few times and pulled herself up straight. "By the way, I showed my client"—oh, so he wasn't Bernie anymore?—"and he approved one of your samples. Now I'll need to see colors. We have to get that just right. Could you drop by his house with samples of off-whites and beiges?"

"Of course. When would you like me to drop by?"

"How about tomorrow morning, say around nine thirty?"

I agreed. She said a quick good-bye and pushed her cart down another aisle.

As I headed home, it occurred to me that Bunny had just made it back on to my list of suspects. If she was staying right across the street from the Coffee Break, she could have spied on the McDermotts and found just the right moment to strike. The only problem with my new theory was that I still had no motive for her.

The next morning, as I was walking over to Al's Garage, I noticed a red Jeep parked in front of his shop. I went over and peeked inside. On the backseat was a basket with pink and white spools of yarn. This was my car, all right. I turned toward the office and stopped. A heated argument was going on inside.

"I don't want to hear about it anymore," a male voice was yelling. *Ricky's?* "Not one word. Do you hear me?" It *was* Ricky, I thought, arguing on the phone with someone. But to my surprise, a female voice replied.

"I don't know where you get the idea that you own me. I don't belong to you. I have the right to make my own decisions, to live my own life."

"I'm telling you, Emma. If you move to New York, you'll be sorry." I could picture him, his face contorted with fury, eyes flashing, and I was filled with dread for the girl.

"Is that a threat?" she was saying. I wondered if maybe I should walk in, interrupt the argument somehow.

"You can think what you want, sweetheart. But let me tell you this. I ain't going to sit around and wait for you. If you go, me and you are through."

"Oh, yeah? Well, we're through whether I go or whether I stay. I'm sick and tired of your bullshit." It didn't sound as if she feared him, at least not physically.

The voices were getting louder and the argument was escalating. Any thought I'd had of walking in was gone. At this point, my interference would only make things worse. But I very much wanted to hear every word. I stepped closer.

"So that's how you thank me," Ricky was yelling, "after everything I've done for you?"

"What exactly do you think you've done for me?" *Yes, what exactly* did *you do for her?*

"You know what I'm talking about. I took risks for you. If I go to jail, it'll be your fault." *What risks?* I wanted Emma to ask.

"You and I both know I never asked you to do anything. You decided it all on your own." *Decided what?* "If I'd had any idea what you were planning, I would have told you not to."

Don't stop now, I wanted to scream. *You would have*

told him not to what? *Not to kill McDermott? Not to break into his studio?* The door flew open and Emma stormed out. She was so upset that she didn't notice I had been listening. I put on my best smile. "Hi, Emma," I said.

She stopped. "Oh—er—hi, Della." She struggled for calm. "What are you doing here?"

"I'm just picking up my car. I dropped it off yesterday. My wheels needed balancing. If you want to give me a minute, I can give you a lift wherever you want to go."

She scowled. "I doubt you'd drive me all the way to New York," she said, and all at once, fat tears rolled down her cheeks.

"Stay right there," I said. "I won't be a minute." I hurried inside and paid my bill. Ricky glared at me as if I were responsible for everything wrong in his life.

He handed me my receipt. "Your keys are under the mat," he growled and stomped off into the garage.

I hurried back out and looked around. Emma was gone. *Shit.* I hopped into my car and took off, scanning up and down the street as I drove. She couldn't have gotten very far. I'd been inside for only a few minutes, three or four tops. But she was nowhere to be seen.

I walked into the store and was greeted by the wonderful aroma of freshly brewed coffee. *Oh, God, do I need a cup.* I popped my head through the beaded curtain. Jenny was filling her display case with fresh pastries.

"Morning," I said. "Spare a cup of coffee for a friend?"

"I have a fresh pot on right now. Ed gave me a lift to work on his way to the hospital."

I stepped inside. "Oh, he did, did he? I take it you two spent the night together?"

She grinned, flushing with happiness. "He's been hinting at sharing an apartment."

"Already? But you've been dating only, what? Two months?"

"About that. But"—she shrugged—"at our age, people know what's right for them."

"Whoa. Not that I don't like him. Quite the opposite—I think he's wonderful—but don't you think you should slow down a little?" I wagged a finger at her. "And if you tell me you know he's the right one because you read his aura, I swear I'll . . . I'll . . ."

She gave me a cocky grin. "You'll what?"

I smiled. "I'll . . . be your matron of honor at your wedding?"

"Who's putting the cart before the horse now?"

I laughed along with her.

"All right," she said. "I promise it's not because I read his aura. Don't you know I can't read the auras of people close to me? But if we ever do decide to get married, you'll be the first to know. However, you will definitely *not* be my matron of honor." My face fell until she continued. "You're way too young to be a matron. But you can be my *maid* of honor."

I grinned. "We've got a deal."

I had already collected my color samples and was halfway through a second cup of coffee when Marnie walked in. I was surprised to see her wearing an almost normal outfit for a change. Her Lucille Ball hair was tied up in a loose bun. Her eye shadow was heavy, but brown rather than electric blue. And instead of a jungle of animal prints, today she wore black pants and a bright pink peasant blouse. She looked lovely.

"Here," she said. "I've got a few more place mats for you." She waddled over and dropped a bag onto my desk.

I opened it. "Oh, Marnie, these are beautiful." I fingered the fabric. It was woven with thick yarn in a simple basket-weave pattern and edged with a cotton strip. I counted them—four.

As if she could read my mind, she said, "I know there aren't many, but I'll work on making more of the same while I'm here."

"Thank you. Four is better than none." I pulled out my tags and my stock book. "You sure finished these fast. How do you do that?"

"Insomnia," she said. "It's wonderful for production. Also, I always use extra-thick yarn for place mats. It takes a fraction of the time."

"If you don't mind, I'll let you tag them. I have to run. I promised Bunny that I'd stop by the Whitby house to do some color matching before I order the yarn."

She beamed. "See? I knew you'd need me."

"I do need you. But it's not fair for you to work for nothing, so here's what I propose. Whenever you mind the store, I'll pay you by the hour for your time."

"That's fair," she said, taking the tags from me. "I hope you go out a lot."

I laughed, grabbed my purse and car keys and took off with my samples.

*   *   *

I had seen the Whitby house only once, in early evening. Now, as I drove up, the place looked even more imposing by daylight. Perhaps it was because the long drive was empty of cars, but somehow the estate seemed bigger, the house whiter and more elegant.

I parked my car to the side, at the edge of the circular drive, and hopped out. The doorbell sent peals of ringing echoing through the house. A few moments later the door opened.

"Ye-e-e-s?" said the butler, stretching that one syllable into four. He looked at me the way I might look at a reptile.

"Hi." I beamed him a smile that did nothing to melt his icy demeanor. "I'm Della Wright of Dream Weaver. I have a nine-thirty appointment with Bunny Boyd."

"Oh, yes," he said, excruciatingly slowly, as if the mere mention of Bunny Boyd were painful to his ears. He stepped aside and I walked in.

Without the party crowd, the foyer looked even larger, more like that of a hotel foyer than that of a private home. For the first time, I noticed the columns that supported the two spiral staircases. They were either real marble, or painted in a faux-finish marble. I was dying to get a closer look.

"If you'll come with me," the butler said. I followed him up the stairs and to the study from which the gun had been stolen. I looked at him, wondering how difficult it might be to extract information. Probably like

a muffin right about now—butter pecan, if there are any left."

Marnie marched off to the back, disappearing behind the beaded curtain. I picked up my calculator only to put it down again when the phone rang.

I picked it up. "Dream Weaver, Della speaking. How can I help you?"

"You can help yourself by minding your own business." The voice was raspy, almost a growl. I looked back, but Marnie had already disappeared behind the beaded curtain. The voice continued. "If you don't stop sticking your nose where it doesn't belong, what happened to McDermott will happen to you." There was a click, followed by a dial tone. I stared at the receiver in my hands.

Suddenly Marnie was standing next to me, holding a tray laden with coffee cups and muffins. "Are you all right? Who was that?"

"I—I don't know." I thought fast. "I'm pretty sure it was a man, but whoever it was disguised his voice." I pushed the call display button—unknown number, of course.

"Disguised his voice, why? What did he want?"

"I just got a warning," I said, dazed. "Seems I'd better mind my own business. Otherwise what happened to McDermott will happen to me."

Her face fell. "Oh, my God. Somebody has just threatened to kill you. You have to call the police."

I thought this over. "And tell them what? That I got a crank call? What do you imagine they'll do?"

"What if it was the killer?"

I was wondering the same thing. "I think it might have been Ricky Arnold."

"Emma's boyfriend? What makes you think that?"

"I told Emma she shouldn't allow her boyfriend to stand in the way of her dream. If she repeated to him what I said, he'd definitely think I was sticking my nose where it doesn't belong. He probably blames me for her decision to move to New York."

She scowled. "And Emma, like most eighteen-year-olds, probably couldn't wait to throw in his face that other people agree with her."

I picked up the phone and punched in Emma's number again.

"Oh, hi, Della," the girl said when I identified myself. "Sorry I didn't wait around for you. I just needed to get out of there."

"Don't worry about it. By any chance, did you tell Ricky about the advice I gave you to live your own life?"

She hesitated. "I might have. Why?"

"And you told him that I encouraged you to pursue your dream of modeling?"

"Yes. Why? Is everything all right? Ricky didn't do anything, did he?"

"Somebody just called me, warning me to mind my own."

"Was it Ricky?" she asked, sounding worried.

"It could have been, but I can't be sure. Whoever it was, he disguised his voice—deep and raspy."

There was a short silence. "I got some calls from

someone who sounded exactly like that," she said. "I'm pretty sure they were from Mrs. McDermott. She's the only person I know who hates me. Maybe she was the one who called you too."

"Mrs. McDermott," I repeated, stunned. Could that have been her? "Well, don't worry about it. It was probably just a crank call." I wished her good luck on her trip again and hung up.

Marnie stared at me. "Did I just hear right? You think Mrs. McDermott made that crank call?"

"That's what Emma believes, but I can't see why she would do that." I repeated what Emma had said. "She sounded pretty sure." I was quiet for a moment as a thought occurred to me. "You know, I've been wondering if money could have been a motive for McDermott's murder."

She gasped. "You think Rhonda killed Philip?"

"I don't think anything right now. I'm just looking at all the possibilities."

"Well, as much as I don't like the woman, I doubt she is capable of murder. In fact, I'd probably be more likely to kill someone than she would. She's such a wimpy, whiny, dishcloth of a woman."

The telephone rang again. I looked at it, wondering if this was going to be another threat. I snatched it up before I lost the nerve.

"I just saw an ad on craigslist about an apartment for rent," a girl's voice said. "Is it still available?"

Next to me, Marnie looked even more worried than I'd been. I threw her a reassuring smile. "As a matter of fact, it is."

"I'd like to make an appointment to come and see it. Would it be possible to come by today?"

"No problem. I work in the same building, right downstairs, so you can pop by anytime." I gave her the address.

"Great. I'll be there in half an hour or so."

"That must have been good news. You're grinning from ear to ear."

"Somebody's coming over to see the apartment. She sounded young, but nice." I frowned. "I hope she can afford the rent."

"You listed the price in the ad?"

I nodded.

"In that case, don't worry. And if she asks you to lower the price, you don't have to agree." She picked up her coffee and muffin and returned to her loom.

"It's not like people have been lining up to rent it."

"Bah, don't worry about it. You'll rent it in time."

I was sure I would, but every month the apartment remained empty was another month of rental income I would never recover. I picked up the notes I'd taken at the Whitby estate, pulled out my calculator, and began punching in the length and width of the fabric I needed to produce.

Planning a weaving project consists of counting the amount of yarn needed. First one needed to calculate the amount for dressing the loom, then the amount for the weft. This project was so large that when I completed my calculations, the total was way more than I'd imagined.

Could this be right? I went over the figures once

again. This time the total was even higher. After repeating the calculation half a dozen times, I was confident that I had arrived at the correct amount. "I hope Bunny won't be put off by the advance I'm going to ask."

The bell tinkled and I looked up. "Oh, hi," I said, surprised to recognize the girl from whom I'd bought my wide loom. "I'm sorry. I've forgotten your name."

"Margaret," she said, coming forward, hand extended. "Margaret Fowler." Margaret was in her late teens or early twenties, with short brown hair. Her eyes were a deep shade of gray. They were arrestingly beautiful. The only flaw in her otherwise lovely face was a rather unfortunate nose. It dwarfed the rest of her delicate features. Still, her smile was so engaging that it made up for the graceless trait.

She came forward. "I had no idea when I called about the apartment that I was talking to you."

"You're here for the apartment?" I said, surprised. "When I saw you walking in, I thought you were dropping by to take a peek at my store."

"I'd love to do that too, if you don't mind."

Marnie came over and introduced herself. "I'm Della's store manager."

I suppressed a chuckle. If she considered herself the store manager, she had to be the worst-paid manager in history.

Marnie continued. "You're going to love the apartment. It's just beautiful."

"It sounded lovely in the ad. It's a little more than I wanted to pay, but that won't be a problem for long. I'm sure I'll find a job soon."

My hope deflated. The last thing I wanted was an unemployed tenant. I needed someone who could afford the rent and pay it on time.

I turned to Marnie. "Margaret used to have a weaving studio."

Marnie's eyes widened. "You're a weaver? Why, that's just too fortuitous to be a coincidence. Della just picked up a huge contract and will be needing help. Maybe you could work for her."

Margaret turned and looked at me with such hope that I was tempted to agree. That could solve her money problems and, at the same time, assure me of getting the rent.

"It's still a bit premature to be talking about hiring anybody. I don't even have a signed contract yet." Now that I was looking at her again, I had the impression she reminded me of someone, but I couldn't for the life of me think of whom. I pushed that thought away and turned to Marnie. "Would you mind the shop while I run upstairs with Margaret?"

Marnie beamed. "No problem. Take your time."

Margaret followed me out of the shop and up the stairs. I pointed to the second door down the hall. "I live right there."

"Do you own the building?" she asked, looking impressed.

"Well, right now I think it would be more accurate to say that the mortgage company owns it."

"I really hope I like it," she gushed.

"I hope so too," I said and then was struck with an unnerving thought. If Margaret and I became friends, as I had a feeling might happen, that could present a problem. I was notoriously bad at saying no, and if she had financial difficulties, it would be impossible for me to ask her for the rent if she fell behind. One more reason for me to hire her as soon as the contract with Bunny was signed.

"Why are you moving?" I asked, pausing in front of the door. "I saw your apartment. I thought it was lovely."

"It is," she said. "And I love it. But the place is huge. Now that I've sold off all my weaving equipment and closed my studio, I should really find something much smaller and less expensive."

The place was huge, I remembered. And even as large as it was, the old loom I'd bought had taken up the entire living room. The rest of her equipment was in her dining room, the setup similar to the way I'd designed my space when I was using Matthew's house.

"You sold off everything?" I was surprised.

"I still have tons of yarn—enough to last me a lifetime—and a lot of woven goods." She chuckled. "And even more that are only in the planning stage. Actually, I kept one loom for my personal use." She stood aside while I unlocked the door. "I love weaving, but I wasn't able to earn a living at it."

I wasn't surprised. It was difficult enough to attract clients with a shop right smack in the middle of Main Street. With a studio in her home, it must have been near impossible. "That's too bad." I opened the door and let her in. "What kind of work are you hoping to find?"

She stepped into the main room: a kitchen, living and dining room combo. Her eyes widened. She forgot all about my question and made a beeline for the stove.

"Oh, I love it. I've always wanted one of these." The stove was an antique Wedgewood gas range, more than sixty years old and still in impeccable condition.

"I have a thing for antique stoves too," I said. The more she and I spoke, the more I found myself liking her. She was so nice, so very likable.

She looked at the refrigerator and chuckled. "I guess that's almost old enough to be an antique too."

"I'm planning to replace the refrigerator. These old things use up way too much electricity. It's more economical in the long run to buy a modern appliance."

"Really? A new refrigerator? That would be wonderful." She trailed her hand along the countertop, which was made of black Formica and trimmed in aluminum, just like mine. She grinned. "The kitchen is gorgeous. I wouldn't change a thing—except the fridge."

"I'm glad you like it."

She wandered over to the living area, standing in the center of the room. She looked around, tapping her chin with an index finger as she furnished the apartment in her mind. "I could put my sofa there and my table over by the window." She looked outside. "Nice view."

She turned to me. "Can I see the bedroom and the bathroom?"

I showed her down the hall to the bedroom and opened the door.

She walked in, gave it a cursory inspection and

moved on to the bathroom, which like mine, had an old claw-foot tub with a nickel-plated showerhead and a wraparound rail for the curtain. The floor was tiled in small white lozenge-shaped tiles and edged with a black border.

"Everything is so beautiful," she said, awed. "It looks like everything is original to the building."

I nodded. "That was one of the first things that attracted me to this building. The owner was meticulous in its upkeep."

"It sounded lovely in the ad, but it's even nicer than I expected." She turned to me. "I'll take it." And then, hesitantly, she added, "If you'll have me, of course. I can give you the first and last month right now if you like. Oh, and I have a dog. Is that a problem?"

Before I had a chance to think, I blurted, "It's not a problem at all. I love dogs. What kind is it?"

"She's a French bulldog. She's not very big, only twenty pounds."

"You're kidding. A friend of mine has one too. I dog-sit him in my shop every day. We'll have to introduce them. What's her name?"

"Clementine."

I laughed. "Wasn't that the name of Winston Churchill's wife?"

"Most male bulldogs are named Winston, so that's why I chose Clementine."

"You're right. My friend's dog is named Winston." I grinned. "I can't think of anyone I'd rather have as a neighbor. Come, I have a lease downstairs. I'll have you fill it out."

"You mean it?" I nodded, and she whooped and danced a few steps.

"You can look around while I fill out the landlord's section." I only hoped she found a job soon.

I jotted down the terms on the agreement while Marnie showed Margaret around the shop. She was full of compliments. "Oh, I love this monk's cloth throw. I've always wanted to make one like this, with a country heart design."

Marnie nodded. "It is nice. That's one of Jenny's projects. You'll meet Jenny in a few minutes." At Margaret's quizzical expression, she explained. "Jenny operates the coffee shop in the back, Coffee, Tea and Destiny. Didn't you see the sign outside?" At that moment, a trio of women left the coffee shop, cutting through my store on their way out.

"Oh, that's why it smells so good in here. I was wondering where that came from."

"I have the lease ready," I called to her.

She picked up the document, nodding silently as she read it through. And then she signed it. "I'll write you that check before I forget."

"You don't have to worry about that. I'd remind you."

She laughed, rummaging through her bag and pulling out a checkbook. "Here you go—first and last month." I handed her a copy of the lease in exchange and folded mine safely into my drawer.

"Hello. Am I interrupting?" Jenny asked as she joined us.

I turned. "Jenny, meet my new neighbor and tenant, Margaret Fowler."

They smiled and shook hands, and then Jenny said, "So you're renting the apartment. Congratulations. It's a beautiful place. When are you moving in?"

Margaret looked at me. "As soon as possible. I'd like to start bringing in furniture right away, if you don't mind."

"I don't mind at all," I said. "We're still a week away from October, but the place is empty, so you might as well use it."

"Well, that's definitely a cause for a celebration," Jenny said. "How about a cup of tea or coffee for everyone? My treat."

"Sounds great, but the treat is on me. It's only fair. A new tenant means more income for me."

"Go ahead and pay for the coffee if you like, but how about you bring over a few muffins. Those are on me," Marnie added. To Margaret, she whispered, "Jenny's muffins are homemade and to die for," and then, chuckling, "I bake them myself."

"It's quiet back there for now." Jenny glanced at her watch. "But it's bound to start getting really busy soon. I'll bring everything out here." She went to her shop, returning with a tray laden with mugs and goodies.

I'd already had one just a short while ago. I hesitated. *What the heck,* I thought, picking a lemon-poppy muffin. I could never pass up Marnie's baking.

She passed the coffee around and raised her cup. "To Margaret. May your new home bring you much luck and happiness."

Margaret smiled. "I could use some good luck for a change. I've had nothing but bad luck lately, but after finding this great apartment, I'm beginning to think things are about to turn around." She took a swallow of her coffee and then added, "All I need now is to find a job."

I was only half paying attention to the conversation. From where I stood, I had a clear view of anyone who came to the door. A movement had caught my eye. It was Bunny Boyd. She walked up, put her hand on the doorknob and froze. In her eyes was an expression I couldn't quite identify. Fear? Anger? I followed her gaze. She was staring at Margaret. And then she spun around and hurried away.

What the heck was that all about? Why would Bunny Boyd want to avoid Margaret?

"Della?" I snapped back to what Margaret was saying. "Maybe I can show you some of my woven items. If you like them, I could leave them on consignment with you."

It was a question more than a statement. "That's a terrific idea. I'm always looking for new suppliers and new stock."

Jenny had been studying Margaret for the last few minutes. "What sign are you?" she asked. And then she held up her hand. "No, don't tell me. Let me guess." She squinted at her.

Margaret squirmed, looking from Jenny to me nervously. "What is she doing?"

"She can see auras," Marnie explained. "She can tell

a lot about a person that way. And if she reads your tea leaves, she can tell your future too."

"You're a Virgo," Jenny said. "You are strong willed and determined. You've just suffered a great disappointment, but you're not letting it get you down." She smiled. "Am I right?"

Margaret nodded, impressed. "I am a Virgo. How did you know that? And I just had to close my business, so you're right about a recent disappointment too." She shrugged. "But I tell myself that everything happens for a reason. Something better is bound to come along."

I chuckled. "That was not very difficult to divine. You just told her you'd had nothing but bad luck lately."

Jenny gave me an epic roll of the eyes. "Della is our local skeptic. She never believes my predictions." She turned to me. "For your information, what I told her is what I saw in her aura. I didn't even think about what she'd just told us."

"Sure, sure," I said.

She shook her head dismissively. "Does anybody want a refill?"

Margaret looked at her watch. "I'd better get going." Grinning, she added, "I have some packing to do. If you need to reach me for any reason, don't hesitate to call."

As soon as the door closed behind her, Marnie gushed, "She's terrific. Della, if you decide you need help in your shop, you should hire her."

"I thought you wanted the job. Now you're telling me that I should hire her. What gives?"

Marnie scowled. "You're right. That was stupid of me. But she sounded like she needs a job more than I do."

"I might have the solution." Jenny said. "The way my business is going, I can barely keep up with all the work. I need to check with my accountant and make sure I can afford it, but if he gives me the go-ahead, I'll hire her right away. I have a good feeling about that girl."

"You're doing that well? That's wonderful," I said. "I'm so happy for you."

Jenny picked up the cups, lining them up on the tray. "Don't tell her until I'm sure. I'd hate to disappoint her." She marched off toward her shop, and just in the nick of time. At that moment, the door flew open and half a dozen people walked in and headed directly to the back. The door had barely closed when one more woman walked in. She looked familiar. And then it came to me. She was the maid who had served the drinks at Bernard Whitby's party.

She came to the counter, fiddling with her purse. "Bunny Boyd asked me to drop off this envelope for her. She's sorry she couldn't come in person, but she'll give you a call and arrange to pick up the signed document later."

Now Bunny's behavior had gone from odd to completely ridiculous. She was sending the maid to do her errand rather than risk running into Margaret. That was just plain stupid. Or was I jumping to conclusions?

"Thank you." I took the envelope. "I met you at Mr. Whitby's party, didn't I?"

She studied me. "Perhaps," she said apologetically. "I'm sorry. I'm not good with faces, and there were so many people."

I nodded. "There certainly were." And before she could walk away, I continued. "Have you worked for Mr. Whitby very long?"

"Thirty-two years," she replied. "We worked for the Whitbys all of our adult lives. We worked for his father when we first started."

"We?"

"My husband and I."

"You mean you're married to Sweeny?" I shouldn't have been surprised. It wasn't unusual for married couples who both worked as servants to be hired in the same household. "Sweeny was telling me about Mr. Whitby's missing gun—an old Colt, right?"

Her mouth dropped open. "Jimmy told you about that?"

From the corner of my eye, I could see Marnie rising from her chair. I gave her a warning look and she sat back down.

"Oh, we didn't talk for very long," I answered vaguely. "I just feel so awful for poor Mr. Whitby. He cares so much about his collection. I hope that Colt wasn't too valuable."

She was already shaking her head. "Oh, no, not at all. It was one of the least important in his collection. I mean, it was still valuable, but the gun right next to it was worth ten times as much. It was just lucky the thief took that one instead."

"I hope the collection is well insured."

She nodded. "The police were already there to take down the report. They left black fingerprint powder all over that room. Such a mess." And then, leaning in, she whispered, "I've been wondering if that poor man— you know, the one who was murdered—might have been killed with Mr. Whitby's gun." So Mrs. Sweeny liked to gossip, I thought. Well, I was not about to disappoint her.

I adopted a whispery tone. "I've been wondering the same thing. If it was the murder weapon, it would mean one of the guests at the party is the killer. Does anybody have any idea who could have taken it?"

"Nobody has the faintest idea. It's a mystery. I've been going over and over in my mind the people I saw going upstairs. There were so many of them—at least two hundred."

"Two hundred." I scowled. "That's a lot of suspects. I'm surprised Mr. Whitby allowed guests to walk around the house."

"That was not his idea. It was Miss Boyd's." She grimaced at the name. "He normally never allows people to walk about like that. He hates people nosing around his house." She sneered. "But she wanted to show off, no doubt."

Bunny's idea—how interesting. I stored this new tidbit of information. "It just gives me goose bumps to think that the killer might be somebody I know," I said, widening my eyes dramatically.

"It does me too," she said, and then, as if suddenly realizing that she was participating in gossip, she straightened up. "Well, then," she said stiffly, "I'll let Ms. Boyd know I gave you the envelope." She turned and walked out.

I tore open the envelope and pulled out the agreement. After reading it carefully, I bent down to get the fax machine from under the counter. It was time to place that yarn order. And then I stopped. As excited as I was about starting this project, I had to be smart. I had to get the deposit first.

I turned my thoughts to something Mrs. Sweeny had said. The gun next to the one that had been stolen was worth ten times as much. This suggested the Colt was not stolen for its value. If not for that, then what? Its practical value? Yes, it was possible that whoever took it had stolen it to use it.

Marnie wandered over, eyeing me suspiciously. "*Poor* Mr. Whitby? Really? The man is a gazillionaire."

"Was I being very obvious?"

She smirked. "I'll say. I was surprised she didn't see through you right away. What did you hope to find out?"

"Nothing in particular. I was just gossiping. You never know what you might find out from gossiping."

She tilted her head, repeating, "So, what did you find out?"

"I think it's interesting that of all the guns, the one that was stolen turns out to be not terribly important."

"I'd say it was lucky rather than interesting."

I didn't comment. After a few seconds of silence, she said, "Are you going to sign that contract?"

I rolled my eyes, laughing. "You sure are nosy."

She didn't bat an eye. "Why would you ever think otherwise? Everybody knows I'm curious." She regarded me suspiciously. "You're not sure you want the job anymore, are you?"

I laughed. "Don't be silly. I just want to go over it carefully a second time and make sure it's right before I sign it."

"Good idea," she said, and returned to her loom.

Matthew answered on the first ring. "Well, if it isn't my very own personal informant. I take it you have some new and important information to share with me?"

"As a matter of fact, I do."

"Good timing, I just had lunch and was about to take Winston for a walk. Why don't we meet in the park behind the church? We can chat without risk of anyone overhearing."

"Where are you going?" Marnie called as I grabbed my sweater and headed for the door.

"I'm joining Matthew for a walk."

Her frown morphed into a grin. "Have fu-un, and for heaven's sake, flirt," she called out as the door swung closed behind me.

The church was a block down the street, right next to Briar Hollow Mercantile, almost equidistant between Mathew's house and my shop. I walked briskly, figuring my pace would be close to Matthew's and Winston's so we should meet about halfway. Sure enough, as I approached the church, I spotted them coming toward me from the opposite side. Suddenly, Winnie spotted me and took off at a gallop, his lead whipping along behind him.

He threw himself at me, almost knocking me down. "Whoa there, big boy." I took hold of his leash and handed it to Matthew as he caught up.

"Bad boy," he said firmly. Any other dog would be squirming with guilt. Not this dog, though—he stared up at Matthew, wagging his nonexistent tail.

I chuckled. "Sometimes I wonder about you, Winnie. With an ugly mug like yours, you should at least be really smart." Winston gave me a happy bark, proving my point exactly. "You're not even smart enough to know when you're being insulted."

Matthew gave him a pat on the head. "Don't you mind what Della says, Winston. You're not ugly at all. And I know you're smart. You're the hero who saved my life last summer."

Winston looked up at him, as confused as ever.

"He doesn't understand a word you say. To him, people talk is just as incomprehensible as barking is to us. Isn't that right, big boy?"

He looked back at me. "Woof."

I grinned at Matthew. "See?"

We strolled along the sidewalk bordering the church and picked a bench at the edge of the park.

"Out with it. What did you find out?"

"A couple of things." I didn't want to mention the crank call I'd gotten. He'd only worry. But I told him that I'd run into Bunny last night and learned that she owned the Longview. "Which means she had not only the opportunity to steal the gun, but also the opportunity to get inside the Coffee Break without anybody seeing her."

"Good job," he said.

"That's not all. It turns out that giving tours of the Whitby house during the party was her idea. Whitby never allows it. So if she wanted to steal the gun herself, what better cover?"

"Maybe she just wanted to show off her work."

"That's what Mrs. Sweeny said." I shrugged. "It's true that I still don't have a motive for her, but I don't want to take her off my list, at least not yet."

"Listen to you," he said, chuckling. "Your list. By the way, I have news too. The police have agreed to make copies of McDermott's photos."

"Great. When can I look at them?"

"They won't be ready until tomorrow. They're having them cropped so all I get are the head shots."

"That makes sense." I nodded. "Oh, and before I forget. I overheard an argument between Emma and her boyfriend." I tried to repeat it as best I could. "I have no idea what he did that was so terrible that he could be in jail, but whatever it was, Emma had nothing to do with it."

"You're good at this," he said.

I beamed. "Do the police know what kind of gun killed McDermott?"

"I'm sure they do. But they're keeping that information from the public."

"How difficult would it be to get ammunition for an antique gun?" I asked. "The butler told me it was more than a hundred years old, a Colt, a model 1908." He gave an incredulous look. "What? I was a business analyst. I have a memory for numbers."

"Good for you. God knows I don't. Right offhand, I have no idea what kind of ammo it would use. I'll have to look it up."

"And here's another thing. Mrs. Sweeny said the stolen gun was not terribly valuable. It was sitting right next to one of the most expensive weapons in Whitby's collection. Why would somebody steal a relatively inexpensive gun when there's another, worth ten times as much, right next to it?"

Matthew nodded. "Interesting."

I continued. "I think it was stolen by the killer because he intended to use it."

"It could be," he said.

I planted both hands on my hips. "I hate when you're vague like that. Tell me what you're really thinking."

"It's still early to jump to these kinds of conclusions. We have to keep in mind that we still don't know what kind of gun was used. All I know is that McDermott was shot four times from a distance of about fifteen feet, and all the bullets hit him in the heart, within an inch of one another."

"So whoever shot him was good with guns."

"So it would seem."

I groaned. "There you go again. You never commit to an opinion. No wonder you're still unmarried. You can't commit to a woman either." Just as soon as the words were out of my mouth, I wanted to bite them back. I felt the heat rise to my face. Rather than sit there

and suffer more embarrassment, I jumped to my feet
and hurried away.

Stupid, stupid, stupid. Why did I always do things
like this? Maybe Jenny was right. I was afraid. Rather
than risk getting hurt, I was subconsciously pushing
Matthew away. I headed back to the shop, feeling like
an utter failure.

At the newspaper vending machine, I picked up a
copy of the *Belmont Daily* and walked on. I opened the
door, stepping aside to let in a trio of women. They
made a beeline for the coffee shop. One of them was
telling her friends about the amazing prediction that
Jenny had told her that had come true.

To each her own, I thought.

Marnie looked at me as I walked in. "Hey, why the
sullen face? Or am I being nosy again?"

I was so upset, I was near tears. "I really messed up
this time."

She got up from her loom. "Uh-oh, what did you do?"

"Me and my big mouth—I couldn't have made things
worse." Suddenly tears were quivering on my lashes,
and before I knew it, I was spilling out the whole story
to Marnie.

She clucked along sympathetically. "Sugar pie, that's
not so bad. Sure you feel silly, but you can make things
right very easily. But you have to do some changing.
Everybody knows you're head over heels with him—
everybody, that is, except him. When he's around, you
start behaving like somebody else. You're not yourself
anymore. You have to start being nice to the man. You
know what they say about attracting flies with honey."

I groaned. "You're telling me to flirt again, aren't you?"

She widened her eyes. "Yes. And what's so bad about that? I happen to think he's in love with you too. But you've been sending him such mixed signals, the guy probably doesn't know whether he's coming or going." She wagged a pudgy finger at me. "If you want that man, you're going to have to go after him."

In love with me. What crock. "I must be the most awkward woman in the world when it comes to attracting a man."

Marnie regarded me without the least bit of sympathy. "I'm going to give you your first lesson."

I looked at her. Marnie, with her carrot hair and outrageous outfits, was going to give me lessons on how to attract a man. I would have protested if I hadn't been so bummed out. Instead, I said, "What do you suggest?"

"The most intoxicating thing to a man is a woman who shows interest in him. The few times I've seen you with him, you're so busy talking about clues and investigating and all your suspicions that he probably has no idea you even like him."

That was almost word for word what Jenny's boyfriend had said, and she had nabbed him within months of being single again. Is that how she'd done it? Maybe I should start taking her advice—at least about this.

"It's the easiest thing in the world," Marnie continued. "Ask him about his day. Show some interest in his activities, in things that are important to him. Try to look at him adoringly, for a change."

"What do you mean, for a change? How do I normally look at him?"

"Sweetie, you look at him the way a big sister might look at a younger, idiotic brother."

"I do not." I tried to think back on how I usually behaved around Matthew. It was true that I constantly worried that I might inadvertently show my feelings. Perhaps that fear did tend to make me seem distant. But the thought of exposing the way I felt . . . I gave myself a shake. Maybe Marnie was right. I grimaced. "What if he tells me he doesn't feel the same way? Or worse, what if he laughs at me?"

Marnie scoffed. "Don't be silly. Take my advice— you know, flutter your lashes and flirt with him a little. And remember, you can't do worse than you are right now."

I *so* didn't see myself doing the flirty thing. I was an intelligent woman, cerebral. Or at least I wanted to see myself that way. I was not the silly eyelash-fluttering type. But nonetheless, I said, "Okay, fine. I'll give it a try."

She gave me a hard look. "Don't *try. Do.*" And then, turning on her heel, she went back to her weaving.

Bat my lashes and flirt? I could just imagine how Matthew would react to that. He'd fall over laughing. I pushed that image out of my mind and glanced at my to-do list—order the yarn for Bunny's project and start dressing the wide loom. I had already filled out the order form and had almost faxed it to the distributer. I was tempted to do so now. But I hadn't even looked at the contract a second time yet. I'd do that tonight. I'd go over it line by line and make sure it protected me.

Glancing around for something to do, I picked up a pad and pencil and went to the shelves of yarn along the far wall. Even if I decided to not take it, it wouldn't hurt to take inventory of the skeins of white linen I had on hand. And I could dress the loom. If things went horribly wrong and I lost the contract, I could still use it for other projects. I got to work, and soon I had counted the skeins and was ready to start measuring the warp.

This presented an entirely new challenge. I had a number of measuring racks, but none of them was nearly big enough to prepare for a loom of this size. I looked around and my eyes fell on the chair behind my dobby loom. *Chairs, they would work.* I pulled two chairs into the center of the shop, placing them eight feet apart. And using their backs, I began winding my warp around one, then crossing between the chairs before winding around the other. Normally I would have measured for the entire project at once, but in this case it was easier to do the dressing in stages. Back and forth I went until I had no more yarn. And then I carefully tied small pieces of ribbon around each group of yarn to make sure the cross remained intact. When I removed it from the chairs, the measured warp looked like a giant rope.

Customers began streaming through my shop on their way out from Coffee, Tea and Destiny. Lunchtime was over. The aroma of vegetable soup and grilled bread had been driving me mad since I'd come back from my short meeting with Matthew. Now that the shop was emptying, I wouldn't feel so guilty taking up Jenny's time. My stomach rumbled.

From her loom, Marnie said, "Come see what I've got so far."

I coiled the rope of warp on top of my loom and went over for a look. She was working on place mats in a classic fire stitch in blue, white and yellow. "They are gorgeous," I said.

"I was hoping you'd like the design." She beamed. "I measured enough warp to make twelve, but I'm thinking of making only eight and weaving a couple of runners to match, instead. What do you think?"

"That's not a bad idea. A lot of people use runners instead of trivets. Why don't we test them? If they sell well, we'll make place mats and matching runners a regular stock item." I started back toward my own project and stopped. "I don't know about you, but I'm starving. I'm going to ask Jenny to fix me a sandwich. Can I get you something while I'm there?"

She got up from her bench. "I'll go. What kind of sandwich do you want?"

While Marnie disappeared into the back, I gave my counter a cursory wipe and pulled out Bunny's contract, going over it again. The terms were exactly as we'd agreed, except that it made no mention of a deposit. I picked up a pen and at the bottom of the document, I wrote, "Client agrees to a nonrefundable deposit of"—I checked my calculations and entered the amount—"which will cover materials needed to complete the project, plus a percentage of the labor." I initialed the line and signed at the bottom. Unless Bunny agreed to this clause, accepting the job would be risky. Surely she would agree. I returned the contract to its envelope, put it away and unfolded the newspaper.

The first page was devoted to the murder of McDermott, as it had been since his death. The police, I read, were no closer to solving the case than they had been on the first day. My eyes swept through the article, which told me nothing I didn't already know. The last paragraph mentioned that McDermott was an amateur photographer and even that he had a photo studio in Belmont. I wondered if this information might encourage tips from the public. The police must have been hoping for exactly that because two lines later the paper gave the number of a tips hotline and a plea for anyone with information to call in.

I thought of Mrs. Anderson. If she read the article, she was probably beside herself with worry. Impulsively, I pulled out my laptop, turned it on and searched the online phone directory for Jeffrey Anderson of Belmont. The number popped up.

I glanced over my shoulder. There was still no sign of Marnie. I picked up the phone and punched in the Andersons' number.

A woman came on. "May I speak to Mrs. Anderson please?"

"Speaking."

"Oh, hello, Mrs. Anderson. I hope I'm not calling you at a bad time. This is Della Wright of Dream Weaver."

I imagined, more than heard, the small gasp. "What can I do for you, Della?"

"I hope you don't mind my calling. I thought you might be happy to know that the police searched the photo studio and found pictures of dozens of women, but none of you." There was a long silence. For a moment I thought she had hung up. "Hello?"

"I'm here," she said, and then nervously, she asked, "Are you absolutely certain?"

"I am. I have a friend helping the police, and he saw all the pictures. There were none of you among them."

Horrified—"You mean, you told somebody?"

"Not at all. He gave me the names of the women he knew. And he would have recognized you if your picture had been there." I was lying again, but I just saw no point in upsetting her more.

There was a long silence as she digested this. "That doesn't make me feel any better. Now I have to worry about where those pictures disappeared to. Somebody must have taken them."

"Are you absolutely sure your husband didn't know about them? When he heard about Mr. McDermott's murder, he might have sent somebody to get rid of them."

"Impossible," she said. "My husband would never condone anything illegal. And furthermore, he would have come to me. No. I'm afraid if those pictures are missing, it's more likely they were taken by somebody planning to use them against us."

I hadn't thought of that. I felt worse for having called her.

She continued. "If you find out any more, please let me know." And suddenly I heard a click followed by a dial tone. She had hung up. I stared at the receiver in my hand and returned it to its cradle.

Behind me, footsteps approached. Marnie was returning.

"I got you a bowl of vegetable soup and a chopped egg sandwich." She set them on the counter and went back to her loom, already biting into her submarine.

"Thanks. Are you going to work right through lunch? You can join me if you like."

She shook her head. "That's nice, but I want to get back to those place mats. I aim to finish them as soon as possible."

I swallowed a spoonful of soup. It was good. And I flipped to the second page of the newspaper, where I was surprised to find an article about Jeffrey Anderson. He had just announced his candidacy for governor. My eyes widened. That made him Whitby's political opponent.

I read on. Anderson's decision had been announced at a press conference the previous evening—only one day following the murder of McDermott. No wonder Mrs. Anderson had been so frantic to get her hands on those pictures. A few pages later, I found McDermott's obituary. The deceased had been fifty-one years old, I

read. He left behind his wife of twenty-eight years and
a sister who lived in Virginia. There was no mention of
children. The article went on to announce that a short
memorial service would be held at St. Pat's Church at
seven o'clock the next evening. That got me thinking.

It was likely that the killer would have been someone in the community. I wondered if he or she would
attend the funeral. You never knew what you could
learn from watching people mourn.

I turned the page to an article about the local grade-
school spelling bee. The next page was all about a Belmont gardener's prizewinning roses. I tuned another
page—the Social Scene. I stopped.

LOCAL MILLIONAIRE SEEN OUT AND ABOUT WITH
TELEVISION PERSONALITY, the headline of the column
read. It went on to say that a certain local millionaire
had been seen at a Belmont restaurant in a tête-à-tête
with a television interior designer. The writer hinted at
a romance between the two, describing them as "gazing into each other's eyes over a candlelit dinner, in a
discreet corner of the restaurant." Nowhere were
names mentioned, but who else could it be but Whitby
and Bunny? There weren't dozens of millionaires in
these parts and even fewer television interior design-
ers.

I chuckled to myself. How much of the short article
was true, I had no idea. I read the paragraph a second
time. And then I saw, just below that little piece of gossip, another article, this one about Bunny Boyd, the celebrity designer working on restoring one of North
Carolina's most famous historical homes. The story went

on to describe Bunny as one of best decorators in the country and the house in question as belonging to Jeffrey Whitby, who was running for governor. How the newspaper imagined its readers would not make the link between the two gossip pieces was beyond me.

A few lines later, the writer mentioned that the beautiful Bunny Boyd had never married. That was odd. I paused to think about that. Neither Bunny nor Bernard Whitby had ever been married. I wondered if maybe their affair had been going on for many years. Come to think of it, it was a bit strange that he had never married either. Over the years there must have been dozens of women vying to capture his heart, or at least his bank account. Which of the two was Bunny really after?

I had finished my soup and was halfway through my sandwich when the phone rang, and speak of the devil, the call display showed none other than Bunny Boyd's number.

"Della, hi. I'm sorry I didn't drop by. I got so busy. Time just ran away from me. Did you have a chance to look over the contract?"

I was tempted to mention that I'd seen her come to the door, but that might not be a good idea. "I looked at it. It all seems fine, except that it makes no mention of a deposit."

"That's not important. If you tell me the amount, I'll draw up the check and drop it off this afternoon, tomorrow at the latest. I hope you placed that order. You need to get going if you're going to finish on time."

Not important to her maybe. But to me it was crucial. "I've already calculated the amount of yarn I'll need, and I was planning to place the order as soon as I get the deposit. In the meantime, I'll start calling weavers today, so we can work in shifts."

"You haven't placed the order yet? That can't wait. I promise I'll stop by and drop it off before the end of the day. And please make sure you order the entire amount of yarn. Otherwise we'll end up with different dye lots. We can't have that."

She was so insistent I found myself unable to argue. "I always order the full amount I need for a project, and the company I order from is very good. They usually deliver the next business day."

"Oh, that's good. I'll want to double check the color before you start production. Call me the second the order comes in. If they deliver within a day, there's no point in dropping by today. I'll come by tomorrow to check the color and drop off the deposit at the same time. Two birds with one stone. See you then." And before I could utter a word, she had hung up.

I stared at the receiver in my hands. She had promised to drop off a check and then reneged on it, all in one short conversation. And she still expected me to have all the materials for the project within twenty-four hours. Now what was I supposed to do?

"Who was that?" Marnie asked, pausing in her weaving.

"Bunny Boyd," I said. "I all but promised to order the yarn, but if I place the order and she reneges on the deposit, I'll be stuck with an immense amount of yarn. It would take me years to go through all of it. My only other option would be to return it to the distributor and pay a hefty restocking fee. Damn it. I should have been more insistent."

"If you want to know what I think," she said, rising from her chair and stretching her back, "don't take the chance. You have too much at risk."

I had already arrived at that decision. Still . . . "What if I lose her contract?"

"Don't sell yourself short. How many weavers have the competence to produce the quality she's looking for? And how many do you think have the right kind of loom?"

Marnie had a good point. "You're right. She'll just have to understand." I stared down at the loom again, gathering my courage. What was it about the woman that intimidated me so? "This brings up another problem."

"What?"

I picked up the rope of warp. "I've already measured all this yarn. What am I supposed to do with it? Discard it? She said she wants to check all the dye lots to make sure they're identical. I've never seen one plain white linen yarn look any different from another—as long as they're the same weight. But I wouldn't put it past her to insist that she can see a difference." Marnie laughed. "I'm glad you see the humor in this, because I sure don't," I said, scowling.

"Sometimes, sugar pie, there is some money that's just not worth the effort."

I groaned. That was not what I wanted to hear. I wanted her to tell me not to worry, that the contract was mine and that everything would work itself out. Well, the only thing left to do was pray Bunny would be understanding and that she dropped off the deposit and signed the agreement including the clause I'd added.

My weavers were a varied bunch. Four were experts, middle-aged ladies who had wandered into my store, looking for yarns. They had little else but time on their hands. I had no difficulty getting them on board. Of my three younger weavers, Lydia Gerard was close to my age—in her midthirties—and taught English at the local high school. I'd met her when she walked through on her way to Jenny's shop. She'd stopped and we'd chatted for a few minutes. A couple of days later she'd dropped by again to show me a few of her weaving projects. I picked up the phone.

"That's wonderful," she exclaimed, when I told her about Bunny's project. "I have fewer classes this semester, so I have a couple of free periods back-to-back during the week. I'd be happy to help if you need me."

I still felt nervous talking about the contract as if it were a done deal. "Whether I get it or not, I hope you can weave me some place mats. I can't keep them in stock."

"Sure," she said. "But from what you tell me, that new loom of yours is a monster. Is it dressed?"

"Not yet," I said.

She was quiet for a minute as she went over her schedule. "Tomorrow's Saturday. I can stop by in the morning if you like. I could give you a hand dressing

the loom. If you get that contract, you'll need it ready
to go, and it could take you weeks."

"That's true, but the yarn hasn't arrived yet. If you
want to come in and take a peek at my new loom,
you're more than welcome."

"Great. I'll see you tomorrow, say ten thirtyish?" We
said good-bye, and I called another of my weavers, this
time getting only an answering machine. I left a voice
mail and made my last call.

Mercedes Hanson was the youngest of my help-
ers—a teenager. A few months ago she took a few
weaving classes and developed a love of the craft. Since
then, Mercedes had made a few items beautiful enough
to show in my shop and had been thrilled to get a check
once they had sold. She was not proficient enough to
work on a project like Bunny's, but there were other
things she could do to help. There would be bobbins to
fill, warp lengths to measure and probably a half dozen
other small chores.

"You want me to help produce handwoven fabric
for a designer?" Her voice was filled with equal mea-
sures of excitement and concern. "Do you really mean
it?"

"I'll keep you busy helping in little ways, and you
could learn a lot just from watching."

She sounded relieved. "I'd like that. How big is the
loom?"

"It's ninety-eight inches wide and six feet tall, with
two sets of treadles and eight harnesses." I pictured her
trying to imagine the size.

She gasped. "It sounds like a loom on steroids."

I laughed. "That's an excellent way to describe it. It is a bit imposing when you first see it."

"How many yards of fabric do you have to produce?"

When I told her, she gasped again, exclaiming, "You don't have a cottage industry anymore; you're going into the manufacturing business."

I chuckled. "It does feel a bit like that. But once this contract is completed, I doubt I'll ever land another one near its size. I'll be back to weaving afghans, coverlets, tea towels and place mats."

"Can I come and see it?"

"Of course you can. I have a weaver coming over to look at it tomorrow. Why don't you come around the same time? And then we can check your class schedule and decide when you can work." She agreed on the time and hung up.

When I looked around, Marnie had left her loom and was pulling on her jacket. "I think I'm going to head home," she said. "I have a lot of baking to do. Was that Mercedes you were talking to?"

"Yes. She'll be coming in to help whenever she can."

"That was nice of you to ask her to help. I know she's been dying to drop by the shop, but she's afraid of being a pest."

"That's just silly," I said. "She should know better than that. I like having her around. I'll make sure she feels welcome when she drops by tomorrow."

Marnie nodded. "Good. That'll make her happy." With that, she marched toward the door, calling over her shoulder, "See you in the morning."

The door closed behind her, and suddenly the shop felt very lonely. I glanced at my watch—six fifteen. It was more than an hour later than my usual closing time. No wonder the place had been so quiet for the last hour. I glanced toward the back, wondering what Jenny was still doing here. She should have left an hour ago too.

"Yoo-hoo," I called as I headed for her shop. I pushed the beaded curtain aside. "What are you still—"

Jenny had climbed on top of her counter and was struggling with a light fixture. "I'm changing this bulb. Here. Hold this." I moved closer and took the old bulb while she twisted in the new one. "Done." She hopped off the counter. "So, any new developments on the murder?"

I let out a long sigh. "Every time I turn around I discover something new, some element that throws new light on the case. I have so many suspects now, I'm more confused than ever."

"I have no doubt that you'll figure it out."

"This time I'm not so sure."

She picked up her bag and hooked it over one shoulder. "Were you just about to leave?"

"You bet I am. I'm tired." I tapped my watch. "It's twenty past six. Want to come up for a glass of wine?"

"That's the best offer I've had all day." She grabbed her sweater and followed me out.

Upstairs, I pointed her toward the fridge. "You pick a bottle and I'll be right back." I hurried to the second bedroom, which I'd turned into my office. I carried the twenty-four-by-thirty-six-inch whiteboard back to the kitchen, where Jenny was struggling with the cork from a bottle of pinot grigio. It came out with a soft pop.

"Here we go." She noticed the board and frowned. "What is that for?"

I set it up next to the kitchen table. "You are going to help me look at all the suspects and analyze their motives."

"Gee. I can't think of anything I'd rather do," she said sardonically. From the cupboard, she pulled two stem glasses and filled them. She handed the first one to me. "I knew I'd have to pay for this wine somehow." She pulled up a chair. "Go ahead. I'm all ears."

I picked up a felt marker. "I spoke to Mrs. Anderson today. I guess I didn't tell you about the photos I found of her having a romantic dinner with—you won't believe this—Bernard Whitby." Her eyes went from bored to total disbelief as I filled her in.

"Mrs. Julia Anderson? The one who's married to the mayor?" she asked, shocked. "I can't believe it. I always thought they had such a great marriage. Mind you, I used to think the same about my marriage, and look at what happened there."

"Even politician's wives sometimes make mistakes."

"But having an affair with your husband's political adversary? That's suicide. It's crazy."

"Hold on. Those pictures were taken a long time ago, maybe as much as twenty years ago. Back then her husband was probably not involved in politics, and if he was, Whitby was not his adversary. He wasn't even involved in politics until—what—just a few days ago."

"That's true," she said, more calmly.

I shrugged. "And who knows what was going on. Maybe the pictures look more incriminating than the situation really was. Or maybe she and her husband were separated for a while. Or maybe he was having an affair. We shouldn't judge. The point is that those pictures disappeared. When the police went in, they were all gone—every last one of them. And just the night before, there were at least a dozen of them. I saw them myself."

Jenny's eyebrows bobbed. "When you turned her down, maybe she got somebody else to steal them."

I discarded that as a possibility immediately. "She swears she knows nothing. And rather than relieved, when I told her the pictures had disappeared, she sounded more worried. She's convinced they were stolen by someone planning to use them against her. What I wonder is, does somebody want to cause trouble in her marriage? Or is this a politically motivated maneuver?"

Jenny's mouth dropped. "Jeffrey Anderson just announced his candidature for governorship."

I nodded. "And his opponent is Whitby—"

"Maybe he stole the pictures."

Again, I shook my head. "I thought of that, but Whitby is in the running himself, and those pictures don't exactly shine a flattering light on him."

"All the more reason for him to want them gone."

"Normally I might agree with you except for two things. How would he have known about the pictures? Also those pictures wouldn't hurt him nearly as much as they would Jeffrey Anderson. Don't forget. Whitby was a bachelor."

Jenny nodded. "Yes, but a bachelor having an affair with a married woman isn't exactly guiltless either."

That was a good point. I turned to the whiteboard and made a series of horizontal lines. At the top left corner, I wrote, "Suspects." Then, along the same line, in the center, I wrote, "Motives."

"My first suspect is Emma." I marked down her name, and under motive, "desperate to keep her boyfriend from finding out about her nude photos."

"Do you really think she could have killed McDermott and then broken into his studio to steal her photos? It doesn't make sense. She gave you the key so that you could get the pictures for her."

"That's true. However, that doesn't mean she didn't kill McDermott." I thought out loud. "She might have worried that if the cops found her pictures there, they'd know she was the killer. But she might have been afraid to go there herself in case the cops were already there." At Jenny's incredulous look, I continued. "You told me yourself, not very long ago, that we never really know what goes on in another person's mind. Everyone is always shocked when somebody they know turns out to be a killer. It is traumatizing when a neighbor, a friend or a relative turns out to be a murderer. But some of the worst murderers in history were highly respected people. Look at John Wayne Gacy. He was a pillar of his community. Yet he had murdered dozens of victims, some of whom he'd buried in his own backyard."

She shuddered. "I can't imagine what his aura must have looked like."

I suppressed a smile. "Back to my list—then there's the boyfriend, Ricky Arnold." I scribbled along as I explained my theory. "Who knows? He might have known about those nude photos all along, never telling Emma. He could have killed McDermott out of jealousy or anger."

Jenny was beginning to enjoy the process. "He could have killed McDermott and stolen the pictures for a number of reasons. A: He's possessive. He sees Emma as his property and didn't want anybody else to see her naked. And B: After killing McDermott, he had to get rid of the pictures because they gave him a motive for the murder."

"I hadn't even thought of that scenario." I wrote it down. "My third suspect is Mrs. McDermott. She could have killed her husband out of jealousy or anger. I suspect they didn't have a very good marriage if he was having affairs. Another possibility is that he had life insurance. In that case, money could have been her motive."

Jenny stared into the distance. "I wonder if either one of them was thinking of divorce."

I widened my eyes. "You are good at this."

"It's all those years of living with a cop."

Before his death, Jenny's ex was not only a policeman, but the local chief of police.

"Now the question is," I said, "how do we find out whether he had life insurance and whether one of them wanted a divorce?" I turned back to my whiteboard and wrote down the name of my next suspect, Mrs. Anderson. "We know she had a motive to kill McDermott. The man was blackmailing her. And even though she says she had nothing to do with the disappearance of her pictures, she could be lying."

"Somehow I doubt that," Jenny said. "I just can't picture her skulking around in the middle of the night."

"I agree that it's not likely, but it's not impossible." I continued. "And then there's her husband. He could have known about the photos. Maybe McDermott was blackmailing him too. After all, he had as much to lose as his wife did—probably more. If those pictures became public, he could kiss his political career goodbye." I paused. "If he knew about his wife's indiscretion, then he certainly had motive to get rid of both the blackmailer and the evidence."

Jenny seemed unimpressed. She took a sip of wine, looking at me skeptically over the rim of her glass. "Any other suspects?"

"There's also Bernard Whitby."

This time, Jenny laughed out loud. "I can't wait to hear your reasoning on this one."

I shrugged. "I can't really find a motive for him wanting to kill McDermott. But he had a motive for wanting those photos, maybe not a great one but a motive nonetheless."

Jenny nodded. "Amazing, isn't it? But we have to remember that in politics, any semblance of impropriety is enough to turn the voters against a candidate.

And newspapers love sex scandals. They can stretch out a one-line story into months of headlines."

"My next suspect is Bunny."

Jenny frowned. "I know I told you the woman was trouble, but how does she fit into all of this?"

"I might be stretching somewhat, but it occurred to me that if she wants to be the next governor's wife strongly enough, she might have wanted to get rid of Whitby's competition. Didn't you see how she was sidling up to Whitby at the party? Maybe she knew about those photos and took it upon herself to get them. That would be one way of making Whitby owe her."

Jenny gave me a sardonic look. "Much as I don't like the lady, I think that theory is pretty weak. That doesn't give her any kind of motive for killing McDermott. And how would she have known about those pictures? The way I see it, whoever broke into his studio was probably also the killer, or at least working with the killer."

"My last suspect is the woman McDermott was having the affair with." I shrugged. "But so far, I have no idea who she is."

"Or if she even exists," Jenny added. "For all you know, Emma could have made her up."

"You're right." I scribbled a few words onto the whiteboard and crossed my arms. "All of these people were at the party, maybe even the mistress. Any one of them could have stolen the gun. Any one of them could have lain in wait for McDermott to open the shop that morning. And any one of them could have broken into the studio. But since Mrs. Anderson's are the only pictures we know for certain are missing, I think the whole case somehow revolves around her photos." I put the felt marker down. "Those are the only suspects I have for now, unless you can think of someone I forgot."

"You are forgetting one important person." I waited.

"You," she said. "You were there when Mrs. McDermott walked into the shop. You could have come in quietly, killed McDermott and then returned to the entrance, called hello a few times for Mrs. McDermott to come in. That way she would have been a witness for you."

I nodded and played along. "Not a bad scenario. What's my motive?"

She thought for a second. "You did it out of friendship for Marnie and me. You wanted to get revenge for them hurting Marnie's feelings, and for me, so my shop wouldn't have any competition."

"Wasn't that nice of me?" Laughing, I pulled out a chair and sat. "I'm glad you're not working for the police. You'd have me arrested in a New York minute." I took a sip of wine and put my glass back down. "All kidding aside, there is one possibility we haven't considered. McDermott was a blackmailer. Who's to say he wasn't blackmailing other people too?"

"How would you find out?"

"Matthew got the police to give him copies of all the photos they found in the studio. There were more than a dozen women. Our first step will be to identify them."

"You've been here less than a year. You couldn't possibly know all of the people from around here."

I took another sip of wine and set down my glass. "If I can't, maybe you and Marnie can."

"Me?" She thought this over and nodded slowly. "I've never tried it, but I wonder if I might get a reading, or an impression of some sort, just by looking at a person's photo."

This time I couldn't hold back. I gave her the mother of all eye rolls.

Chapter 10

The next morning, I picked up a newspaper and glanced across the street at the darkened windows of the Coffee Break. I wondered what Rhonda's plans for the future might be. She'd probably take some time off to mourn and then she might continue the business on her own, or maybe sell it and retire. I didn't know her well enough to like or dislike her, but I felt sad for the woman all the same. I headed to work with the paper under my arm and was just about to walk in when I heard the sound of a car door slamming.

"Della, hi." I turned around. It was Margaret. She was dressed in jeans and a sweatshirt as she came around a beat-up Honda, carrying a large cardboard box. "I decided to bring over my weaving projects. I was just going to drop them off upstairs and ask you when you'd like to see them, but—"

"I'm here now. Why don't we do it right away?"

"Gee, thanks." She grinned and followed me inside. I walked around the shop, turning on lights, while she dropped the box on the counter and pulled open the flaps. "I hope you like them."

"I'd be surprised if I didn't."

She unfolded sheets of silk paper, revealing a beautiful light blue wrap. She lifted it out carefully. The yarn was fine, the weave tight and perfectly even. "Is this what I think it is? A pashmina?"

She beamed. "Yes. Do you like it?"

"It's beautiful."

She touched it gently. "It's actually silk and cashmere, not real pashmina, but I think it's just as lovely."

"How many of these do you have? I'm sure I can sell them—and for a good price."

She parted the box flaps again and took out a small pile. "I have four more—white, cream and two black."

"Would you be willing to leave them with me on consignment?"

"Willing?" she gushed. "You bet."

"How much do you want for them?"

The bell rang, interrupting our conversation. I turned. Jenny was walking in, carrying a box of pastries.

"Hi, Margaret. Hi, Della. What are you two doing here so early?"

"I was showing Della my weaving, and she's agreed to sell them on consignment."

"Her work is beautiful," I added.

"I can't wait to see. I'll get the coffee going and be right back." She disappeared behind the curtain, and I returned to the girl's beautiful pieces.

"What else have you got in there?" I asked.

She dove back into the box, this time bringing up a pile of fine linen hand towels. "I know these aren't so popular anymore, but I love making them."

"I disagree. They sell reasonably well in my shop. Many of my clients use them as fancy dish towels, or they display them in their powder rooms."

"That's what I would do with mine if I had a powder room." She went back into the box and brought out a stack of place mats.

"I could kiss you," I exclaimed. "I never have enough of these. They sell out faster than I can get them in."

"Really?" she said. "That's so great. I have piles more at home. They're one of my favorite things to make. They're so easy. I didn't want to bring in too many in case I'd have to cart them all back upstairs."

"Bring them all, please. I'll be happy to take them." I glanced into the box. "Any other surprises in there?"

"No. That's all I brought with me. But I can show you more when I bring my next load."

"That would be great. The sooner, the better." I pulled out my stock book and store tags, and for the next few minutes we discussed pricing. We had just come to an agreement when Jenny appeared, carrying a tray with coffeepot, mugs and a basket of muffins. "Coffee's ready."

I looked into her basket of goodies. "What kind have you got there?"

"Marnie and I are trying a new recipe. I'm not charging for these. They're samples. If everybody likes them, I'll make them a regular item on the menu."

Margaret hesitated. "They all look delicious. What is this one?"

Jenny glanced at it. "Raspberry chocolate." She nodded toward the basket. "The other one is blueberry and white chocolate."

"Oh, good heavens, this is sinful," I said between mouthfuls. "If I don't stop eating muffins, I won't be able to fit into any of my clothes anymore."

Jenny waved away my comment. "Don't be silly. You look great." She poured two cups of coffee, handed them over, and then came around to the other side, where Margaret's items were stacked. "Show me everything."

Margaret handed her the blue pashmina.

Jenny fingered it. "This is absolutely divine."

"Jenny is a weaver too." I pointed in the direction of one of my displays. "The rugs over there are hers."

"I noticed those yesterday. I love them."

"So do the customers," I continued, giving Jenny a teasing look. "Unfortunately, once those are gone, I won't be getting any more. Since Jenny got herself a new boyfriend and opened her business, she has no more time for weaving."

Jenny chuckled. "And Della has been trying to make me feel guilty ever since."

She continued to admire everything until Margaret glanced at her watch. "I'd better get back to work. I have half a dozen boxes to bring upstairs, and then I have to run back and get changed so I can go job hunting." She gulped down the rest of her coffee, thanked Jenny and hurried out.

From the window, I watched her grab an open box of pots and pans and head for the side door leading upstairs to the apartments. "She's very talented," I said. "Maybe I should ask her to work on Bunny's project."

"Why do I get the feeling you're not sure about wanting that project anymore?"

"What are you talking about? I can't wait to get started. The only thing holding me back is I need the deposit and for her to sign the contract."

"I hope you won't be making a mistake." She picked up the tray. "I'd better get back to work."

Jenny disappeared into the back just as Bunny appeared in the entrance. To my surprise, she was dressed with considerably less flash today. She wore a knee-length beige skirt and matching jacket over a pearl silk blouse. Her makeup was softer, her eye makeup more subdued. She looked . . . elegant. Somebody must have given her a few tips about how a politician's wife should dress. Now she looked the part.

"I was just on my way to do a bunch of errands," she said, "and decided I might as well stop by to pick up the contract and give you your deposit." She walked over and pulled out her checkbook. My eyes landed on her left hand and nearly popped out of my head.

"Whoa, that is one beautiful diamond." It was the size of a doorknob.

She preened and wiggled her fingers. "It is beautiful, isn't it?"

"Is it what I think it is? An engagement ring?"

She smiled, and I had the uncanny impression I was watching a satisfied cat licking its paws after dining on a mouse. Her next words came out as a purr. "It is." She smiled. "And before you ask—no, I can't tell you who. He wants to make the announcement himself." And if those words weren't enough of a clue, she continued. "I would hate the papers to get ahold of the story before he announces it officially."

"Of course," I said, but I couldn't help adding, "I'm very happy for you and Mr. Whitby."

She was making a big show of denying it when suddenly the door opened and Margaret breezed in. "I just wanted to let you know I'm leaving," she called from the doorway.

Bunny turned, and Margaret froze. A moment stretched into two as both women stared at each other, neither saying a word. Then Margaret spun around and stormed out, the door swinging shut behind her.

What was that all about? When Bunny looked at me, the gleam of satisfaction in her eyes had given way to a worried frown.

Her voice was tight. "How much did you want for that deposit?"

I gave her the sum, half expecting her to argue the amount. But she didn't say a word. She scribbled fast, tore out the check and handed it to me. "Call me the minute the yarn comes in. I don't have to come back. I'll trust you to make sure they're all from the same dye lot. Then you can bring a sample to the house to compare to the original drapes and upholstery." She turned on her heel and walked out.

"Wait. You forgot the contract," I called after her, but she was already striding down the street.

How incredibly odd. I must have been already living

in Briar Hollow for too long, because I had the sudden uncontrollable urge to gossip. I hurried through the store to the back. Jenny was behind the counter, setting out fresh muffins on trays and sliding them into the display case.

"Jenny, something really weird just happened." I wasn't sure why I was whispering. Except for her and me, the shop was empty.

She stared at me. "What are you talking about?"

I told her about the confrontation Bunny had narrowly avoided with Margaret yesterday. "And now it just happened. Bunny was inside, showing off her diamond engagement ring—"

Jenny's eyes popped. "Hold on. Her *engagement* ring? Who is she marrying?"

I raised my brows. "Take a wild guess."

"You don't mean Bernard Whitby?"

"She didn't come out and say it, but she gave enough hints that only an idiot wouldn't have guessed." I continued my story. "She was at the counter, having a grand old time showing off her ring, when Margaret walked in. When they saw each other, they both froze. You could have heard a pin drop. They must have stared at each other for a full minute, neither one saying a word. And then Margaret spun around and stormed out."

"Did Bunny say anything after Margaret left?"

"Not a word. I mean, she pretended nothing had happened, but she looked livid. She just went on, talking about business."

She scrunched her forehead. "What do you think is going on?"

"That's what I'd like to know."

The bell rang again, and I hurried to the front. It was a group of women, customers of Jenny's. They called out hellos and good mornings as they walked on through to the back. Then I was alone again, with nothing to do but ponder my new questions.

How did Margaret and Bunny know each other?

What was the meaning of their odd behavior?

I couldn't question Bunny, but surely Margaret would tell me.

Chapter 11

I wasn't alone for long. At nine o'clock, Marnie arrived.

"Good morning, Marnie. I have a favor to ask. Would you mind keeping an eye on the store for a few minutes while I run to the bank?"

"Go," she answered brusquely.

Ignoring her mood, I grabbed my jacket and gave her a peck on the cheek. "You're the best."

"How did you ever get along without me?" she replied, sounding a bit mollified.

"And you'll rub it in, no doubt," I called as I hurried out.

I had Bunny's check in my hot little hands, and it had been written on an account from the Briar Hollow Savings and Loans, which was where I also banked. I could deposit it and have the full amount credited to my account immediately, without the usual two or three days' freeze on the money. That way I could pay for my yarn order up front and get a 5-percent discount. With an order as large as the one I would place, that 5 percent would amount to a lot of money.

I pushed through the door and went straight to the first wicket. The pretty young teller greeted me with a smile.

"Good morning, Della."

I smiled. People were beginning to know me around here, and that felt good. I placed the check on the counter. "I'd like to make a deposit." I pulled out my bank card.

She picked up the check and glanced at it. "Nice."

I smiled. "And it'll all be gone before you know it."

She turned to her computer, punched a few keys, frowned, and punched a few more. She stared at the screen for a moment and then turned to me apologetically. "I'm sorry, but that account doesn't have sufficient funds to cover the amount on this check."

"What!" I picked up the check and studied it. Was it dated today? It was. Was it properly filled out and signed? Everything looked fine to me. I was astonished.

"Maybe the account holder meant to stop by and make a deposit before you cashed it?" the teller suggested.

I nodded. "That must be it," I said, wanting very much to believe it. "I'll give her a call and find out when I should come back."

The teller smiled. "I didn't stamp it, so as long as the money is in the account, you can use the same check."

"Thank you." I walked out, still staring at the check in my hands. Was this a simple mistake? Or was it something else? Bunny must have known I'd go straight to the bank to deposit the check. She wouldn't have purposely given me a bad one. Or would she?

Maybe she'd meant to date the check for tomorrow. Or maybe she'd meant to go straight to the bank from my shop. I searched for an explanation. Maybe her unexpected run-in with Margaret had unraveled her even more than I'd thought. That had to be it. As soon as I got back I'd give her a call and she'd fix the problem. Everything would be fine.

If I really believed that, why did I feel as if I'd just swallowed an anvil?

"That didn't take long," Marnie greeted me as I walked in. And then, noticing the look on my face, she frowned. "What's wrong?"

I pulled out the check and waved it. "There wasn't enough money in the account to cover it."

"Who's it from?"

"Bunny Boyd."

She hurried over and glanced at the amount. Her eyes widened. "It's a lot of money. But why is she writing checks she can't cover? Unless she wrote it on the wrong account by mistake."

That was a possibility I hadn't thought of. "I'm sure it's just a mistake," I said with more conviction than I felt. "Thank God I decided to make the deposit before placing the yarn order."

"Call her. And demand that she replace it with a good check right away. If she thought she was going to get you to do all that work and then not pay for it, she's got another think coming. She's not dealing with a fool."

I nodded, feeling uneasy at the idea of confronting someone who would likely be my biggest client ever. I stared at the phone.

"Go on," Marnie insisted. "Call her. Or are you going to let her walk all over you?"

"You're right." I picked up the receiver and punched in her number. The phone rang once, twice and then her voice mail answered. I listened to her ten-second message and then left mine. "Hi, Bunny. This is Della at Dream Weaver. Could you call me back? I just stopped by the bank to deposit your check, but there seems to be a problem with your account." I hung up.

Marnie was looking at me with a mocking smile. "Chicken," she said. "Give me the phone. I'll tell it like it is."

"Don't you dare. What if it was just a mistake? I don't want to risk insulting her. She'll call me back, I'm sure."

She sneered. "Women like that don't get insulted. They're too busy manipulating."

Marnie returned to her loom, throwing me disapproving looks, which I was ignoring. The bell above the door tinkled and my weaver friend, Lydia Gerard, walked in. Lydia was a shapely brunette a few years younger than me, with dark eyes and the kind of sultry looks most men find irresistible. What made her just as likable to women was that she never seemed to notice her effect on the opposite sex.

She called out a hello to Marnie and looked around, her eyes stopping at the loom. "Good gracious, that is a huge loom," she exclaimed. "I'm almost afraid to try it. Are you sure it's not too big?"

I chuckled. "I know how you feel. I was worried about the same thing when I first saw it. And then the

owner showed me some of the work she'd done on it.
She let me try it, and it's no different from working any
other loom."

"Where did you find it?"

I told her about Margaret. "All I know is that she
decided that weaving as a career wasn't bringing her
the financial security she needed. She sold off everything except one loom. Now she's looking for a job."

Lydia frowned. "Margaret? Is her family name
Fowler? I know her. She's young, right? In her early
twenties? Lives in Belmont?"

"That's right," I said.

"Did she tell you what happened, why she lost her
business?"

"She didn't say much and I didn't want to pry. She
mentioned something about a big contract that fell
through and getting stuck with a lot of—" All at once,
it hit me. The contract must have been from Bunny
Boyd. That explained everything. No wonder Margaret
had been shocked to see her in my shop. And no wonder Bunny wanted to avoid running in to her. Suddenly, I couldn't wait to call Margaret.

Lydia was looking at me quizzically. "What is it?"

"I was just wondering. Would you happen to know
who that contract was from, or what it was for?"

"I have no idea. All I know is she is an excellent
weaver and has a great reputation. I can't imagine why
she would have lost any contract."

"She just rented my upstairs apartment."

"Oh, so you'll get to know her really well. She's nice.
You'll love her."

That was good to hear. It confirmed my own opinion of her. At that moment the bell rang and Mercedes walked in.

"Hi, Della," she called out as she came through the door. And then noticing Marnie, she waved happily. "You're here too? Does that mean you're working for Della now?"

"That I am. I'm her store manager."

"Mercedes, so nice to see you," I said. "Come meet my friend Lydia Gerard."

Mercedes smiled shyly. "Hi, Miss Gerard. What are you doing here?"

"Hi, Mercedes. Della asked me to help her on a project. Are you into weaving too?"

"You two know each other?" I gave myself a mental head thump. "I keep forgetting, everybody knows everybody in Briar Hollow." After living in Charlotte for most of my life, I still found that strange.

Lydia laughed. "That might well be, but I know Mercedes from school. She's one of my best pupils."

Mercedes smiled shyly. "That's because Miss Gerard is one of my best teachers."

I couldn't help remembering how different Mercedes had been when I'd first met her. Instead of wearing her hair its natural blond, she had it dyed black. She'd worn black jeans, black sweaters and heavy black eye makeup. Even her jewelry had been the skull-and-bones variety. Her transformation was like night and day. Now she wore pretty clothes and soft makeup. She was beautiful. I wondered if her schoolwork had seen a similar transformation.

Marnie waddled over, putting an end to my mus-
ings. Together, she, Lydia and Mercedes studied the
loom, discussing its similarities and differences to other
looms on which they'd worked, until a short time later,
Mercedes left hurriedly to join her mother. "She's taking me shopping in Charlotte," she said. "See you
soon."

She opened the door, stepping aside to let someone
in. It was Matthew, dropping off Winston.

Standing next to me, Marnie elbowed me gently.
"Remember what I told you. Bat those long lashes of
yours."

"Hi, Marnie," Matthew called out. "Della, when you
have a minute." And then he noticed Lydia, and his
serious expression melted into a grin. "Lydia, I haven't
seen you in ages."

She beamed back at him and hurried over. "You look
great," she said and gave him a quick kiss on the cheek.
Winston dropped onto his butt, staring up at Lydia
adoringly. What the heck? Even Winnie loved her. *Trai-
tor*. I threw him a dirty look.

Next to me, Marnie whispered, "Take a good look at
Lydia. Now, that girl knows how to work what she's
got."

"If you're trying to make me feel better, it's not
working," I snapped back.

Matthew grinned down at Lydia, and my heart sank.
She said something and he laughed, the little lines at
the corners of his eyes crinkling. And then he put his
hand on her arm, and I almost had a meltdown.

"Maybe this is just the kick in the ass you need,"

Marnie whispered. "Judging by the way those two are looking at each other, you'd better figure out how to get that man real soon, because he ain't gonna stay single forever."

Lydia and Matthew chatted on for a few minutes, which felt more like hours, and at long last, she left, calling out a friendly, "Give me a call sometime. I'd like that."

Hopefully he'd forgotten about my blowup yesterday. I wandered over wearing my best smile. "Hi, Matthew. I'm so happy you dropped by." I stopped and petted Winston.

Matthew looked surprised. "You are?"

"Yes," I said, and then, not knowing what else to say, I added, "I have some interesting information."

"Ah, that explains it. You want to talk about the investigation."

From across the room, Marnie rolled her eyes. "Actually," I said, searching for something nice to say that wouldn't be too embarrassing. "What I really want is to invite you over for dinner. You know that beef bourguignon recipe of my mother's that you like so much?" He looked at me warily. I continued. "Well, she sent it to me and promised to talk me through the steps while I prepare it for the first time." Behind him, I could see Marnie nodding her approval and blinking furiously. Oh, she wanted me to bat my lashes. I blinked a few times.

"Do you have something in your eyes?" he asked, looking concerned.

"Oh, er, I'm fine." *So much for fluttering my lashes.* I

gathered my courage and prattled on. "So, what I'm trying to say is, I'd like to cook your favorite dinner for you."

He laughed. "That's sweet, kiddo. Tell you what. Let's do that. You cook, and I'll bring over a bottle of wine and—just in case the beef bourguignon doesn't turn out—I'll bring a pizza."

With that, he turned and headed for the door.

I called him back. "Hey, what did you want to speak to me about?"

Still laughing, he stopped with his hand on the knob. "Oh, right. I wanted to ask you if you planned to go to McDermott's memorial service this evening." And already knowing what my answer would be, he added, "I'll pick you up at a quarter to seven. After the service, we can go over those pictures together." And just in case I might mistake it for a date, he added, "Why don't you ask Jenny to come along?" The door closed behind him, and I turned to Marnie.

"Well, sugar pie, I'll give you an 'A' for effort."

"And an 'F' for failure. Oh, Marnie, what am I going to do? You saw how awful I am at flirting. He laughed at me."

"Keep trying. You'll get better at it with time."

Getting better *with* time was all very nice, but the question was, would I get better *in* time—in time to snare Matthew before some other girl did?

Chapter 12

Marnie returned to her loom, calling out to me that she'd have a few place mats finished by the end of the day. I set Winston's cushion in its usual spot behind the counter and went through my drawer for the business card I'd put away a few days ago. I picked up the phone and punched in the number.

"Hi. I can't come to the phone right now. Leave a message," her voice mail said.

I left my name and number and hung up. Damn it, I really needed to speak to her, and the sooner, the better. I still had Bunny's uncashed check, and if Bunny was the cause of Margaret losing her business, there was a good chance I'd never get the money up front.

"Marnie, can you mind the store for a few minutes? I'll just run upstairs and be right back."

"Sure. I'm getting paid, so take your time."

I ran up the stairs as fast as my four-inch heels allowed. I knocked. "Hello, Margaret? It's me, Della." A few seconds later, I heard footsteps and then the sound of the latch unlocking. The door opened.

"Hi, Della. Come on in. I just brought over a second

carload. I've already started putting some of my stuff away."

I stepped in and looked around. The kitchen counter was covered in pots and pans, dishes and glassware. On the floor were half a dozen boxes waiting to be unpacked. Good heavens, how I hated moving. Suddenly I noticed the French bulldog. "Well, hello, Clementine. And how are you?" The dog lumbered around me, sniffing at my hand as I offered it—the doggy version of a handshake. "She is so cute. How old is she?"

"She's two years old." Margaret frowned. "I hope you don't mind that I'm already unpacking."

I gave Clementine a head scratch. "Of course I don't mind. I already told you to go right ahead."

"It's a mess right now, isn't it? But don't worry. I'll have the place looking wonderful in no time. What's up?"

I cleared my throat, wondering how I should broach the subject. I was never very good at roundabout ways, and as usual, I went straight to the point. "If you don't mind, I'd like to know what happened between you and Bunny Boyd."

Margaret turned away abruptly, but not fast enough to hide the emotions that played over her face: dismay, embarrassment, fear. She walked back to the kitchen, picking up a stack of dishes, and hefted them inside a cabinet. When she turned to me, she seemed to be struggling for words.

"Margaret?"

She stared down at her hands in silence.

"It was pretty obvious that you two know each

other," I said. "I couldn't help but wonder whether Bunny had anything to do with you closing your weaving studio. The reason I'm asking is because I might be dealing with her for a large contract too, and now I'm concerned." She raised her eyes, still saying nothing. "That contract you talked about, the one that was pulled away from you suddenly, was it from Bunny Boyd?"

Her sigh was full of misery, her voice so low that I guessed the yes more than heard it.

"But why? I saw your weaving. You're incredibly talented."

She shook her head. "My ability had nothing to do with it. It was for personal reasons."

I searched her face, unable to bring myself to ask the details.

"Della, please don't take this the wrong way. But I really don't want to talk about it. This is a private matter." And then, worried that I might get the wrong idea, she added, "Don't worry. I didn't do anything wrong, if that's what you're worried about."

"I don't doubt that for one second. I knew you were a nice person the minute I met you." I stood uncertainly for another minute. "I feel awful. Now that I know you had the contract—I just bought your loom, and—"

"Don't worry about it. It's not your fault. If anything, I'm glad it's you."

"But how will you feel if I take on the contract you lost?"

"I'd be happy for you. I promise."

I turned to leave, and stopped. "Should I worry about her pulling the same kind of stunt on me?"

She didn't even have to think about it. She shook her head. "No. As I said, it was personal. I'd be careful, but no more than with any other contract. I know she sincerely wants that order delivered, and her client has the money to pay for it."

I was more confused than ever. "If only I didn't need the money—"

She interrupted. "Don't be silly. That kind of contract can be important, not only financially but for your reputation too. I'd feel terrible if you turned it down on my account."

I nodded. "Thanks. If there's anything I can do to help, just let me know." I was halfway down the stairs when I turned and ran back. "What about if I hire you to work on the contract? Do you think that would just be too weird?"

"I think Bunny might have a conniption."

I grimaced. "I was afraid you might say that. Anyhow, for all I know Bunny might not even give me the contract. I'm asking for the deposit to be nonrefundable if she changes her mind."

Margaret gave me a thumbs-up. "Good luck."

Back in my shop, two ladies were looking at one of the cashmere afghans, debating whether the color would clash with the older woman's living room sofa. Marnie stood by, ready to help. The younger of the two, a brunette, examined it closely.

The older woman standing next to her said, "Maybe I should bring in one of the cushions before I decide."

"I have a suggestion," Marnie said. "Why don't you take it home and see if you like it. If you don't, you can bring it back and choose another color. If we haven't already got it in stock, we'll make it for you."

"You don't mind?"

"Not in the least."

"In that case, I'll take it." She picked it up and carried it to the counter. I wrote out the bill, put the purchase on her credit card and wrapped the afghan carefully in silk paper, attaching one of my lovely Dream Weaver tags to it. "Here you go. I hope you enjoy it."

"I'm sure I will," she said, and together, the two women exited.

I turned to Marnie. "You handled that very well."

"If a client is interested, you have to get them to buy right away. If they say they'll be back and walk out without buying, nine times out of ten you'll never see them again."

"You have great sales techniques for somebody who never worked in sales."

"I'm an old lady," she said, grinning. "I've learned a lot over my lifetime. Now, how about a cup of coffee and a muffin?"

"Great idea," I said. "I'll get them." I crossed the store and parted the beaded curtains. I was happy to see that three of the six tables were full. Jenny was doing good business. She spotted me and waved.

I reached the counter, and without preamble, she said, "Two coffees coming right up."

"Gee, maybe you're not just a card reader but a mind reader too."

She smirked. "Very funny. One of these days you'll take my gift seriously; you'll see."

I planted my elbows on the counter, looking through the glass top at the pastries below. "And I'll have one of those and one of those." I pointed to the caramel-pecan and the cranberry-lemon muffins. "And those. By the way, Matthew was wondering if you and Ed were planning to go to the memorial service tonight."

"I'd feel weird going, seeing as he was a competitor and all." She handed me the cups of coffee and the bag of muffins. "You can drop by my place after if you like."

"I'll take a rain check on that. Matthew has those photos we want to go over together."

I hurried back to my shop, getting there just in time to answer the phone. "Hi, Mom."

"I was just calling to chat," my mother said. I didn't believe that for one second. My mother never called to chat. She had something on her mind.

"Good timing," I said. "I have a favor to ask. I want to make a beef bourguignon, and I was hoping you could give me the recipe."

"*You* are asking me for a *recipe*?"

"Come on, Mom. It's not as if I never cook."

"Ha!"

I disregarded that. "And besides, if it looks too complicated, I thought maybe you wouldn't mind talking me through the steps when I make it." From his mat next to me, Winston raised his head and stared at me, looking very much as if he understood I was talking about food. Maybe he wasn't so dumb after all.

"You? Make beef bourguignon? What's the occasion?"

"I don't need an occasion to—"

She cut me off, suddenly excited. "You're cooking for Matthew, aren't you? That's his favorite meal. Oh, I'm so happy. You're finally taking my advice."

"Mom, if you don't stop this right now, I'll cancel the dinner."

She calmed right down. "No problem. I'll be happy to give you the recipe. It's actually very easy. And you should make it with mashed potatoes instead of roasted potatoes. That's how he likes it best. And get a nice bottle of—"

"I have a pen and paper now," I interrupted. "Can you give me the ingredients right away?" I wrote them down and then the instructions. Actually, it did sound easy. But if anybody could ruin a recipe, it was me.

"When are you planning to make it?"

"I was thinking of tonight, but seeing as it takes four hours in the oven, I guess I won't have time. Maybe I'll make it tomorrow, or the day after."

"If you want an easy recipe for tonight, you could always make—"

"No, I think I'll stick to takeout pizza tonight. One evening of cooking is enough for one week."

"Oh, all right." She hesitated, and I guessed that what she would say next was the real reason for her call.

"Della, please tell me you're not getting involved in the investigation of that poor man who was murdered."

"If you're asking because you're worried for me,

don't be. I would never do anything to put myself in danger."

"I seem to remember not so very long ago, some-body was shooting at you."

"He never fired, just aimed."

"Oh, Della, don't you see? That's the same thing. Another second and you could have died. Please don't get involved. Back off. Let the police take care of it. That's what they're there for."

"Oh, Mom, you're so sweet," I said, deciding the nice approach was the better one. "You've been worry-ing about me my whole life. I think that's probably why I'll never have children."

This shut her right up. "What do you mean?"

"I see you worrying all the time. If that's the price of motherhood, I think it's not for me."

"Oh, I don't worry so much. In fact, I don't worry at all. I know you're an intelligent woman and that you can take care of yourself."

"Really? Thanks, Mom. I'm happy to hear that." And before she figured out that she had totally been played, I told her I loved her and hung up.

"That was cute," Marnie said, laughing. "I take it your mother is a tiny bit controlling."

"To put it mildly. She's been on a campaign to get Matthew and me together practically since we were toddlers. And recently I found out that Matthew's mother has been playing the same number on him."

"Ohhhh. *That* explains it."

"That explains what?"

"What self-respecting man will date the woman his

mother has chosen for him? No wonder Matthew is immune to your charms."

"That's not good. In that case, no matter what I do, I won't stand a chance."

"The situation is not entirely hopeless. You're just going to have to try even harder. As for your beef stew, you could have asked me. I'm a pretty good cook, in case you forgot. If you want to use your mother's recipe, I'll be happy to give you a hand all the same."

"You really want Matthew and me to get together, don't you? Why?"

"I must be an incurable romantic." She winked. "If you have to contend with his mother, you'll need all the help you can get."

I was looking around for something to do when, all at once it seemed, the shop was full of customers. Marnie left her loom to help. By the time the rush was over, I had made four sales, two of Margaret's pashminas, four of her place mats—she'd be happy to get the money—one of Marnie's afghans and a set of tea towels from another of my weavers. I added up the total. The amount wasn't huge, but it was at least double what I used to sell on a typical day before I moved to this new locale. Business was definitely improving.

"How did we do?" Marnie asked.

I told her. "Not bad. Not bad at all. But there's still room for improvement." She came over to the counter, took a pair of scissors from the drawer and returned to her loom. "I have eight place mats just about ready. I'm taking them off the loom now."

The phone rang and I glanced at the display—Bunny

Boyd. I gestured to Marnie frantically. "You take it. Tell her I'm not here."

Marnie waddled over, looking at me as if I had just sprouted a second head. "One minute you want to talk to her and the next you won't even take her call. I don't get you."

"Be polite," I whispered just as she picked up the receiver.

"Dream Weaver, Marnie Potter speaking. How may I help you?" She listened a few seconds. "Della is out at the moment. May I take a message? Yes. No. That's right. I'll tell her." She hung up and returned to her loom.

I chased after her. "What did she say?"

"You know what she said. She asked to speak to you. I told her you were out, and she said to ask you to call her back."

"That's all?"

"Oh, and she might have mentioned something about the money now being in her account and that you wouldn't have any problem when you make the deposit."

I stared at her. "She might have?"

She ignored my little barb and added, "Why aren't you already on your way to the bank?"

I gave her a half smile. "I know. I should be. Maybe I have rocks in my head, but I seem to have lost my excitement for that project." Knowing that Bunny was behind Margaret's losing her business had dampened my enthusiasm.

For once, Marnie had the grace to not say, "I told you so."

The next customer to walk in was Emma, looking as if she'd just lost her best friend. "I thought I'd say good-bye before I left."

"You're going to New York?" I asked.

She nodded. "I am."

Marnie waddled over. "Good for you. I'm sure you'll take the city by storm."

Emma smiled, but a tear glistened at the corner of one eye. "It's not easy saying good-bye. I won't know a soul in New York."

"How is Ricky taking it?" I asked.

She shrugged. "Not well. But it doesn't really matter because he was just arrested by the police."

I gasped. "What?" Ricky was the murderer? For some reason, I was sure that couldn't be right.

"He was stealing cars and breaking them down for parts, and he had the nerve to say that he did it for me— so he could get us a nice apartment." Her eyes watered again. "That made my decision very easy." She paused. "And he admitted that he was the one who made that crank call you got."

"Really?" I said, although I wasn't the least bit surprised. "When are you leaving?"

"I'm taking the bus from Charlotte tomorrow."

Marnie patted her on the arm. "The next time we see you, it'll be on the cover of *Vogue*."

Emma laughed. "That would be nice." She looked into the back. "Is Jenny here? I want to say good-bye to her too."

"Go on. That'll make her real happy," Marnie said.

Emma disappeared behind the beaded curtains, reappearing a few minutes later, brandishing a bag of cookies. "For the road," she said, smiling. "Jenny insisted."

The rest of the day went by with no more than a trickle of sales, giving me ample time to review what I had just learned. The fact that Ricky had been arrested for car theft did not mean he couldn't have killed Philip McDermott, but it did explain the argument I'd overheard between Emma and him. It also convinced me that Emma was innocent. If the girl would break up with her boyfriend because he stole, she couldn't possibly be a killer—at least not in my opinion. I was relieved to strike her off my list of suspects.

At five o'clock, I put up the CLOSED sign in the window and added up my daily sales. The total was not bad at all. It was reassuring to know that if things continued improving at this rate, if worse came to worst, I could survive without the Whitby job. I'd debated all afternoon whether I should ask Bunny to come in and sign the contract or not. It was high time I stopped being a wimp and called her. I stared at the phone, gathering my courage. What the heck was I waiting for? I used to be a big-city career woman who let nothing stand in my way. Before I could change my mind, I picked it up and dialed. Once again, my call went straight to voice mail.

"Hi, Bunny. Della here. I'm sorry I missed your call. I looked over the contract you gave me and I added a small clause to protect myself. I hope you'll understand that I can't start work until you sign it. Please call me." I hung up and looked at Marnie.

She was grinning widely and gave me a thumbs-up sign. "Good girl. There's hope for you yet." She gathered her bag and headed for the door. "See you tomorrow."

"See you tomorrow, Marnie," I called back. I was happily surprised at how much she enjoyed working in the shop. Over the last couple of days, her attitude had undergone a remarkable change. She still came in grumpy occasionally, but by midday she radiated. She was right. Working from my shop, rather than her home, was therapeutic for her.

"And being here is therapeutic for you too, isn't it, Winnie?" He looked up at me with his eternally puzzled eyes. "And having you here is just as good for me."

He blinked and went back to sleep while I prepared my deposit. "Ready to go for a walk, big boy?" He hopped off the sofa and clickety-clacked to the door. I called out a good night to Jenny, and we took off.

Winston had a lot of qualities, but obedience was never one of them.

"No, Winston. I don't want to go that way." But no matter how much I tried to direct him toward the bank, he marched on determinedly, dragging me along. I gave up and let him lead, until suddenly I found myself in front of the Coffee Break.

"Winston, stop," I ordered, and for some odd reason, this time he obeyed, plopping his butt onto the sidewalk. I peered inside the darkened shop. It had been only a few days since McDermott's murder, but the place already looked abandoned. The food counters in the back were empty, the magazine racks bare.

I was about to continue on my way when, from a second-floor window, I heard Rhonda's voice. She sounded excited. "How dare you even ask?" she shrieked. "Of course I mind. You and my husband had an affair for years and I'm not about to forget it." Who was she talking to—or rather, screaming at? "Sure it was a long time ago, but wives don't forget that kind of hurt. I was never able to have children. If you show up at his funeral, I swear I'll have you thrown out. And you can try and explain *that* to your boyfriend." *Boyfriend?* Maybe she was talking to Bunny. But if she were, wouldn't she have used the word "fiancé" rather than "boyfriend"? On the other hand, maybe she didn't know about the engagement. As to her comment about never having children, I couldn't make heads or tails of it. What did that have to do with anything?

As I stood there in the middle of the sidewalk, staring at the window above, I became aware that to anyone watching I would have looked as if I was spying—which, granted, was exactly what I was doing. I dropped to one knee, pretending to fix a nonexistent shoe problem. The conversation—by now I had guessed that it was on the telephone—continued.

"You can call it blackmail if you want, but frankly, letting everybody know what kind of a woman you are is exactly what you deserve."

Blackmail. Mrs. McDermott had actually used the word. Did that mean what I thought it did? Had she picked up where her husband had left off? If so, that would explain how Mrs. Anderson's pictures had suddenly disappeared.

Rhonda McDermott had probably always known about her husband's studio. She probably also knew of his nude photography, maybe even of his little blackmail sideline. If he really had been hiding it from her, then she must have been spying on him. How ironic.

My mind was spinning with new theories and fresh suspicions, and it was a few minutes before I noticed that the conversation had ended. I looked up and was shocked to find Mrs. McDermott staring down at me.

"Let's go, Winston." I was in such a hurry to get away from there that it wasn't until I'd walked another block that I remembered—damn—I still had my daily bank deposit to make.

At just about six thirty, I was freshly showered and made-up. I had piled on the mascara and now stood in my bra and panties, riffling through my closet, looking for something that would be appropriate for a memorial service. I pulled out a dress and studied it. It was the navy number with the turtleneck collar and long sleeves. Even though it covered a lot of skin, it was formfitting. From the corner of the room, Winnie watched approvingly.

"You like this one, don't you, big boy? This is the one you wanted me to wear to the party. Maybe you were right." His bat ears flicked forward and then back. "If I'd worn this dress instead of the red one, who knows, maybe Matthew would be in love with me by now."

He gave me a "woof," as if to say, "That's right."

"I sure hope you know what you're barking about." I took the dress off the hanger and pulled it on. I closed the door, posing this way and that for the mirror behind it. I stepped into a pair of four-inch heels and nodded with satisfaction. "I have to hand it to you, Winnie. I guess you were right. This dress makes me look mighty fine."

By six thirty, I was ready and waiting . . . and waiting . . . and waiting. My heart skipped a beat every time a car went by. I picked up the phone a dozen times to make sure the line wasn't dead. At seven o'clock Matthew had still not arrived and hadn't even called to explain.

"What do you think of that, Winston?" I asked. "I've been stood up, and on an outing that isn't even a date. How pathetic is that?" Winnie struggled to his feet and strolled over to lick my hand. "I love you too, big boy."

Well, I was not going to sit here and wait all night. I'd go by myself if I had to. I gathered my purse and my car keys, gave Winnie a pat on the head and left. I had just reached the street when a green Jaguar came to a screeching halt not ten feet away.

"I'm sorry I'm late," Matthew said, jumping out of the car. He hurried to the passenger side and held the door open. "I was writing, and I completely lost track of time."

"I wondered what happened."

He closed the door behind me and jogged over to the driver's side. "You weren't really leaving without me, were you?" he asked, buckling his seat belt. "If that ever happens again, don't just leave. Call me."

"It's a deal," I said.

The service was being held at a funeral home in Belmont. Along the way, I told Matthew about Mrs. Mc-Dermott's conversation that I'd overheard.

"She actually used the word 'blackmail'?" he said, keeping his eyes on the road.

"She did. Her exact words were, 'You can call it blackmail if you want.'"

"And you have no idea who she was talking to."

"None. At one point she said something like 'try explaining that to your boyfriend.' I thought it might be Bunny, but then she would have said 'your fiancé.'" From the look on his face, I realized I'd never told him about Bunny's engagement ring. I filled him in.

He was quiet for a few seconds. "The only thing we can conclude is that Mrs. McDermott must have known about her husband's blackmail scheme. Maybe she picked up where he left off. Now the question is, who is she blackmailing, Julia Anderson or somebody else?"

"I came to the same conclusion. But because of the 'boyfriend' comment, I doubt it would be Mrs. Anderson—unless she's having an affair with someone. After all, it's her pictures that are missing."

"True."

"It sounds as if she was telling someone to stay away from the service tonight. We'll soon see who is missing." I was quiet for a second. "I'm not convinced that Rhonda killed her husband, but I'm pretty sure she was the one who stole the pictures from the studio. After she found his body and finished answering the police's questions, I think she hightailed it over there and went through those pictures. Who knows? Maybe she got others at the same time."

"Didn't you tell me the person who bumped into you was a man?" He paused. "Oh, you mean the second person, the one who showed up while you were in the darkroom."

"Yes. You know, there's one possibility we never considered," I said. "Maybe McDermott was never behind any of the blackmail. Maybe it was his wife all along."

"I never even considered that," he said. "Who knows? You could be right."

We got off the highway and onto a country road. Soon, clusters of houses went by and then the sign for Belmont. Matthew slowed. More houses went by, and then we were in the downtown commercial area. A few blocks later, I spotted the sign, PEACEFUL MEADOWS FUNERAL HOME, and Matthew drove into the parking lot. It was packed with cars, as if every car in town were there.

"McDermott must have been well liked."

He slowed to a crawl, looking for a spot. "In small communities like Briar Hollow, it's normal for all of the townspeople to show up to pay their respects." He slid into a parking space and we made our way to the building's entrance.

The parlor was packed. We snaked through the crowd to the far end, where, in lieu of the usual casket, since the body was still in the hands of the Charlotte ME, a large photo of the deceased was displayed. Around it were dozens of smaller pictures. A few feet away and dressed in black, Mrs. McDermott cried softly into a tissue. A woman whispered in her ear, and she looked up with red-rimmed eyes.

Matthew approached. "I'm so sorry for your loss," he said. She nodded and thanked him. He moved aside, and I stepped in front of her, saying the same thing. She looked at me. Her mouth tightened, but she didn't say a word.

I moved away. Was her coldness my imagination? Or had she guessed that I'd been listening in on her conversation earlier? She'd seen me being questioned by the police after finding her husband's body. She probably suspected that I was helping them again. But why would that upset her? Wouldn't a wife want her husband's killer found?

I made my way through the crowd, nodding and smiling hello to familiar faces as I took note of those who were absent.

Jenny had already told me she wouldn't be here, but I'd wondered whether Marnie would come. There was no sign of her. Across the room I noticed Jeffrey Anderson chatting with an elderly couple. I looked around for his wife, but she was nowhere around. Maybe she *had* been the person to whom Rhonda had been speaking. I wandered farther and noted Mr. Whitby surrounded by a small group of people. To my surprise, Bunny was nowhere around either. That was more than odd. I would have expected her to latch onto her fiancé's side and not let go for a second. A few steps later, I spotted the Sweenys, both looking very stiff and proper in black suits. Who was missing? Emma Blanchard wasn't here, obviously, since she was on her way to New York. And neither was Ricky Arnold, who was enjoying the hospitality of the local police. Mrs. Anderson's and Bunny's absences were the only two I noted as suspicious. Didn't political wives and fiancés always accompany their men for such occasions? Who else? I glanced around the room one more time and came up blank.

I scanned the room for Matthew and discovered him near the entrance chatting with Officer Bailey. I was surprised to see Bailey dressed in civilian clothes— making his presence less conspicuous, I guessed. A few feet away were two other men I recognized as policemen, also not in uniform. So the police were here. Were they keeping track of everyone who came? I was tempted to tell them that what they should really take note of was those who weren't.

Matthew looked around and saw me. He wandered over.

I leaned in. "I forgot to ask you. Did you find out if Mr. McDermott had life insurance?"

Matthew's smile stiffened. I turned around and found myself face-to-face with Mrs. McDermott. She was staring at me through narrowed eyes. And then she turned and walked away.

"Uh-oh. Do you think she heard that?" I whispered.

Matthew bobbed his brows. "I'd say that was pretty obvious."

"How about we get out of here?" I said. "I don't think she'll be very happy if we stick around."

We wove our way out through the crowd, and minutes later, we were back at the car. Matthew slid into his seat, pulled out his cell phone and punched in a number. "Who are you calling?"

"Bottoms Up," he said to me, and then into the phone, "One extra-large pizza with the works, extra cheese, to go. Matthew Baker. I'll pick it up in ten minutes." He dropped his iPhone into his pocket. "I take it beef bourguignon is not on the menu tonight?" He winked, and my heart fluttered.

We took off.

"Did you notice that neither Mrs. Anderson nor Bunny Boyd were there? Don't you think that's suspicious?"

"I suppose," he said, sounding unconvinced. "But there could be countless reasons for them not being there."

"Why do you think the police were there? Do you think they were keeping track of who came and who didn't?"

"That's standard procedure. They always show up for services and funerals of murder victims."

"In that case, they might be forgetting about the one person who had to be there whether she killed him or not—Mrs. McDermott."

He glanced at me. "I'm sure they didn't forget about her."

"How sure are you that she overhead me ask about her husband's insurance?"

"Of course she heard. Didn't you see the look on her face?"

I shivered. "For a moment I wasn't sure what she'd do."

"Put yourself in her place," he said in a pacifying

tone. "If she's innocent, how do you think she feels, overhearing someone ask about her husband's life insurance? Losing a loved one is difficult enough without being subjected to everyone's suspicions. Under the circumstances, I think anybody would have reacted the same way."

Matthew was right, and I felt a pang of guilt for suspecting her. Poor woman. She had looked completely devastated after finding her husband's body. Still . . .

"All I'm saying is, let's not forget about her. By the way, you never answered my question. Did you find out whether her husband had life insurance?"

"The police already questioned her about that. She admitted to owning a fifty-thousand-dollar policy on her husband's life, which he bought when they first got married, more than twenty-five years ago."

"Fifty thousand dollars? That's all? I'd expected it to be for a larger amount."

He slowed and looked both ways before turning onto the highway. "People have been killed for less. Anyhow, the cops are not taking her word for it. They're still looking, but it's a lengthy process. It means contacting all the insurance companies. They're also monitoring her bank account for any unusual activity. So far, they've found nothing suspicious."

I pondered all of this for the rest of the drive, and ten minutes later Matthew pulled up in the parking lot of Bottoms Up. He ran in, returning with the pizza, and we were on our way back to my place, where Winston greeted us with his usual overexuberance.

Matthew dropped the pizza box on the counter and

crouched to Winston's level. "I know. I know." He scratched his back. "I'm happy to see you too." He stood. "I forgot something in the car." He ran out, returning moments later with a thick file, which he dropped on the dining room table.

"What's that?"

"The pictures of McDermott's models—we'll go over them later."

He opened a bottle of wine and I set the table. My eyes kept going to the file. I could barely wait to see who else might be in there.

As last, he returned and handed me a full glass of Pinot Noir.

"Thank you." I waited for him to sit, and then I served us each a slice of pizza. I took a bite. "Sorry," I said, reaching out for the file. "But I've been waiting for this for two days. I can't wait any longer." I opened it.

The first picture was a head shot of Emma. The girl was truly gorgeous, her features incredibly photogenic. Her eyes were large and widely spaced, her cheekbones high and her lips generous.

"She really could make it in modeling," I said. "I'm glad she didn't let that boyfriend of hers stand in her way."

"What are you talking about?"

"I guess I didn't tell you what happened." I told him about the vibration in my steering wheel and my visit to Al's Garage the next day. "When I went to pick it up the morning after, I overheard Ricky and Emma arguing." I repeated what I'd heard. "She dropped by the store earlier to say good-bye. She's on her way to New

York. And get this. Ricky is in jail for car theft. I suspect she might have turned him in."

"I knew about his arrest," Matthew said. "And you're right. Emma was the one who reported his thefts to the police."

"And you didn't think of telling me?"

He ignored the jab and continued. "The police also searched Al's Garage and found parts from tons of stolen vehicles."

"So Al was in on it too?"

"He claims that Ricky drove into Charlotte for parts every other week and that he had no idea they were stolen."

"A likely story," I said. "Getting back to Emma, I'm convinced she had nothing to do with McDermott's murder or the stolen pictures."

"I agree."

"Well, isn't this a refreshing change? I don't think I've ever heard you voice a firm opinion, especially not one that agrees with mine."

He chuckled and picked up Emma's photo, studying it. "I guess one could say she's attractive. She's just not my type."

My pulse quickened. "What is your type?" I asked, trying to sound casual.

He looked at me and his dark eyes lightened. "Oh, I don't know. Maybe I just prefer brunettes." He was looking at my hair. My mouth went dry. And then he continued. "Lydia Gerard—now, there's a beautiful woman."

My heart sank, and I struggled to keep my smile

from dropping. "She is, isn't she?" I said as if I didn't care in the least. I couldn't quite meet his eyes.

The next dozen pictures were of Emma. "The cops were thorough. They didn't need to give us so many head shots of the same models."

Then there was a picture of a pretty redhead. "Who's she?"

He gave me a name I'd never heard before. "She used to live in Belmont but moved to Los Angeles about ten years ago. The police checked and she was at her job the day McDermott was killed. There is no way she could have made it here, killed McDermott and gotten back to LA in time for work."

"What about the gun? Any news from the examiner on what type it was?"

"They've confirmed that the gun was a Colt semiautomatic."

"So it wasn't Whitby's gun."

"We still don't know that."

I looked at him, puzzled. "What do you mean you don't know for sure? Whitby's Colt was more than a hundred years old, and you just said that the murder weapon was a semiautomatic."

He smiled. "Colt semiautomatics already existed a century ago. So it could have been the same weapon."

"Oh. I had no idea. I always thought semiautomatic meant modern." I thought quickly. "If it was the same weapon and they never find it, can they still make a case?"

"Presumably, but it will be much harder. Without the murder weapon, the prosecutor will claim it was

Whitby's missing gun, and unless we can prove beyond any shadow of a doubt who stole it, the defense will point out that anybody at the party could have taken it."

"So this might turn out to be the perfect murder."

"Perfect murders don't exist. With forensic science, nowadays even decades-old murders are being solved." He gave me a crooked smile. "It ain't over till it's over, kiddo."

He picked up another photo, this one of a brunette. This picture also looked as if it had been taken during the seventies or eighties. "Beatrice Mallory," Matthew said. "Happily married and living in Charlotte. And she also has an unshakable alibi. She was nowhere near here the day of the murder." He set that picture aside along with the dozen or so more shots of the same woman. He continued on, identifying and setting aside model after model until he got near the bottom of the pile. "This one is still unidentified." He handed it to me.

"I noticed this one in the darkroom." The shot was old, like so many of the others. The model was rather plain, with brown hair, brown eyes and unmemorable features, yet there was something familiar about her. "I have the feeling I've seen her before but I have no idea where."

He nodded. "Bailey said the same thing. She reminded him of someone, but he couldn't think of who."

"Can I borrow it? I'll show it to Jenny and Marnie. They might recognize her."

"I don't see why not." He handed it to me.

"Give me a few more of her. She might look different from other angles."

"That's the only one the police found of her."

"That's odd. McDermott had dozens of pictures of every other model. Are you sure?"

He glanced at me. "If I say there is only one, that's because there is only one." He answered my silent question. "She wasn't very photogenic. He might not have taken more than a few pictures of her to begin with."

It was true that the girl certainly wasn't very attractive. He pulled out the picture, studied it again and set it aside. We continued through the pile until I had seen them all.

He picked up the stack and shoved them all back into the folder, all except the unidentified girl. "Every woman in those pictures has an alibi except for Emma and this unknown woman."

"And we've already eliminated Emma as a possibility. What about Mrs. Anderson? Even though her pictures weren't there, she's still a suspect."

"Nobody's eliminating her."

I turned over a new idea. "I'm beginning to think that maybe McDermott's murder had nothing to do with the nude photos," I said, plopping back against my chair.

"Could be," he said vaguely, eyeing the last piece of pizza. "You want it?"

I waved it away. "You go ahead. I'm full." Two minutes later it was all gone except for a small piece on my plate. I picked up the plates and carried them back to the kitchen with Winston hot on my trail. I threw him the piece and he lunged for it.

From the dining room, Matthew called him back. "Ready to go home, Winston?" Winston galloped back.

"Don't look so happy to leave, big boy," I said, joining them in the foyer.

Matthew was already clipping on his leash. "All he knows is that he's going for a walk—his favorite thing, along with food, belly rubs and head scratches." As if to confirm this, Winston wiggled his butt, barking happily. "Sorry to be leaving so abruptly. I want to get an early start on my writing tomorrow."

I might have been tempted to suggest he stay for another glass of wine, but after his comment about Lydia, I was not about to.

"I'll see you when I drop off Winston in the morning," he said, and a minute later he was gone. The downstairs door closed, its sound reverberating under my feet. Suddenly I was alone, and the apartment felt incredibly lonely. I wondered idly if Margaret had already moved in next door. It would feel reassuring to have someone living close by. I shrugged off the unease as normal after a visit to the funeral parlor. I poured myself a second glass of wine as I got ready for bed.

The next morning was miserable, wet and cold. I slipped on a raincoat and made a mad dash to pick up my paper, throwing a quick glance at the empty coffee shop across the street. The lights of the McDermotts' living quarters were turned on, but the shop was still dark. Maybe Rhonda would never reopen. If she sold her shop, maybe Jenny would consider buying it. I slipped the paper under my coat and hurried back to my shop. I wiped my feet on the entrance mat and dropped the paper on the counter.

"Hello-o. Anybody here?"

From the back came the sound of the coffee grinder. Coffee would be ready in a few minutes, thank goodness. I shook the rain off my coat and picked up the phone. I dialed my message code. "You have zero messages." Bunny had still not returned my call—what a surprise.

"Who was that on the phone?" asked Marnie from the doorway.

"Oh, hi. I didn't hear you come in."

"I just walked in." She shook the rain off the zebra-print umbrella, which matched her zebra-print rain-coat. She closed it, leaning it against the doorframe.

"I was just checking my messages. Sill no news from Bunny." I walked around the counter. "I'm getting myself a cup. You want one?"

Marnie chuckled. "Yes, please. If I don't get one soon, I'll turn into a worse grump than you."

"What is that supposed to mean?"

"Put a smile on your face, child."

I headed toward the back. Jenny greeted me with a cheerful "Good morning."

"How do you do it? You're in a good mood no mat-ter what the weather."

Her lips tilted at the corner. "If you'd had the night I did, you'd be happy too."

I wiggled an eyebrow. "I take it you're talking about a night with a certain good doctor?"

She blushed. "No, I mean I had a really good night's sleep."

"Sure you did." I picked up the cups she handed me and winked. "Or maybe you were *dreaming* about the good doctor." I hurried to the front before she could think of a smart retort.

Marnie had slipped out of her raincoat. I noticed the bag in her hands.

She carried it over. "I have another four place mats."

"So fast!"

"I've been weaving so many years, it's as easy as pie for me." She snapped her fingers. "And speaking of pies, I gave Jenny an apple-cranberry pie I want her to test with customers. You'll have to let me know if you like it."

"There's no question I'll like it. The question is, will I still fit in my clothes afterward?"

Marnie rolled her eyes. "You are so fat—why, you're practically obese."

The bell rang, and Matthew came in followed by Winston. "Hey," he said, walked over and planted a kiss on my cheek.

"Hey to you too." He unclipped Winston's leash and the pooch jumped up at me. I pushed him off. "Down, Winnie. You're getting me all wet." The dog trotted away, dropping onto his cushion. He glanced back at me, looking insulted.

"Did you show Jenny and Marnie the picture?" Matthew asked.

"Oh, shoot. I forgot it upstairs. I'll run up and get it."
I hurried to the door. "Be right back."

I was halfway up when I heard a door close. A moment later, Margaret appeared at the top of the stairs.
"Hi, Della."

"Hi." And then I noticed her French bulldog on a leash. "Hi, Clementine. How are you this morning?"

"She had a good night. We slept here for the first time last night."

I reached the landing and petted her. "Hello, pretty girl. Are you going to visit Winston downstairs?"

"Is he there now?" Margaret asked.

"He is. You should stop by. I'll be only a minute." I hurried to my apartment and raced back down.

Back in the shop, I looked around. The only person there was Marnie. "Where's Matthew?"

"He was in a rush to get somewhere. He said to tell you he'd pick up Winston around two. Oh, and Margaret's in the back with Jenny." She pointed behind the counter. "And guess who's got a girlfriend."

I walked around. There was Winston nuzzling with Clementine. "Ah, that's so cute. Now the only one around here who needs a boyfriend is me."

"And me," Marnie quipped, planting her hands on her ample hips.

I stopped myself from laughing. "I didn't know you wanted one."

"Hey, I may be middle-aged, but I'm not dead. I still have needs, you know." I must have looked shocked because she added, "I'm talking about affection—you know, like hugging—and company." She glanced at the file I'd just dropped on the counter. "What's that?"

"Matthew got copies of all the models McDermott photographed over the years. The police already identified all of them except for one. Matthew thought you might recognize her."

Marnie came closer. I handed her the picture. She stared at it for a long time.

"What do you think? Have you ever seen her before?"

She put it back in the folder and handed it to me with a shrug. "I have no idea who she is. She looks somewhat familiar, but it could be she just reminds me of somebody."

I let out a long breath. "She looks familiar to me, but I can't place her. I was thinking that she might be someone local. A person can change a lot after ten or twenty years."

"True, but I think I'd recognize that nose. That's quite a honker she's got." It wasn't a very nice comment, but I was used to Marnie's blunt ways. She paused. "The person you really should ask is Jenny. She's lived in Briar Hollow her whole life."

"Didn't you?"

"I was born here, but when I got married I followed my husband to Charlotte. I didn't move back here until ten years ago. Whoever that girl is, she might have lived here during the years I was away."

I picked up the file. "I'll go ask her now."

"She's got a shop full of customers, and Margaret is

with her. A bunch of people came in while you were upstairs."

I'd been gone for only a minute. "Good for her." I picked up Marnie's place mats and studied them. Each was woven in a different color against the same white warp. One was navy, one red, one forest green, and the last one was a golden yellow. "An odd set; how pretty."

"I thought it might be interesting to make something different for a change."

I placed my white coffee mug on the red mat. "Look at that. They'll look great on a breakfast table, especially with white dishes."

She headed for her loom and settled comfortably in her chair. Soon a few customers walked in. I slid the folder with the picture of the unknown model under the counter and hurried forward.

"Welcome to Dream Weaver. Can I help you?" The women were lookers. They strolled around for a few minutes, and just when I was sure they were about to leave, one of them picked up the new place mats Marnie had just brought in.

"These are so colorful. What do you think?" she asked her friend. "Aren't they fun?" She looked at the tag. "I'm taking them." She picked them up and marched over to the counter. A few minutes later they had left. The shop was empty again.

I waved my sales book to Marnie. "We're out of place mats again."

"I saw that. You're right. I can't make them fast enough."

"I'd better call all my weavers and tell them to get going on place mats." I picked up the phone. A few minutes later, I had promises for eight sets, and there were still two weavers I hadn't been able to reach.

Marnie chuckled. "Eight sets should last you at least a couple of days." Her next question was one I'd been asking myself. "What are you going to do when you hear from Bunny?"

A group of Jenny's customers walked through the shop at that moment, and I waited until they had left. "I think her silence is speaking loud and clear. She doesn't want to sign that agreement, and I can't afford to work with a customer like that."

"So you've made up your mind?"

I hesitated. "Oh, God. I just don't know."

"Don't know what?" Jenny asked from behind me.

I turned around. She had a tray in her hands. Margaret was standing next to her, wearing a grin. She placed a platter of fresh muffins on the counter.

"Bunny Boyd still hasn't come in to sign that contract."

"You should see that as a sign," she said. "Don't work with her. I told you. You'd so regret it."

Margaret frowned. "I hope you're not hesitating on my account?"

Marnie and Jenny looked at her, puzzled. "Why would it have anything to do with you?" asked Marnie.

I explained. "I found out that Bunny gave Jenny the contract and then pulled it away from her suddenly, leaving her with all the yarn she'd already purchased for the project. That's why Margaret had to close her studio."

They looked at her for confirmation. Margaret nodded, but added uncomfortably, "It isn't as bad as Della makes it sound."

"It sounds plenty bad to me," Jenny said.

"Don't worry. If I turn her down it will be for my own reasons."

Marnie nodded. "It's true. She gave Della a bad check."

"To be fair, she made good on that check right away. It was just a mistake. The reason I don't want to deal with her is that she isn't reliable. I've asked her more than once to agree in writing that if she changes her mind, the deposit is nonrefundable. Maybe I'm just being paranoid, but if she decides to sue me for that deposit, she can afford a lawyer much more than I can. I can't order that amount of yarn without feeling safe."

"I have an idea," Margaret said. "Why don't you buy the yarn from me? I already have the full amount you'd need to fill the contract. You can pay me when you get paid, and if Bunny pulls a number, then you can sell the fabric you've already produced, return the rest of the yarn and pay me only for what you've used." She saw my hesitation. "Think about it," she insisted. "It's a good idea. It would benefit both of us."

It was a great idea, but for some reason I still hesitated. "Let me think about it."

"On another note," Jenny said, putting an end to the subject, "I have good news. Della, Marnie, meet my new employee, Margaret."

Margaret laughed. "Not only her first, but also her only employee."

"That's wonderful." I said. "Good for you. When do you start?"

"Right now," she said.

Jenny passed coffee all around and we clicked mugs.

Margaret took a sip and then excused herself. "I have to get back. I can't stand around chatting. I have a job to do, you know." She hurried to the back.

"She's going to be great," Jenny said. "I have a good feeling about her."

I suddenly remembered the picture. "I have something I want you to take a look at." I pulled out the file and handed it to Jenny. "Do you recognize this woman?"

She studied it in silence for a few seconds and then shook her head slowly. "I can't say that I do. Is she supposed to be from around here?"

I shrugged. "I have no idea. I told you about the photographs I found in McDermott's studio. They've all been identified except for this one. Nobody knows who she is."

Jenny studied it again. "Do you have any other pictures of her, maybe one from a different angle?"

"No. That's the odd thing. There are dozens of pictures of every other model, but only this one of her. Matthew thinks McDermott might not have been as inspired by her."

"Because of that honker," Marnie said.

"This picture looks like it was taken decades ago," Jenny said.

I nodded. "Judging by the hairstyle and the makeup, it looks to be about twenty years old to me."

Marnie came over and stared down at the picture.

"Della thinks she reminds her of somebody, but she can't figure out who."

"I don't know. I could be wrong about that."

At that moment, Margaret returned. "I just wanted to ask you how—" Her eyes fell on the open file on the counter. She stared at the picture and blanched.

"What is it?" I said. "Are you all right?"

"I'm fine," she answered in a tight voice. "I'd better get back." Before anyone could say another word, she whirled around and hurried to the coffee shop.

Marnie stared after her. "What the heck was that all about?"

Puzzled, I said, "I have no idea."

Jenny was quiet for a moment. "All I know is the minute she laid eyes on that picture, her aura went from soft blue to a dark gray."

Marnie frowned and stared down at the picture. "Do you think she recognized the woman?"

It hardly made sense to me. "She's a bit young to have known her. She couldn't have been more than a baby when that picture was taken. But I think she does know something." I turned to Jenny. "Give me a minute with her." I hurried to the back.

Margaret was sweeping the coffee shop floor. She saw me and scowled.

"Tell me," I said, putting a restraining hand on the door handle. "You recognize that woman, don't you? Who is she?"

Something like fear flashed through her gray eyes and she looked away. "I have no idea who she is. I'm sorry, Della. I can't talk now. I'm working."

"Come on, Margaret. Jenny won't mind. Please, tell me—"

"Maybe this wasn't such a good idea after all," she said, whipping off her apron. "I should find another job." She threw it on the back of a nearby chair and stormed through the beaded curtains. A moment later, I heard her snap a command at Clementine. "Come, Clem." Then the bell above the door tinkled.

Jenny came in, looking bewildered. "What the hell just happened?"

"I think she just quit." I shook my head, baffled. "It's my fault. I must have pushed her too hard. I'll go talk to her."

I hurried after Margaret, taking the stairs to her apartment as fast as I could. I knocked on the door. "Margaret. Please don't quit. Jenny needs you. I promise I won't question you again."

My pleading was met with silence. I stared at the door for a long time. What could Margaret be so afraid of?

Chapter 13

I returned downstairs, puzzled. When I walked in, Jenny had returned to her shop and Marnie instantly bombarded me with questions.

"Why did she run away like that? Does she know something? Did she recognize the girl in the picture?"

"She wouldn't answer the door," I said, staring at the picture before shoving the folder into the drawer. "Maybe it was my imagination, but I could have sworn she looked scared. She ran into her apartment and locked the door."

Jenny wrinkled her nose. "What the heck is going on?"

The bell above the door tinkled, and a moment later Matthew walked in. I looked at my watch—eleven. What was he doing back here so early?

"Hey there, gorgeous," he said, putting all thoughts of unknown models, of murder and of suspects out of my mind.

I widened my eyes in mock surprise. "Are you talking to me?"

"Don't be silly," Marnie said, striking a pose. "You're talking to me, right, handsome?"

"Right," he said, the crinkles around his eyes deepening. "I like that blouse you're wearing."

"I was hoping you would," she said, batting her lashes.

I dropped down and petted Winston. "I don't care that Matthew likes Marnie better, just as long as you like me, right, Winnie?" I glanced up at Matthew.

He grinned back at me. "I was wondering if you'd mind keeping him a little later this afternoon. I could pick him up around six or so."

"Great, and then you can come up and have dinner with me—beef bourguignon."

His eyes lit up. "That's an invitation I won't turn down. I'll bring the wine."

I glanced at Marnie, who was nodding furiously and batting her lashes again.

I smiled at Matthew. "Mashed or roasted?"

"Mashed, by all means."

"Great, dinner will be ready at seven."

"Perfect," Matthew said. "And just to prove I trust your cooking, I won't bother bringing the pizza." He headed for the door, threw me a smile and left.

The door swung shut and Marnie threw her hands in the air. "By God, she's got it." She turned to me. "You actually did it right this time. You flirted."

"I did?"

She raised a hand and high fived me. "That proves it. There's hope for you yet."

She returned to her loom, singing, or rather, screeching some old love song—something about a fellow needing a girl in his arms. Winston, who was lying in front of the counter, sat up and howled along with her.

I laughed. "I think he's telling you not to quit your day job." I pulled his cushion from under the counter and fluffed it up. "Come, Winnie." He stopped howling and dropped back down. I threw him a piece of jerky and soon he was snoring contentedly.

The day flew by with a constant stream of customers. The shop was so busy that I didn't have a minute to slip into the back to order a sandwich until nearly two o'clock—good thing, considering Jenny had lost her new employee and was running herself ragged.

By then I was famished. But when I walked in, the tea shop was still packed. Ever since the Coffee Break had been closed, Jenny's business had doubled almost daily. I waved at her from the beaded curtain, and she signaled that she'd get back to me. I walked back out. Damn, if her shop continued being that busy, I'd have to start bringing in my own lunch. And I wasn't even any good at making sandwiches. That thought suddenly reminded me that I'd promised Matthew beef bourguignon for dinner. *Shit*.

I ran to the front, shouted at Marnie that I was going grocery shopping and I'd be right back. I grabbed my coat and was about to tear out of there when Julia Anderson walked in. I threw Marnie a panicked look.

As if on cue, Marnie hefted herself off her seat. "I'm heading out to do that shopping you wanted," she said. She counted on her fingers. "Two pounds of beef chuck, two cups of pearl onions, one pound of cap mushrooms, garlic, beef broth and potatoes. Am I forgetting anything?"

I must have looked confused because she called over her shoulder as she headed toward the door, "I'll give you a call from the grocery store. If I'm forgetting anything, you can tell me then." The door closed behind her and Mrs. Anderson and I were alone.

"What can I do for you?" I asked.

"I know you turned me down when I asked you before, but I'm hoping this time you might feel differently." I waited for her to continue. She took a deep breath. "The blackmail has started again," she announced.

My eyes widened. She continued. "Whoever took the pictures from Philip's studio has picked up where he left off. I got this in the mail this morning." She rummaged through her purse and pulled out an envelope. It was addressed to her with a printed label, the generic stick-on type used in laser printers. She opened the envelope and handed me the note.

The message consisted of three lines of pasted words cut from newspapers and magazines. It read: "I have the pictures. For ten thousand dollars I will give them to you instead of to the newspapers. Get the money ready and I will contact you with further instructions."

I looked into her frightened eyes and my heart went out to her. The poor woman was terrified.

"It came yesterday morning. I got a call last night with instructions to drop off the money tonight."

"Tonight?"

She looked near tears. "I'm to meet this person in the park behind the church at eleven o'clock tonight. He warned that if anybody else came along, he would send the pictures to the newspapers right away."

"You heard the blackmailer's voice? You're certain it was a man?"

She hesitated. "It was difficult to say. The voice was deep and raspy, but it sounded like somebody changing his voice."

"Could it have been a woman?"

She looked taken aback. "You think a woman might be behind this?"

"I have no idea whether it's a man or a woman. I'm just looking at all the possibilities. Do you have any idea who it might be?"

She shook her head. "None. The only thing I can tell you is, if my husband ever finds out, it will kill him." She closed her eyes suddenly and wavered on her feet as if she might faint.

"Mrs. Anderson, are you all right?"

She swallowed and pulled herself up. "I'm fine."

"I don't understand what you think I can do. If this person told you to come alone—" And then it hit me. "You want me to go in your place?"

Her eyes watered. "I know I have no right to ask you—"

Call me crazy, but all at once, I did want to go in her place. "What were the instructions?" I asked.

"I'm to sit on the bench at the edge of the park behind the church and wait. When the blackmailer sees me, he'll give me the signal to leave the envelope on the bench and walk to the opposite side of the cemetery. I'm to wait there until he picks up the money, makes the drop and leaves. As soon as he's gone, I can pick up the pictures."

I knew very well I shouldn't get involved, but I felt compelled to help the woman. "You and I are the same height," I said hesitantly. Her eyes brightened with hope. I continued. "He'll never be closer than about twenty yards, and in the dark he won't be able to see your face any more than you can see his." I was using "he" as she was, but I suspected the black-mailer was none other than Mrs. McDermott, which was another reason I wanted to go. The woman might be a blackmailer, but I was convinced she wasn't dangerous.

"I can't tell you how much I would appreciate it."

I thought of the nice dinner I was planning for Matthew. I thought of the snuggling and kissing I was hoping to do on the sofa in front of the fireplace. If I timed things right, I could still spend a nice evening with him. I'd just have to cut it a bit short. And if I went, I might not see the blackmailer's face, but I'd at least see his figure. I'd know whether it was a man or a woman. All at once I made up my mind. "I'll do it," I said suddenly.

"Thank you. Thank you." She opened her purse and riffled through it, pulling out two envelopes. "This one is for you."

"I can't take your money," I said, handing it back.

"I insist. There's five hundred dollars in there."

I shook my head. "Please consider coming back and shopping at the store if you like anything. We don't know that I can help you yet."

"It's a deal." She handed me the other, thicker envelope. "This one is in exchange for the photographs." She repeated the instructions. "And remember, he will leave the photos on the bench. Don't forget to pick them up before you go. Do you understand?" I nodded. "Thank you." She turned and left.

As soon as the door closed behind her, I was filled with panic. What had I just done? I had actually agreed to meet someone alone and in the dark. And that person was certainly a blackmailer and possibly a murderer. But even as I berated myself, I knew I wouldn't change my mind. Somebody had to take a chance if this murder was ever to be solved. And if I was right, this might just do the trick.

The phone rang, snapping me out of my thoughts.

It was Marnie. "Do you have that beef bourguignon recipe in front of you?"

I opened my drawer and shuffled around until I located the piece of paper on which I'd jotted it down. "I have it."

"Good. Now read me the ingredients." I did, and then she said, "Got it. I'll get everything you need and I'll stop by my house for a couple of frozen lava cakes. All you'll have to do is pop them in the oven for seven minutes. That and a scoop of ice cream and Matthew won't stand a chance. He'll be yours for eternity." She hung up.

Unfortunately not for eternity, it seemed, since I already had another engagement at eleven o'clock tonight.

Chapter 14

"Don't worry," Marnie was saying. "I'll help you every step of the way—except with the flirting," she added. "You're on your own with that."

It was a quarter to three and we were in my kitchen.

Jenny had knocked on Margaret's door herself, begging her to come back, and the girl had relented. Now she and Jenny were minding both shops while Marnie helped me prepare Matthew's favorite meal. As soon as it was in the oven, we'd both hurry back to the shop.

"Preparation will take twenty minutes at most," Marnie promised.

She lined up the ingredients and pointed to the onions. "The first thing you do is parboil the pearl onions so that you can peel them more easily."

She might as well have been speaking Chinese. "Parboil?"

She stared at me, incredulous. "Oh, boy. I have a feeling this might take a long time. But don't worry. I'll be gone by the time Prince Charming shows up."

"You'd better be gone earlier than that. Jenny will mind the store, but what if she has customers?"

"I have an idea," she said. "I'll call you from downstairs and walk you through the steps. If you have any problems, I can be here in a second."

She threw off her apron and hurried back downstairs. A second later my phone rang. It was Marnie. "Okay, first thing you do is—"

Other than Winnie sniffing around and constantly getting in my way, things were going along great. I threw him a small piece of meat, which he gobbled up in one gulp, and placated, he retreated to his cushion. I cooked on.

An hour later, my beef bourguignon was braising in the oven and already filling the kitchen with a wonderful aroma.

"I can't believe I did it," I gushed. "And it wasn't even that complicated."

"Maybe for you," Marnie grumbled at the other end of the line. "But I came pretty close to a heart attack about a dozen times." I laughed. "I hope you know how to make mashed potatoes," she continued.

"I know how to peel them. I know how to boil them and I know how to mash."

"Thank God for small favors," she said. I could almost hear the eye roll in her voice. "Then you don't need me for that." The phone went dead. It wasn't a second later that it rang again. "Okay, here's how you make perfect mashed potatoes." She gave me a list of ingredients to throw in, salt and pepper, butter and chives. "And my secret ingredient, sour cream. The trick is to mash, add a bit of sour cream and mash again. Keep doing this until you get a nice and creamy consistency. Got it?"

"Got it."

"Then you do the seasoning—just a little at a time and then taste. Keep adding little by little until it's just right. Do you think you can handle that?"

"Of course I can do that. Now, good-bye." This time I hung up.

An hour later, the potatoes were peeled and ready to put on the stove. Marnie's lava cakes were in the refrigerator, the instructions for preparing them on the counter. I had nothing to do for the next hour and a half but make myself beautiful.

"Want to help me pick a dress, Winnie?" He clambered to his feet and followed me to the bedroom. I pulled dresses from the closet, laying them out on the bed. "How about this one?" I held the sleek black knit dress in front of me.

Winston growled.

"You don't like it? I agree. It's way too fancy for a simple dinner at home. I don't want to look as if I'm trying to seduce him"—even though that was exactly what I wanted to do. I put it back on its hanger and pulled out a blue wrap dress with a V neckline. "How about this one?" Winston stared for a moment and then barked. "And we have a winner," I said. "You're getting good at this."

I hurried to the kitchen, checked on the dinner and then took a shower and dressed. At five o'clock Marnie popped in.

"I just want to make sure you've got everything under control." She opened the oven, lifted the lid and put it back down. "It'll be done by seven, seven thirty. Now, remember. You add the pearl onions and mushrooms no more than a few minutes before serving. Otherwise they turn to mush."

"Got it." I wished I felt as confident as I sounded.

"By the way," she said on her way out, "Bunny Boyd called. She wanted to know if your order of yarn had arrived yet."

"She what?"

Marnie smiled. "You told me to be nice in case you changed your mind, and that's exactly what I did."

"Great. The one time I think someone deserves a good talking to, you don't."

"Sugar pie, you have to learn to affirm yourself." She grinned. "Don't worry. I told her you left her a message yesterday, and when she pretended that she never got it, I repeated it to her word for word, without giving her a piece of my mind."

"What did she say?"

"She said that unless you place that order today, you can forget about the contract."

My eyebrows froze somewhere near my hairline. "She did, did she? Fine. I don't even want her stupid contract."

"Don't get yourself all riled up. Right now you have to think nice thoughts so that you can be in a good mood when Matthew arrives."

"You're right. I can already feel my blood boiling." Unless I put my mind on something else I would be tense all evening. I took a deep breath and exhaled slowly.

"That's better," she said. "Now, do you need any last-minute help with anything?"

I glanced around. Everything in the kitchen was done. The dining room table was set. Cheeses were already mellowing on the counter for appetizers. I shook my head. "I can't believe I'm saying this, but no. Everything is done. I made dinner, and it's all under control."

Marnie nodded. "Just don't forget how to flirt, and you'll be perfect." She headed toward the foyer. "See you tomorrow, cupcake." Suddenly I had nothing more to do but wait—and be nervous.

At six o'clock, Matthew buzzed from downstairs, and I let him in. He came up, taking the steps two at a time and carrying a bottle of red wine in one hand and flowers in the other. He handed me the bouquet.

"Pink roses. Oh, Matthew, I love them."

"There are lilies and asters in there too," he said. "I thought you'd like them. They reminded me of you somehow."

"They did?"

He didn't answer, bending down to pet Winston. "Hey, boy. Did Della spoil you too?" He stood back up. "Where do you want the wine?"

"How about you open the bottle in the kitchen." He trailed after me and made appreciative noises as I checked on dinner.

"It's not every day I have a beautiful woman cooking me my favorite meal," he said, rummaging through the drawer for a bottle opener.

I had already cooked and mashed the potatoes following Marnie's directions. I had tasted them and they were perfect. They were now sitting in a pot on top of the stove. All I would need to do was pop them in the oven to warm up at the same time I added the pearl onions and mushrooms to the stew.

"Everything will be ready in an hour. In the meantime, we can have wine and cheese in the living room."

He looked around. "I'm impressed. You don't even look nervous."

"Why should I be nervous?" I said, thankful he couldn't hear my heart thumping against my ribs. I opened the cupboard, grabbed two glasses and handed them to him. He poured and carried them to the living room. I followed with the tray of crackers and cheese.

I checked my watch. I'd planned everything down to the details. I had forty-five minutes to relax. Then, at six forty-five, I would complete the last step and serve dinner at seven. I would pop the lava cakes in the oven at seven thirty and serve them at seven forty-five. At eight thirty we would move to the living room again and sip our wine until around ten. With any luck, there might be a bit of canoodling during that time. And then I would have to make some excuse—exhaustion or something—and Matthew would leave early enough for me to change into jeans and make it to the park before eleven.

We sat. "How's your book coming along?" I asked, determined to take Marnie's advice and get Matthew to talk about himself. Easy enough since I was interested in his life.

"It's coming along. I've been working on inserting anecdotes, the way my editor suggested, and I have to admit, she knows what she's talking about. The book is a lot less dry. I think even people in the industry will like it better."

"That's wonderful. I can't wait to read it. You'll have to sign my copy."

He laughed, and the way he looked at me told me Marnie was right. The more interest I showed in him, the more he seemed to like me.

Soon, the timer I'd set for the beef bourguignon rang, and I excused myself, added the pearl onions and mushrooms, put it back in the oven for a few minutes, along with the mashed potatoes. Fifteen minutes later, we sat down to eat.

"This is every bit as good as your mother's," he said between bites. "If I didn't know better, I'd think she was hiding in your bedroom right now after having cooked it herself."

I laughed. "Go check for yourself if you don't believe me."

Lava cakes were the perfect dessert. By the time dinner was over, I was basking in the glow of success, made all the more pleasant by the two glasses of the smooth merlot Matthew had served me. Everything had gone perfectly. I had even flirted. Marnie would have been proud of me. Now we were back in the living room. Matthew sat across from me, studying me through golden eyes.

He got up and refilled both our glasses and then walked around the coffee table toward me. For once I hadn't put my foot in my mouth. I dared believe that he was going to sit close to me, maybe even wrap his arm around my shoulders. In a few minutes we would be kissing.

Suddenly he tripped. "What the hell?" He had regained his balance. Now he stared at the object on the floor—my purse. Uh-oh.

It lay open, with a pile of hundred-dollar bills—ten thousand dollars' worth of bills—spilling onto the floor.

He tore his eyes away from them and looked at me. "I think you have some explaining to do."

I scrambled for an answer. "I—I was going to tell you." That was a complete lie, and from the tightness of his mouth, I could tell he already knew as much. "It's not mine. It's blackmail money. Mrs. Anderson's payment in return for those pictures of her with Mr. Whitby."

He frowned. "What the hell are you talking about?"

I told him. "Please don't be mad at me. She was so desperate, Matthew. I felt sorry for her. I couldn't say no."

He stood with his hands on his hips, glaring down at me, his eyes ablaze. "I can't believe—I take that back. I am not in the least surprised. I should have known you would do something like that." He shook his head in frustration. "Do you have any idea what kind of danger you'd be putting yourself in? If the blackmailer also happens to be the killer, you could end up with a bullet through that pretty head of yours." At least he'd called me pretty—sort of. "I absolutely forbid you to go."

My eyebrows bobbed. "You *forbid* it?" Now *I* was starting to get angry. "You have a lot of nerve thinking you have the right to tell me what I can and cannot do. Who do you think you are?"

His jaw hardened, and his eyes darkened. "You're right. Only somebody close to you would have the right to worry about your safety. And God knows you and I are anything but close." He turned to Winnie, who was watching, puzzled, from the corner. "Let's go, Winston."

Winnie jumped up and scampered after Matthew. The door slammed shut behind them.

Stupid, stupid, stupid. I had done it again. I had spoiled the perfect opportunity to set this friendship on fire. Judging from the way he'd looked at me before leaving, I wasn't sure I even had his friendship anymore.

Chapter 15

The streetlamps threw golden pools of light along the dark street. For the second time in days, I was wearing running shoes. I hurried toward the church, uncomfortably aware of the ten thousand dollars in cash inside the envelope stuffed in my Windbreaker's pocket.

People get killed for much less.

I looked around. The street was quiet, not a soul around. I wasn't sure if that made me feel better or not. I wished Matthew were here. Hell, I'd even be happy to have Winston with me.

I reached the church and followed the walk to the back, where the park and cemetery were. It was one thing to come here during the day, but it was entirely different at night. There were no streetlights here, the only lighting from the moon. I squinted and spotted the park bench. I rushed over and settled into the wait . . . and wait . . . and wait . . . hoping that I was right and that the blackmailer was Rhonda McDermott. Otherwise, I might be in as much danger as Matthew had warned.

All around me shadows loomed. They seemed to grow larger, closer with every advancing minute. Every crack, every snap startled me, and I had the uncomfortable feeling that somebody was watching. I couldn't be certain—it was too dark to check my watch—but I thought I'd been waiting for a long time, much longer than I should have. I suddenly remembered the light at the end of my key chain. I fished through my pocket for it and flicked it on—eleven thirty. He was half an hour late. How long was I supposed to wait?

Maybe he was watching now, making sure there was nobody else around. I'd wait another few minutes, I decided, already imagining how disappointed Mrs. Anderson would be if the blackmailer didn't show up. I'd return her money, of course. In fact, I felt so uncomfortable carrying such a large sum that I couldn't wait to get rid of it.

Suddenly a shadow appeared. This one was definitely moving toward me, and quickly. Hold on. Hadn't Mrs. Anderson said that the blackmailer would keep his distance? That seeing his face would put me in danger? He was now no more than ten feet away and still advancing. I sprang to my feet and ran.

"Wait, Della. It's me."

I stopped and turned. "Matthew?" The figure came closer. It *was* Matthew. "What are you doing here? You scared me half to death."

"Sorry, kiddo. After I left your place, I decided I couldn't let you come here by yourself. If something happened to you, I would never forgive myself."

Luckily it was dark, so he couldn't see the blush rising to my face. "You were worried for me? That's so sweet." I looked around. "Do you think the blackmailer saw you?" I whispered. "Maybe that's why he didn't show up."

"He couldn't have. After leaving your place, I went straight home, dropped off Winston and came here. I've been here for nearly two hours. If anybody had come anywhere near this place, I would have seen them. You were the only person the whole time."

We locked eyes, and the gaze held.

I cleared my throat. "I'm glad I don't have to walk back home on my own. I don't like carrying all that money."

He wrapped an arm around my shoulders and steered me toward the street. "I shouldn't have gotten so angry at you," he said.

Was that an apology? Was Matthew actually apologizing? "I guess I shouldn't have tried to keep a secret from you."

He chuckled. "What you should have done is turn down this stupid errand in the first place." He squeezed my shoulder affectionately, and my heart skipped a beat. "Every time I turn around you're doing something else that keeps me up nights worrying about you." A lump settled in my throat. This was as close to an admission that he cared as I'd ever heard.

"I guess I'm just a sucker for people in distress. She looked so miserable that I couldn't turn her down. But you're right. It was stupid of me."

A few minutes later, we were at my door. He turned me around until I faced him, and our eyes locked again.

I was fed up with our eyes locking. What I really wanted was for our lips to lock. He tilted my chin up with a finger, bent down, and my knees nearly buckled. And then he *kissed* me—on the cheek, damn it. But it was a kiss nonetheless. And it made the whole scary evening totally worth it.

"Good night, gorgeous," he said, and then he walked away.

Chapter 16

I slept like a log, so much so that when I looked at my alarm clock, it was already eight o'clock. I'd overslept by more than an hour. I threw back the blankets and hopped out of bed.

I scrambled into the first outfit I grabbed, did a three-minute makeup job and then spent ten minutes looking for a safe spot where I could hide ten thousand dollars and feel safe that nobody would find it. I opened the can of coffee beans and hid it in there. No, too easy. I pulled it out and slipped it behind the gallon of ice cream in the freezer. I changed my mind again and shoved it inside the bag of dog kibble.

I was halfway out the door when I changed my mind again and went running back. This time I slid the envelope between the Rice Krispies cardboard box and its wax paper bag. Nobody would think of looking there.

No matter how late I am, there are certain things I simply cannot forgo. One is my coffee, the other my newspaper. I hurried down the street to the newspaper dispenser and was just about to head back to work when I noticed that the side door to the McDermotts' building—the entrance to their private quarters'—was ajar. How strange, especially on a gray day like today. I stayed rooted to my spot for a few minutes, certain that Rhonda would show up to either close the door or step out—but no. The door remained open. Suddenly a gust of wind came, flapping the door back and forth.

The little voice that had been niggling that something was wrong was now screaming. I crossed the street and stuck my head in the doorway.

"Hello? Anybody home?" Silence. That same voice was now quite insistent that I walk away *now*. I disregarded it and stepped inside. "Hello? Mrs. McDermott?" Still nothing. I wandered farther.

The McDermotts' home looked old and tired, in my books synonymous with sad and loveless. The hallway paper was peeling at the corners and seemed to date from the seventies. I popped my head into the kitchen. I noted a worn and graceless yellow oak table and matching chairs and walked on. In the living area, the walls were old rose—an awful color—the chintz sofa and armchair shapeless. On the floor, the pastel Oriental rug was gray from age and too few cleanings.

"Hello? Is everything all right?" I stepped to a doorway—a bedroom, I realized—and peeked in. "Mrs. Mc-Dermott?" As my eyes adjusted to the dimness, I could see the shape of a bed, a dresser and a bundle on the floor. I blinked.

That was no bundle.

It was Mrs. McDermott.

The woman was twisted in an unnatural position with one arm flung over her head. I felt along the wall for the switch and flicked it on, flooding the room with light.

"Mrs. McDermott? Are you all right?" But even as I said this, I knew from her sightless stare that the woman was dead. I stepped closer and touched her wrist—ice-cold. My hand sprang back. And then I noticed the dark circle that had pooled around her—blood. I jumped up and ran out of the room, afraid I might be sick. I stuck my head out the door and took a few deep breaths, and my good sense caught up with me. I couldn't just leave. I had to call the police. I scrambled through my purse for my cell phone and dialed 911.

"I'm calling to report a murder." As soon as I mentioned a pool of blood and that the deceased was Mrs. McDermott, the dispatcher's voice rose.

"Stay right where you are. And don't touch anything. I'm sending the police and the coroner."

The second I hung up, it hit me. If Mrs. McDermott was the blackmailer, as I suspected, this could explain why she hadn't shown up at the appointed time last night. She was already dead.

A new thought occurred to me. I had maybe two, three minutes at most before the police got here. It wasn't much time, but maybe just enough for what I wanted to do. I looked around. If I had wanted to hide photographs somewhere in this house, where would I have put them?

I returned to the bedroom, stepped around the body and headed for the closet. My hand was three inches from the handle when I stopped. I didn't want to leave prints. I pulled the sleeve of my sweater over my hand and opened the closet door. I scanned the contents: two hanger rods, one above the other, both crammed, the top one with shirts and sweaters, the bottom one with dresses and pants. On the floor a jumble of shoes. Above, no shelf. I hurried back out. I walked around the body again and moved on to the desk in the living room. I opened the drawers—pens, paper, eraser, stapler, but no pictures. I hurried to the kitchen, pulling open the cupboard doors—still nothing. I stood in the center of the room and looked around.

I was searching in places that were too obvious. The hiding spot would have to be easy access, but not so obvious as to be the first place a person might look. And then my eyes fell on the broom closet. I dashed over.

It wasn't until I was closing the door again that I noticed the corner of a brown manila envelope peeking out from a red plastic bucket. I snatched it, being careful not to leave prints, and opened the flap. Just as I'd suspected, inside were half a dozen pictures of a young Mrs. Anderson gazing adoringly into Bernard Whitby's eyes.

It looked as if I'd been right. Mrs. McDermott was probably the blackmailer.

Suddenly I heard the sound of a siren approaching. I stuffed the pictures back inside the envelope and slipped it back where I had found it. Moments later, when the police came bursting in, I was sitting in the living room, looking innocent.

"Well, well," Bailey said, laying eyes on me. "I take it you called in the murder?"

I nodded. "She's in the bedroom."

At the same time, the second cop, who had rushed by, called out, "She's over here." Bailey gave me a hard look and marched off toward the bedroom.

I stayed put, waiting for the questioning I knew would follow. A minute later, Bailey was back. He sat across from me and studied me through suspicious eyes. "Explain to me again," he said, pen poised to take down my words, "what you were doing traipsing through the dead woman's house."

When he put it that way, I had to admit my actions did sound suspicious. "I was across the street, picking up my paper at the vending machine. I do that every morning." I went on to explain about the side door being open, about the gust of wind that sent it flapping. "At first I thought she'd left it unlatched by mistake. I only popped my head in to let her know. But when she didn't answer, I started worrying."

"So you thought, why don't I take a stroll around her house?"

I held on to my patience. "No. By then I was worried. She'd just lost her husband. For all I knew, she might have been ill, fainted or something."

"Is that all?" the officer said with more than a hint of sarcasm. "I can't help but notice that every time there's a murder around here, there you are. How can one person be involved in so many murders?"

Whoa, "involved" was a big word. "If by that you mean that I happened to find both bodies, then, yes, I'm involved. But if you're suggesting that I had something to do with their murders, then you're way off base."

He was trying to rattle me. I knew I shouldn't worry, but I couldn't help it. Even if Officer Bailey knew I was innocent, he might well have decided to solve the case the easy way—by convicting the convenient bystander, a temptation that might be made all the greater by the fear that unless he arrested someone soon, this same convenient bystander might solve the case before he did.

I made a big show of looking at my watch. "As far as I'm concerned, I did my duty. I called in the murder. If you need to speak to me, I'll be at work. I'd better get going." And since he didn't protest, I got up and out of there, hurrying more with every step, until I was almost running back to the store.

By then I was more than an hour late for work. Still, I went back to my apartment. I picked up the phone and dialed. "Mrs. Anderson, please. Della from Dream Weaver is calling."

In the background I could hear classical music and then, "Hello, Della." I could tell by her tone that she was not alone. And just in case somebody was listening on the line—good grief, I really was becoming paranoid—I spoke in code, praying she would understand. "Hello,

Mrs. Anderson. I waited for that weaver you told me about, but she never showed up. I still have that deposit you left me. Can you tell me when you'll stop by for the refund?" There was a long silence at the other end. "Mrs. Anderson?"

"I'm listening, and I must say, I'm very disappointed." She sounded more furious than disappointed.

"I followed your instructions to the letter, but the weaver never showed up," I said, a bit more insistently. *Not my fault. Get it?*

"Fine," she said, and without another word, she hung up.

I stared at the receiver in my hand. Now what was I supposed to do? I had no idea when she would come get her money. If she didn't pick it up soon, I had a good mind to hand it over to the police. Who was I kidding? I couldn't do that without implicating myself.

I hung up and left the apartment. On my way downstairs, a horrible idea occurred to me. Had I been made a patsy?

I sat on the bottom step, chewing my lip. If Mrs. Anderson knew that the blackmailer was Mrs. McDermott, she might have sent me to meet her, intending on searching her house in the meantime. My blood ran cold as a question popped into my mind. If Mrs. Anderson killed Mrs. McDermott, did that make me an accessory to murder?

I ran back up the stairs, picked up the phone again and dialed Matthew's number. He answered on the fourth ring.

"What?" he barked, sounding irritated.

"Matthew. This is really urgent. You have to help me."

"Della? What's wrong?"

"Did you hear the news? Mrs. McDermott is dead—murdered." I heard his intake of breath. "I found her body." He was quiet for a moment. "Please come. I don't want to tell you the rest on the phone."

"I'll be right over."

I hung up and called downstairs. Marnie answered. "I won't be in for a little while. Can you handle everything by yourself for an hour or so?"

I could hear the smile in her voice. "Ah, hard night, was it? I hope Matthew kept you awake for hours."

I didn't even have the presence of mind to respond. "I'll see you later." Click. I hung up.

I plopped myself in a chair with my elbows on the table and my head in my hands. "I am in such trouble," I said to the walls. And then I hopped to my feet and grabbed the bag of coffee beans from the cupboard. I had to keep busy or I'd go crazy. By the time Matthew arrived, Winston tagging along, coffee was ready and waiting.

We were on our second cup. "Let me get this straight," he said. "You think Julia Anderson played you?"

I nodded.

"You think she sent you to meet the blackmailer—Rhonda McDermott—and during that time, she broke into the woman's house to search for the pictures."

"Yes, but something went wrong. Either Rhonda was late leaving, or Mrs. Anderson got there early. When they came face-to-face, Mrs. Anderson had no choice but to kill her." I paused. "Unless her plan was to kill her all along."

He mulled this over for a long minute. "Before you jump to conclusions, you have to promise me you won't do anything else. Stay out of it, Della. Do not call Mrs. Anderson. Do you hear me?" He did not sound happy.

I squeaked a tiny yes, deciding he didn't have to know I'd already made that call. "Do you think the same killer that murdered Mr. McDermott also murdered his wife?"

"It's a logical assumption," he said.

"In that case, we can eliminate Ricky and Emma. He's in jail and she's in New York. That leaves Bunny and Mrs. Anderson. And since we can't find a motive for Bunny killing either of the McDermotts, that leaves Mrs. Anderson. It's got to be her. Also, I forgot to tell you. I found those pictures of her and Bernard Whitby in the house."

"Are you telling me you searched the place?" he asked, his eyes wide with shock.

"Uh . . . I didn't search it exactly. I just looked around a little while I was waiting for the police. And in case you're worried, I made sure I didn't leave any fingerprints."

"I wasn't worried about that," he said, but in fact, he sounded quite relieved.

"So what do I do now?"

"Do?" he asked, exasperated. "Don't you think you've done enough? I already told you, stay out of it. I'll go down to the station and find out what's going on." He stood, and on his way out of the kitchen, he paused. "I have a good mind to turn you over to the cops myself. That might be the only way to keep you safe." He walked out.

Winston was sitting on the floor next to me. He looked up at me with big, sad eyes.

"He wouldn't do that, would he?" I said.

Winston sighed deeply, shuffled over to his cushion and plopped down. I picked up the empty cups, rinsed them out and popped them into the dishwasher.

"Sorry I'm late," I said as I stepped into the shop. I waited for Winston to come in and closed the door. Marnie came rushing over.

"Jenny's shop is packed, and she's all by herself this morning. Margaret can't be here till eleven," she whispered, wild-eyed. "Everybody's talking about how, since you found both bodies, maybe you had something to do with them being murdered."

I closed my eyes and grimaced. *Damn*. I looked at my watch—ten o'clock. "Maybe I can use that to our advantage. I can try scaring them into spending a lot of money in here."

"Very funny."

"So how do you suggest I handle it?"

"You're innocent, aren't you? Then just behave like normal."

A moment later, a few customers left Jenny's shop, and noticing me, made a dash for the front door. I looked at Marnie. "Gee, you'd think I was aiming a gun at them."

Another group of women walked out of Jenny's shop and scampered away when they saw me. This was not good for business.

When her shop was empty, Jenny came forward, carrying a tray of coffee cups and muffins.

I'd already had two cups this morning, and considering the way my hands were shaking, another was the last thing I needed. But when Jenny handed me a mug, I took it with a sigh of relief.

"I was ready to kill for one of these," I said.

Marnie gave me the eyebrow. "Considering what people around here are saying, that's not something I'd joke about if I were you."

"Maybe you're right." I took a fortifying gulp.

Marnie scowled. "Are you going to drink the whole cup before you tell us what the hell happened?"

I set it down and told them, feeling the horror of it all over again. "I noticed the open door and popped my head in and called her name. When she didn't answer, I got worried and went inside. She was on the bedroom floor, dead."

Marnie looked horrified. "How awful. First her husband and now her."

Jenny frowned. "Was she shot with the same gun?"

"I have no idea," I said. "We won't know that until the ballistics reports come in."

"I don't understand anything anymore," Jenny continued. "Didn't you say she was your primary suspect?"

That's what I'd thought—at some point. "I said she was a suspect. But she was never the only one."

"Who else could it be? We know it's not Emma or

Ricky. Much as I don't like Bunny, I don't think she had anything to do with it."

"I don't really suspect Bunny anymore," I said. "I can't find any motive for her wanting McDermott dead."

Marnie cocked her head. "What I can't understand is why anybody would want to kill Rhonda. If the killer wanted her dead, why didn't he kill her and her husband at the same time?"

"Unless," said Jenny, "Mrs. McDermott found out something." She snapped her fingers. "Maybe she figured out who the killer was."

Marnie nodded, adding her own theory. "And maybe she was blackmailing him."

I decided to let them play detective as much as they wanted and not tell them that I had already come to much the same conclusions. I was especially not about to mention the errand Mrs. Anderson had asked of me. Of all the people involved, she was the one I had least suspected at the beginning. Now, as it turned out, she seemed to have not only the best motive, but also an excellent opportunity, one she had probably planned for just that purpose.

Marnie turned to me, a frown puckering her forehead. "You're very quiet."

"I'm just thinking that . . . I'm utterly confused. I have no idea what to think anymore." They both looked at me as if they didn't believe a word.

Jenny picked up the empty mugs. "I'd better get back." At that moment, the phone rang. I glanced at the call display.

"It's Bunny," I blurted.

Jenny put down the mugs and stared at me expectantly. "Well, aren't you going to answer?"

Marnie planted her elbows on the counter and cupped her chin in the palm of her hand. I took a deep breath and picked it up.

"I'm sorry I didn't get back to you sooner," Bunny said. *Sure, she was.* "I got your message. I'm in New York and won't be back until this evening." Not a word about the message Marnie had relayed to her yesterday. What a hypocrite that woman was. "Now, what's this about you not wanting to place the order until I sign the contract?"

Maybe it was the stress of the morning combined with Bunny's tone of voice, but I suddenly found myself snapping back. "Believe me, I do want to work for you, but I am just a small business. I can't afford to risk ordering such a large amount of yarn without being certain that you won't pull the rug from under me the way you did with Margaret Fowler. So, please come by and sign that contract. Until you do, I won't place that order."

Marnie gave me a huge grin and a thumbs-up. "Atta girl."

Bunny's voice went up an octave. "What are you talking about? I never did anything to Margaret Fowler."

"Oh, no? What would you call what you did?"

"What happened with that girl—"

"What happened with *that girl*, as you call her,

proves one thing. You are not to be trusted," I said, getting more incensed with every word.

"You think I can't be trusted?" She screamed this so loudly into the receiver that Marnie's and Jenny's eyes widened. "I'll have you know one thing. By cashing my check, you committed yourself—"

"I did *not* cash your check," I said with great enjoyment. "I have it right here. You can pick it up anytime you like."

This silenced her. The pause stretched and stretched, and then without another word, the line went dead.

"Woo-hoo!" exclaimed Jenny. "You took my advice. Does that mean you finally believe I can read auras?"

I swallowed hard, suddenly realizing what I had just done. "I wouldn't go that far."

She smiled. "I'll make a convert out of you yet," she said, heading toward her shop.

I gave them a jaundiced smile. "Well, I'd better sell a lot of goods, because I can probably kiss that beautiful contract good-bye."

The door opened and Matthew walked in. "I have some news," he said. Winston scampered out from behind the counter and ran up to him. "Sorry, boy. I'm here to see Della. You, I'll see later."

Winston slunk away.

Matthew glanced at Jenny and Marnie, and I guessed that he wanted to speak privately. "Are you free for dinner tonight?" I asked. "Maybe I can cook you dinner again?"

"That sounds great, but I already have plans."

"Oh? What are you doing?"

"I'm having dinner with Lydia." I struggled to keep my smile from slipping. To my surprise, he thought for a second and said, "But I should be free by nine, nine thirty at the latest. How about if I come over then? Unless you'd rather make it tomorrow night."

Not on your life, buddy. The earlier he came to my place, the less time he'd spend with Lydia. "Tonight is fine. I'll make coffee and if you save some room, I'll serve you dessert."

"Good. See you then." He turned on his heel and left.

Marnie gave me a crooked smile. "Just what kind of dessert do you have in mind?"

"Don't be silly," I said as an image of me wrapped seductively around Matthew flashed through my mind.

"Just so you know," she continued, "I'll be happy to provide cake or pie, but if you're thinking of something racier than that, you're on your own." And before I could reply, she returned to her loom.

"Come on, Winnie. You know me better than that, don't you? I would never throw myself at a man just back from a date with somebody else."

He looked at me. "Ruff," he barked.

Across the room, Marnie laughed. "You should listen to Winston. He just told you he thinks your attitude is rough too."

Winnie was snoring on his cushion behind the counter when the door opened and Margaret Fowler walked in carrying a cardboard box. She dropped it on the counter with a thud.

Looking embarrassed, she said, "I want to apologize for my behavior yesterday. I'm so sorry. I hope we can still be friends."

I was surprised at how relieved I suddenly felt. Obviously, the possibility of being on bad terms with her had bothered me more than I'd realized. "There's nothing to forgive. It was my fault for prying, and of course we can still be friends."

"Oh, good. I promised Jenny I'd be in by eleven. That gives me ten minutes to show you what I have." She pulled open the flaps of the box and pulled out a stack of cloth goods, sorting them into piles: place mats, dish towels, afghans and kitchen rugs.

"They're beautiful," I exclaimed. "I'm so glad you're bringing in some rugs. Now that Jenny isn't doing much weaving anymore, I really needed new inventory."

"I don't know that I can bring them in regularly, but I'll do my best to keep you supplied."

"What I really need are more place mats. I can never keep them in stock."

"Place mats it is."

Marnie wandered over. "By the way, did you know that Della turned down the contract from Bunny Boyd?"

That was not what I had done, but if Marnie had interpreted my words that way, Bunny probably had as well.

Margaret looked from Marnie to me. "Why did you do that? Not because of me, I hope."

Marnie answered. "Of course not because of you.

Because of the way she treated Della. Della asked her a million times to come sign that contract, and she just ignored her. She couldn't take the chance she'd pull the same number on her that she had on you."

Margaret looked uncomfortable, and I changed the subject. "I forgot to tell you I sold a few of your pieces." I opened the drawer and pulled out my stock book, flipping through a few pages. "Let me see. I sold two of your afghans." I continued down the list, checking the items and jotting down the amounts in the margins. I calculated the total and wrote her a check. "Here you go."

Her face lit up. "Thank you so much. I didn't expect to be paid this fast. This is great. I'd better get to work." She turned and hurried to Jenny's shop.

Marnie was staring at Margaret's back as she disappeared behind the curtain. "I just noticed something. Ever since I first met her, I kept thinking she reminds me of someone, but I couldn't figure out who."

"Who?" I asked, only half listening.

"It's her eyes. They're a very unusual shade."

Margaret's eyes were a dark shade of bluish gray circled with black. They were arrestingly beautiful. She continued. "I've only ever seen that shade once before." She paused. "Do you know who else had that color eyes? Philip McDermott."

"Is that so?" I said, not really paying attention. I opened the drawer to put away my stock book, and my eyes fell on the file of the unknown model. For some reason, I pulled it out.

And just as I opened it, Marnie happened to say, "It's too bad. If it wasn't for that nose of hers, Margaret would be a very beautiful girl." My eyes fell on the picture, and I froze. That was who the picture reminded me of—Margaret Fowler.

"Marnie, look," I squeaked.

She waddled over. "What is it?"

"Look at this picture."

She glanced down at it. "You already showed me this one."

"Yes, but look at it again and tell me. Doesn't that model remind you of Margaret Fowler?"

Marnie stared at it and her eyes widened. "Well, I'll be—you're right. It's the same nose."

"And you just said that Margaret's eyes remind you of Mr. McDermott's eyes. Are you thinking what I'm thinking?"

We both stared down at the picture again and then at each other.

Marnie spoke first. "I think maybe McDermott was doing more than just taking pictures of his models."

I nodded. "I think you're right. He was doing a lot more. He was making babies with them. Margaret is his daughter. But who was the mother?" And that's when it hit me. If I imagined the same face twenty years older and with a nose job—"Bunny Boyd," I exclaimed.

Chapter 17

It was five o'clock, closing time, and Marnie had left half an hour earlier. Now Jenny and Margaret were leaving. It had taken all of my self-control to not question Margaret about Bunny and Philip McDermott. I could just imagine what her reaction would have been. No. Whatever her ties to the murders, I would have to figure it out by myself.

"See you tomorrow," Jenny said.

"Tomorrow," I replied. Margaret waved, and they were gone.

There was one more thing I wanted to do before the end of the day. I stared at the phone, wondering if I should call Mrs. Anderson again. Her money was still hidden in my cereal box. I hated to spend another night with it in my apartment. It made me nervous, an invitation for a break-in. Surely the woman wanted it back. If she didn't feel comfortable picking it up herself, I didn't mind dropping it off. I picked up the receiver and dialed her number.

A secretary or maybe a housekeeper answered. "I'm sorry, but Mrs. Anderson is out of town," she said.

"Do you have any idea when she'll be back?"

"No, ma'am. I'm sorry. May I take a message?"

I gave her my name and number and put the receiver down. Now what?

Next to me, Winston barked. "What's the matter, boy? Want to go for a walk?" I grabbed his leash, clipped it on and we left.

Much to my surprise, Winston immediately headed toward the bank, which shouldn't have come as a surprise since today I was hoping to stroll the other way—by the Coffee Break. I was curious to see if there was still police activity going on. "Oh, well. Maybe you know best, Winnie. It might not be a good idea to be seen going back to the scene of the crime." Winnie pulled on the leash, giving his best imitation of a nod.

Ten minutes later we were back. He galloped up the stairs ahead of me and went straight to the kitchen, dropping to his butt in front of the refrigerator.

"Okay," I said. "But only one." I gave him a liver treat, filled his water bowl and then I fished the box of cereal out of the cupboard. The money was still there. I sighed in relief and put it back, shutting the cabinet door.

How could Mrs. Anderson leave town without bothering to pick it up? It made me wonder. She didn't care about the money. Maybe she had every reason to keep McDermott alive. As long as she paid him and he was happy, her secret was safe. Looking at it this way, maybe Mrs. Anderson wasn't the killer after all.

As for Bunny, all along I'd been unable to find a motive for her to have wanted McDermott dead. But now, knowing that she was the unknown model, it changed everything. As Bernard Whitby's fiancé, she had a strong reason to not want that nude picture of her to be made public. And even more important, she didn't want anybody finding out that she'd had a baby out of wedlock, and to make matters worse, from an affair with a married man.

Under any other circumstance, these were incidents that would not have mattered, but as the soon-to-be wife of a politician, all bets were off. How would Whitby react to that kind of information? He might drop her like a hot potato and find himself a new arm-piece. That was a chance Bunny Boyd couldn't take.

There was also the fact that she'd had not only an excellent motive, but also the perfect opportunity. She, better than anyone, had had access to the stolen gun. And living right across from the Coffee Break, she'd also had a perfect view of the comings and goings of both victims.

But why would she have killed Rhonda? I suddenly remembered the conversation I'd overheard Rhonda having on the telephone. That had probably been with Bunny. "You can call it blackmail if you like," she had said. She was blackmailing Bunny. There was the mo-tive. It all made sense.

But what I couldn't understand was how a mother could force her own daughter into bankruptcy. There had to be more to the story. I made up my mind sud-denly.

"Winston, stay," I said. He raised his head from the

pillow and dropped it back down. I hurried out of the apartment.

Margaret answered on the third knock. Without waiting for an invitation, I brushed past her and walked in. "Wow. It looks beautiful."

A sand-colored love seat faced the fireplace. On one of its arms was draped a white afghan. Above the fireplace was a painting of a French bulldog. *Cute*. Instead of curtains, Margaret had draped handwoven tablecloths over an iron curtain rod. There was a small, round bistro table in the dining room, along with two chairs. The decor was simple but tasteful.

"You like it?"

"It's lovely." For a moment I almost decided to forget about my reason for coming. I snapped back. "I know you don't want to, but I have to talk to you," I said. "It's important."

Her shoulders slumped, and she sighed. "Why can't you leave well enough alone? Don't you see? I could get into trouble over this."

"How can you get into trouble? I don't understand."

She turned toward the kitchen. "Can I get you something? A soft drink? Coffee?"

"No, thank you. I just want us to talk for a minute. I need to understand a few things."

She scowled, walked over to the love seat and plopped into it. "You're not going to give up, are you?" Clementine trotted over, placing her head in Margaret's lap. It was the same kind of comforting gesture Winnie might do.

"No, I won't." I sat across from her. "I think I already figured out most of it. For one thing, Bunny Boyd is your mother, isn't she?"

She stared at the floor and nodded. "You have to keep everything I tell you a secret. I signed a confidentiality agreement, and if anybody finds out that I told you, I could be sued for everything I've got." She looked around the room. "It isn't very much, but it's all I have."

My mouth dropped open. Bunny had made her sign a confidentiality agreement and threatened to sue her? I closed my mouth. "I take it you were adopted?"

She nodded. "I love my adopted parents, and the last thing I ever wanted to do was hurt them. But I needed to find my birth mother. So I waited until I was at college, and then I went looking for her. All I knew was that she was from Belmont. That's why I moved out there."

I nodded encouragingly and she continued. "Not long after, I happened to visit Briar Hollow—it's so picturesque—and stopped by the Coffee Break. Funny how things happen," she said as if to herself. "When I went to the counter, I noticed that the woman who served me was looking at me very strangely. She couldn't peel her eyes off of me. I had the impression I reminded her of someone." She paused and picked up Clementine, who had been scratching at her leg. The dog settled in her lap and she continued. "I wanted to talk to her in private, so I went back around closing time, but she was gone. In her place was her husband. The minute he saw me, he turned white. And as soon as I saw his eyes, I knew I was looking at my own father.

"He seemed to compose himself, and he asked me what I wanted. Afterward, I realized that he meant what kind of coffee. But at the time, I thought he wanted to know why I had come. So I told him I was looking for my birth parents and asked him if he was my father.

"You would have thought I'd accused him of a crime. He came storming around the counter, grabbed me by the arm and marched me out of the shop. And then he told me that if I ever came back, he'd call the police."

I was quiet for a few moments as I digested this. "You're certain he was your father? He could have been an uncle or something."

She shook her head and continued. "No, Mrs. Mc-Dermott made that plenty clear later. Anyhow, I was so upset that my own father had kicked me out that for weeks I obsessed about trying to talk to him again. I decided I'd shocked him. I was sure, now that he'd had time to think, he'd want to get to know me. So I decided to write. I sent him a letter with my name and telephone number. I thought he'd give me a call, but he never did. I waited a bit longer and then I went back to his shop. But this time I decided that I should approach his wife first. For all I knew, she could have been my mother." She looked at me with pleading eyes. "It could have happened that way. A young couple have a baby. They're not married, so they decide to put it up for adoption, and then some time later they get married. I convinced myself that once Mrs. McDermott saw me, she'd want to get to know me and we'd have an instant mother-daughter bond." She met my gaze sheepishly. "I know. It was silly."

"Go on."

She sighed and continued. "I waited until she left the coffee shop and ambushed her. I told her that I had been adopted and was looking for my birth parents, and I blurted out that I thought she might be my mother." Margaret gave a strangled laugh. "That didn't go over very well. She made it plenty clear that I was no daughter of hers, that in fact, I was the bastard child of that television slut Bunny Boyd. And that if I had any idea of approaching her husband, she was going to sue me for harassment."

I pictured the scene, imagining Margaret's disappointment. "I'm so sorry. That must have hurt." I almost regretted questioning her.

Clementine hopped off her lap and came to me. I picked her up. Margaret continued. "It didn't hurt at all. She wasn't my mother. And she had just told me who my real mother was. I didn't know how I would find Bunny Boyd, so I went on the Internet and found out that when she wasn't filming in New York, she sometimes returned to Briar Hollow. And then, one week later, she walked into my shop." She stopped as if she had come to the end of the story.

"And then what happened?"

She stared at the floor for a long time. "I've already told you too much. You know everything you wanted to know. Leave the rest alone, please, for my sake. It's really personal." She looked at me so pleadingly that I couldn't bring myself to push. Besides, she was right. I knew all I needed to know.

"Fair enough. I won't bother you about that anymore." I smiled. "But I might bother you to do more weaving for me."

She grinned. "That's no bother. I'll be happy to help you all I can."

I gave her Clementine back and returned to my apartment and to Winnie, who came sniffing and looking at me suspiciously. He must have smelled Clementine on me, because he turned and marched away looking disgusted.

"I'm sorry, Winnie. I held that other dog for only a minute. I promise you're still the only dog I truly love." He stopped and stared at me. *Prove it*, he seemed to say.

"Okay, come." He trotted after me to the kitchen, and I held out a liver treat. His rump hit the floor with a thud. "Good boy." I tossed it at him, and he gobbled it down in one bite.

It was only seven o'clock, and I had two hours, maybe three, until Matthew showed up—hours that felt all the longer because I knew he was with Lydia Gerard. I wondered what she was wearing, probably some sexy little dress. I gave myself a mental thump on the head. The last thing I wanted was to become a jealous wreck. If Matthew and Lydia began dating, the only person I could blame was myself. Instead of showing him that I liked him, I'd spent the last six months trying to prove I didn't care. *Real smart, Della*.

Disgusted with myself, I put the picture of Lydia

and Matthew out of my mind and forced myself to go back to my list of suspects.

I was down to two suspects, Mrs. Anderson and Bunny Boyd, with the latter now in the lead. *But what about Margaret?* I thought suddenly. She might have had a reason to kill McDermott. I hopped back up and raced over to her apartment.

"What now?" she asked, eyeing me suspiciously as she opened the door.

"Don't worry. It's nothing to do with any of that." I flicked my wrist as if waving the subject away. "Did you happen to go to the Whitby party last week?"

She looked at me as if I'd lost all my marbles. "Are you kidding? With Bunny Boyd playing hostess? She would have kicked me out in a New York minute."

"Right," I said. "Okay, I won't bother you again."

"You keep saying that," she said with a smile. "Yet you keep doing it."

I returned to my apartment, laughing. It was only after I closed the door that it occurred to me. How did she know Bunny Boyd was the hostess that night? Certainly she knew that the woman was working for Whitby, but it was a bit of a stretch to expect that she'd be playing hostess at his party—unless she'd lied about not being there. There had been so many people in the house. It wouldn't have been difficult for her to keep out of sight. All she'd have to do was duck behind someone whenever she saw Bunny coming her way. I sat for a long time, trying to come to terms with my new theory.

All this thinking was giving me a headache. I glanced

at my watch and was surprised it was already eight o'clock. If I wanted to make myself gorgeous and eat before Matthew got here, I had better get a move on.

I was halfway through a microwaved frozen pizza when the telephone rang. It was my mother.

"Why haven't you made Matthew that beef bourguignon yet? Don't wait too long or it'll be too late."

I groaned. "Mom—"

She kept right on talking. "I was just speaking to June"—Mathew's mother—"and she told me he had a date tonight with an old girlfriend."

Lydia Gerard was an old girlfriend? *Shit*. Knowing that made me feel even worse. "For your information, Mom, I already made it for him. He was over for dinner last night."

There was a long pause. "Well, it can't have been very good. You didn't even call me for instructions."

"It's nice to know that's what you think of my cooking."

"And with reason. You've never cooked a meal in your life."

"I have too. I can make pasta." Then, realizing this would only prolong the argument, I said, "You're right. I need all the help I can get, and that's why I had a friend come over and give me instructions. The meal was delicious. Matthew had two helpings."

"Oh." She was at a loss for words momentarily. "I hope your friend didn't stay for dinner."

"She didn't. We had dinner alone."

"Oh," she said in a brighter tone. "I hope you wore something sexy."

"Mo-om. Stop it."

"And makeup?"

"Of course. I always wear makeup. Why do you even ask?"

"And did you flirt?"

In a moment of exasperation, I blurted out, "Mom, I feel bad enough that he's out with another girl. You don't have to rub it in that he isn't in love with me."

"I knew it," she squealed. "I just knew it. You're in love with Matthew. Oh, that is so wonderful."

"Oh, for God's sake," I said, already regretting telling her. "I don't see what's so wonderful about being in love with someone who doesn't love me back."

"Just leave that up to me. I'll talk to June—"

I exploded. "Don't you dare say a word."

"I only want to help," she replied plaintively.

"It won't help. If June says anything to Matthew, you might as well forget about him ever wanting to date me."

"I don't understand. Why would it? I think he'd be happy—"

I cut her off. "Think, Mom. How many men do you know who take their mother's advice when it comes to love? Don't you get it? The more you and June push him toward me, the harder he pulls away." For once my comment was met with total silence. "Mom?"

"Yes, dear," she said, sounding deflated. "I understand. I won't say a word. I promise."

"You agree with me?" I was shocked.

"Yes, dear. I don't know why I didn't think of it myself. It makes complete sense."

Now I knew she was just regrouping before another onslaught. I had to end this conversation before she got going again. "I'd better go," I said. "I think that's Matthew at the door now." If she'd thought about this a minute she would have known it couldn't be Matthew. But she wanted so much for us to be a couple that she accepted it.

Her voice went up an octave. "Good luck. And don't forget to flirt."

"Love you," I said and hung up.

I returned to my pizza. But now, try as I might, I couldn't get my mother's words out of my head. *Damn*, Lydia wasn't just a friend; she was an old girlfriend. They used to date. I imagined them cuddled up in a romantic restaurant, gazing deeply into each other's eyes. I gave myself a mental thump on the head. A romantic restaurant in Briar Hollow? Not likely. Chances were they were having hamburgers at Bottoms Up, surrounded by rowdy pool players and beer drinkers. Still, it didn't make me feel one iota better. I wasn't even hungry anymore. I pushed away from the table, and under Winston's horrified eyes, I dropped the pizza in the trash.

I rummaged through the fridge and removed an open can of dog food. "Here, Winnie. This is much better for you than pizza." He did not seem convinced.

I hurried to the bedroom and changed into a blue dress cut on the bias. It was formfitting without being too revealing. "There. You happy, Winnie? I'm wearing your favorite color."

I was halfway through my glass of wine when the

doorbell rang. I glanced at my watch—nine fifteen. Was their date already over? I took that as a good omen.

"Hi." I greeted him with a smile. "Can I get you something to drink?"

He followed me to the kitchen, and I poured him some wine. We clinked glasses. I made a point of making eye contact.

"What's that?" he asked, his gaze resting on the list I'd left on the table.

"I reworked my list of suspects," I said.

He picked it up and headed for the living room. "Let's take a look at this." He scanned it quickly. "You're down to two suspects?"

"Actually, three. I just thought of one more, someone we never even considered. I just didn't add her to the list yet. But before we talk about that, you said you had information for me."

"I do. It turns out that both victims were shot with the same gun—a Colt 1908 semiautomatic, the exact kind that was taken from the Whitby house. If we weren't already convinced the killer was the same in both murders, this proves it."

"And did you find out if it's easy to get ammunition for that kind of old gun?"

"Easy as ordering it off the Internet. Also, both victims were shot within fifteen feet, four .25 ACP bullets in a nice tight three-inch grouping."

"You lost me."

"What that means is that the killer was a good shooter."

I puzzled over this. "How do we find out which of the suspects knows how to shoot?"

He smiled. "I already know that. The police found out that both Bunny and Mrs. Anderson were fans of target shooting."

"Oh, my God. I was right. It's one of them."

"You said you had a third suspect."

I wasn't nearly so sure anymore. Still, I told him about Margaret.

After I had explained at length about what made me think she could be the killer, he picked up the list again. "I'm not convinced."

"Neither am I."

"Let's take another look at this." He perused the list briefly. "So tell me again why you think it could be Bunny Boyd."

"It's simple. She is determined to marry Bernard Whitby. He is a politician, and if it came out that his fiancé had a child out of wedlock from an affair with a married man, he might not be so keen on marrying her. You know how politicians care about the moral majority."

He nodded. "God only knows why something that happened two decades ago would even matter, but you're right. They do go to great lengths to appear unblemished."

"And don't forget that Bunny made Margaret sign a confidentiality agreement. That proves how important it was to her that her past remain safely in her past. If McDermott was blackmailing one political wife, why not also a political fiancé? And if Rhonda picked up where her husband left off, or if she figured out who killed him, Bunny would have had to kill her too. Don't forget, Bunny lives right across the street from the Coffee Break." I had another idea. "Maybe she was watching the house and saw Rhonda leave and then used the opportunity to go in to look for"—I shrugged—"whatever she thought Rhonda had. And maybe Rhonda forgot something and went back. Then they came face-to-face and Bunny had to kill her."

"That's a lot of maybes," Matthew said.

"But that's how murder sometimes is, a bunch of coincidences that add up to somebody getting killed. As for Mrs. Anderson, if she had already figured out that the blackmailer was Rhonda, she might have purposely sent me to that meeting so she would be free to search her house in the meantime. I think either Rhonda was late, or she was early. The point is, they ran into each other and then Mrs. Anderson had no choice but to kill her." I snapped my fingers. "I just thought of something. I always found it strange that there was only one picture of the unknown model. If Bunny murdered McDermott, she probably broke into his studio later and stole her pictures. In her rush, she missed one."

Matthew nodded. "You've put together two excellent circumstantial cases. But you haven't got a shred of hard evidence. I don't know that there's enough here to arrest, let alone convict, anyone. A lawyer could shoot holes the size of canonballs through those theories."

"I know." I let out a long, discouraged breath. "So what do we do now?"

"How about we just enjoy each other's company?"

Had I heard right? I looked at him. He had moved closer on the sofa and was now no more than a few inches from me. I wanted to tell him that I didn't feel like talking, that I wanted him to put his arm around me and his lips on mine. Instead I said, "How was your date with Lydia?"

He picked up his glass of wine. "It was nice. She hasn't changed a bit since high school. Did you know she and I used to date? I was a senior and she was a junior."

I played dumb. "No. How long ago was that?"

"A longgggg time ago," he said with teasing eyes.

"Will you be seeing her again?" I couldn't help it. I had to know.

He shrugged. "She's nice, but . . . I don't usually re-visit old relationships." He raised his eyes to mine. "That was a really good meal you made last night," he said. "I think I should take you out to a nice dinner. Belmont has some nice places."

"Maybe if you tell me what your second favorite meal is, I could learn to make that one for you too."

His dark eyes lightened to a golden caramel shade, and my heart skipped a beat.

"You would do that?"

I said what I thought was light and breezy. "Sure. It's not like I have that many friends to cook for around here." But for some reason Matthew's face fell.

"Right," he said and looked at his watch. "Well, I'd

better be getting home." He downed the rest of his glass in one shot and stood. "Oh, by the way, I have to go into Charlotte again tomorrow. I can either leave Winston with you for the night or drop him off around six thirty tomorrow morning."

I jumped to my feet. "He can stay the night, no problem. But don't leave now. Why don't you have—"

"I have to meet with my agent again. It seems she might have a foreign-rights deal for my book. I don't want to fall asleep halfway through the meeting."

I nodded. "Of course." I followed him to the door and, determined to make up for whatever I had said that offended him, I raised my face for a kiss and closed my eyes—and got a stupid peck on the forehead. And then, to make it even worse, he clambered down the stairs, calling out, "See you tomorrow, kiddo."

Shit! Shit! Shit! What did I do wrong this time?

It was the middle of the night when I awoke with a jolt. I had heard something, a noise that had penetrated my sleep. I rose on one elbow and looked around the dark room—nothing. And then I heard it again—snap. Somebody was in the apartment. *Hide.* I looked around again, this time frantically searching for a safe place to hide. Under the bed? *Of course not.* That would be the first place anybody would look. I scrambled out of bed, pulled back the covers smoothly, tiptoed to the door and slipped behind. As far as hiding places went, this one wasn't great but at least it gave me a small chance of not being seen. A weapon. My eyes paused on the iron doorstop at my feet. I picked it up. It was heavy and could do a lot of damage even to the thickest of skulls. I waited, almost afraid to breathe. The noise was coming from the kitchen. I thought of the ten thousand dollars hidden in the box of Rice Krispies. Well, that did it. If I survived this night, the first thing I'd do tomorrow was deliver it myself to the Anderson house.

One minute stretched into ten, and I was berating myself for stupidly leaving my phone on the dining room table when I heard another noise. This one was louder and followed by a series of scratching sounds, as if somebody were tearing cardboard. How could anybody have known where . . . Suddenly, there was another great tearing sound followed by a low growl—*Winston*? I tiptoed down the hall, holding the doorstop high, and flicked on the kitchen light.

"Winston!" Garbage littered the floor: broken eggshells, coffee grinds, wet paper towels. The kitchen was a mess. "Winston Baker, what are you doing?"

Winnie bowed his head in shame.

"You should be embarrassed. You scared me half to death. What in the world were you trying to do?"

He looked at me with wounded eyes and slunk off to the corner. I reached in the closet for a broom and pail and began the gross task of cleaning up. Two minutes into the cleanup, the mystery was solved when I came upon a few bits of leftover beef bourguignon. I finished sweeping the mess, damp mopped the floor and turned to face the perpetrator.

"I'm letting you off easy this time, but only because you couldn't resist my cooking. I take that as a compliment."

He gave me an appreciative "Woof," and followed me back to the bedroom.

I dropped his cushion on the floor and closed the door. "No more wandering around in the middle of the night for you," I said. I climbed into bed and fell into a deep and dreamless sleep

Chapter 18

Marnie stared at me, discouraged. "Tell me again exactly what you said before he got upset."

I had just told her and Jenny about Matthew's sudden departure and was beginning to feel a bit defensive. "I didn't say he got upset. He just—I don't know—suddenly wanted to leave." Marnie raised an eyebrow. "All right. I suggested I cook something else that he likes—which was perfectly nice of me—and he said something like, 'You'd do something like that for me?' And then all I said was that since I didn't know very many people in Briar Hollow, who else was I going to cook for?"

Marnie wiped a hand over her face. "Sometimes I wonder about you."

"What was wrong with that?"

Jenny put a pacifying hand on mine. "I know you didn't mean to push him away, but you implied that the only reason you were cooking for him is because there's nobody else around. If the man is already sensitive because you've been pushing him away for months, if not years, then that was just the kind of remark to throw him off once again."

"Oh." I mulled this over. "Do you really think he took it that way?"

Marnie rolled her eyes. "Duh."

"It's not so terrible," Jenny said. "Don't worry. I'll think of some way you can make it up to him."

At that moment, the door opened, and Bunny Boyd marched in looking less than pleased. Jenny and Marnie dispersed, leaving me to deal with her in private.

She looked at me haughtily. "I can't stay for more than a minute. Bernie is running a few errands and I have to meet him back at the car in"—she looked at her watch—"five minutes."

Judging by the way she glared at me, I could kiss her contract good-bye. I opened the drawer and got her check. "This is what you want, I presume," I said, handing it to her.

"No, that is not why I'm here. I'm here to clarify a few things." She planted a hand on her hip. "I don't know what Margaret Fowler told you, but whatever she said, it was a complete lie. I did not take any contract away from her."

I was speechless.

Bunny nodded. "I offered her the same job I offered you. Silly me. I should have asked her to sign a contract, but I trusted her. She seemed so happy at the opportunity, and she . . ." Bunny hesitated. "She seemed to want a relationship with me. Then, a couple of days later, I get a legal letter from her, telling me she wants nothing to do with me, that she'll sue me for harassment if I try to contact her again. And along with it she sent back the deposit check I gave her."

I was shocked. I had no idea what to think.

Bunny continued. "You tell *me* who dropped who."

Before I could think of anything to say, the door opened and Margaret walked in. It took a moment for her to recognize Bunny dressed in her new subdued style.

Bunny took a step toward her. "I hear you're spreading stories about me."

Margaret backed up a step and shook her head. "No. I haven't told anybody. I swear. Della just guessed." She looked scared.

"Why are you going around lying, telling people that I took that contract away from you? And that it's my fault that you had to close your business? I never took anything away from you. You dropped me." Bunny's voice was plaintive, hurt. I didn't know who was lying. They both looked so sincere.

"Hold on, both of you." I turned to Margaret. "Bunny says that you sent back the deposit check she gave you."

Margaret nodded. "I did." She looked at Bunny. "You demanded I return it in that letter from your lawyer."

Bunny's face went from hurt to perplexed. "What are you talking about? What letter?"

"The one where you threated to sue me unless I signed the confidentiality agreement."

Bunny looked shocked. At that moment, the door opened and Mrs. Anderson walked in. She looked at Bunny and started to leave.

"Wait," I said. It was like a lightbulb had turned on in my brain. Everything was suddenly so clear.

Everybody turned to me. "I've just figured it out."

Bunny looked annoyed. "Figured out what?" she snapped.

I ignored her tone. "The murder!" I turned to Margaret. "Margaret, tell the truth. You went to the Whitby party, didn't you?"

She hesitated. "Yes." Turning to Bunny, she continued. "It was silly, but I really wanted to see the house you were working on." She turned back to me. "But I swear, I didn't kill anybody."

"I know that." I turned to Bunny. "But you had an excellent reason for wanting him dead."

She frowned. "Me? Kill Philip? Now, why would I want to do that? Sure, I was heartbroken when he walked out on me. I was a pregnant teenager, and the man who had seduced me wanted me out of his life. But that was twenty-two years ago. I've moved on. Besides, I had my revenge." At my astonished look, she continued. "Did you know that the Longview used to belong to his family?" Her eyes brightened. "Well, it did. And I had the satisfaction of knowing that every time he looked out the window and saw the Longview, he'd know that the girl he'd scorned became more successful than he ever was." She planted her hands on her hips. "And I suppose you also think I killed Mrs. McDermott?" she asked sarcastically.

"You had the opportunity to steal the gun and you live right across the street. How better to watch their comings and goings?"

"Wrong again," she said, making an invisible check

mark in the air. "I was in New York when she was killed. And I can prove it."

Damn. So the killer wasn't Bunny. *Okay*. I turned to Mrs. Anderson. "You also had a motive to want McDermott dead. He was blackmailing you."

"That's true," she said. "Except I told Jeffrey about the blackmail." At that moment, Bernard Whitby walked in. Everybody turned to look at him.

"Let's go, Bunny," he said.

She put up a hand. "Hold on a second, sweetheart. You might want to hear this."

He leaned against the doorframe, looking bored. His eyes traveled the group, and when they stopped on Mrs. Anderson, he shuffled nervously.

She stared back at him, and when she spoke, I had the impression the words were for his benefit as well as for mine. "My indiscretion with Mr. Whitby happened almost eighteen years ago, during a bad period of my marriage. Since then, my husband has forgiven me and our marriage is happy and healthy. So there was no reason for me to want the McDermotts dead."

"Ahh," I said, raising a finger. "But you only told your husband after the first murder. And I bet, as much as your husband forgave you, he still wanted all copies of those pictures destroyed, right?"

"If you're trying to accuse me of murder—"

I couldn't help but notice from the corner of my eye that Whitby was nervously signaling Bunny with his eyes and tapping his watch. Why was he in such a rush to leave? Suddenly it hit me. I'd been looking at everything from the wrong angle from the start. All along I'd been searching for a suspect who'd had the opportunity to steal the gun from the Whitby house because everything hinged on the weapon. But what if that gun was never stolen?

"Don't worry," I said. "I know you didn't kill the McDermotts. But the guilty party is right here, in this room."

Bunny planted both hands on her hips. "If you're trying to say I did it, you're dead wrong."

"Actually, I know you didn't do it either." I turned to Bernard Whitby. "You killed them."

He sneered. "That is preposterous."

"You love Bunny, don't you?"

"I asked her to marry me."

Bunny walked over to him and hooked her arm in his.

I gave him a pleasant smile. "I believe you. And I also believe that becoming governor is very important to you—as important, in fact, as Bunny is."

She looked up at him adoringly. "I didn't kill them, Bernie. You believe me, don't you? He tried to blackmail me, but I told him to take a hike. I didn't care if the truth came out or not. All that is ancient history. It was twenty years ago."

"Of course he believes you," I said before he had a chance to answer. "Because *he* did it. He killed Philip McDermott because when he realized you weren't going to pay up, he went to Mr. Whitby. Isn't that right?"

He looked at me, and I detected a tinge of fear in his eyes. I took a few steps toward him. "You killed them because you wanted to be governor very badly, and you wanted to marry Bunny just as badly. And you were afraid that if those pictures hit the press, you'd have to either quit the race or drop Bunny."

The way he grabbed Bunny by the wrist and pulled the door open told me I'd just hit the nail on the head. "Let's get out of here," he said.

Bunny pulled back. "Bernie, tell her that's not true. Tell them you didn't kill them."

"Come, Bunny. We don't have time for this nonsense."

The angry line of her mouth softened to a pout. "I'm not going anywhere until you tell me you had nothing to do with those murders."

"I think it's time I called the police," I said.

He looked stunned for a moment and then he sprang into action. "Fine," he said to Bunny. "You stay if you like, but I'm leaving." He stormed out.

All eyes turned to me.

"I think I just solved the case," I said and picked up the phone.

Chapter 19

One week later

Yes, life is full of surprises. After coming up with all those suspects and all those scenarios, the murderer was somebody nobody had ever questioned. Bernard Whitby himself.

After the police searched his house and found the missing gun, Whitby admitted that it had never been stolen. He had taken it himself. The night of the party, after everyone left, he and Bunny returned to the Longview "to give the Sweenys a chance to clean up," he'd claimed. The next morning, he'd kissed Bunny good-bye, making some excuse for having to leave early, and then he waited in his car with his eyes on the Coffee Break. At a quarter to eight, when Philip McDermott came down to unlock the door, Whitby sprang into action.

It was easy as pie for him. He was a good shooter and he knew that gun well. He'd shot it dozens of times. It didn't take him more than a few seconds to pump four bullets into McDermott's heart inside a three-inch group. Another few seconds and he was back in his car and driving off.

Lucky for me, I was a few minutes late that morning, or God knows, I might have been killed too.

The person who had sneaked into McDermott's studio that night was none other than Whitby. He went there to retrieve Bunny's pictures, and as I'd guessed, in his rush, he'd left one behind. While he was there, he'd come across the pictures of Julia Anderson and him and snatched them at the same time.

Rhonda McDermott didn't have to die. She probably never knew that her husband had tried to blackmail Whitby.

After killing her husband, Whitby began obsessing about Mrs. McDermott and about how much she knew. Rhonda was indeed blackmailing someone—Mrs. Anderson. She had always known about the pictures of Julia Anderson and Bernard Whitby. Her husband had never felt the need to hide those and had kept copies in their home. Those were the copies I'd found in the front closet.

Nobody will ever know for certain what Rhonda's motivation was. What we do know is that after her husband's death, the life insurance company refused to pay until they had proof of her innocence. With the coffee shop closed, Rhonda was short of cash. In my opinion, the woman resorted to blackmail out of desperation. She probably wasn't planning on making a career of it—just a short-term solution for a short-term problem.

As for Whitby, he obsessed about Mrs. McDermott

until he convinced himself that she knew all about her husband blackmailing him. He must have decided that getting rid of her was the only way Bunny's secret would remain buried.

Yes, life is full of surprises. Everybody was sure that Bunny Boyd had wormed her way into Whitby's affections, but it turned out that he was madly in love with Bunny and had been since high school. He was the one who'd pursued her until she'd agreed to be his wife. But, as I'd guessed, the governorship was just as important to him as she was. And when he got the first blackmail demand from Philip McDermott, Bernard Whitby decided on a simpler solution.

"So it was Whitby himself who told Bunny that her daughter had recently moved to Belmont?" Matthew asked.

It was early evening, and we were sitting in my living room, basking in the glow of a good meal and good wine. I'd made coq au vin all by myself. And it was delicious.

"That's right. Philip McDermott sent him the information as proof. And Whitby went to Bunny to find out if it was all true. She admitted everything immediately. She had never tried to hide it. When she'd gotten pregnant at such a young age, her mother had bundled her off to an aunt in New York, so nobody in Briar Hollow had any idea she'd had a child. But when Whitby told her that her daughter was living only fifteen minutes away, she was overjoyed. She had been looking for her for years."

"I take it Whitby wasn't thrilled by that," Matthew said.

"You can say that again. As much as Bunny didn't care who found out, he didn't want a soul to know. He was the one who sent the fake lawyer's letter with the confidentiality agreement to Margaret, and he sent a fake personal letter to Bunny, along with the check he'd made Margaret return."

"Ingenious, really. He might have gotten away with it if it weren't for you."

I beamed at the compliment. "Does that mean you forgive me for all the investigating I did?"

"You mean snooping, don't you?" He gave me a reproachful look. "You could have gotten killed. Honestly, what were you thinking? First you break into McDermott's studio and almost get knocked out . . ."

"That was Ricky, Emma's boyfriend. It turns out he had been following her for a long time, and when he heard that McDermott had been killed, he broke into the studio to steal her pictures so no one else ever would see them."

"That guy was trouble. She's better off without him. Speaking of better off without him, how's Bunny doing?"

"She is still reeling from the shock of Bernie being a murderer, but she's spending a lot of time with Margaret. I think they're building a nice relationship."

I still hadn't mentioned a word to Matthew about my threatening phone call, so there was no point in telling him that Ricky had admitted to it. As I'd guessed, Ricky blamed me for Emma's decision to move to New York, and that call was just his way of getting back at me.

I closed my eyes.

"What are you smiling about?"

"I was thinking about Bunny and how nice she's turned out to be," I said.

After Whitby was arrested, Bunny had surprised everyone by offering to purchase the mansion for herself. Whitby, as it turned out, was not nearly as rich as we all thought since he was desperate for money to fund his defense. He and Bunny had reached an agreement the same day, and now it was only a matter of time before the sale went through. She had then promised me *and* Margaret the contract.

Sure, she admitted, the house was too big for her, but she pointed out that Margaret would get married someday and hopefully give her grandchildren. (At that point I had promised myself to never, ever allow Bunny and my mother to meet.)

Margaret and I were thrilled, especially when Bunny promised to feature our work on one of her shows.

"You're talking about the contract."

I nodded.

"All's well that ends well," he said.

"All's well that ends well," I repeated, looking across the room at Winston, who was nuzzling with Clementine—lucky dog. Why couldn't Matthew be nuzzling with me that way?

As if he had read my mind, Winston seemed to wink at me. "Ruff," he barked.

Weaving Tips

Early Looms

The first looms were crude designs. They usually involved hanging the warp (the vertical thread) over the branch of a tree and holding them tautly down with another branch or some other heavy object. As unsophisticated as those early looms were, the types of weaving produced were not entirely different from the weavings of today, albeit much coarser.

The basic loom had been used in almost every continent before developing into frame looms. Some two thousand years later, complex floor looms were first developed in Egypt.

But what really revolutionized weaving was the discovery of the weaving shed. The shed is the temporary tunnel created by the treadle, which makes it possible to pass a thread through the warp yarns in one go rather than weaving in and out. This made it possible to produce fabric at a much faster rate, which made it less expensive.

Tips for Choosing a Yarn

Apart from the more sophisticated looms of today, the other main difference between the rough weaves of yesteryear and today's finer product is in the yarns we now have available.

Choosing a yarn for your project may sound simple enough, but before you head out to the yarn store, here are some simple rules to remember.

1) Determine how strong your finished product must be and select a yarn with the appropriate strength. For example, if you are weaving a fine scarf, you won't choose the same yarn you would for a strong place mat.

2) Keep in mind how often you will wash your finished item. Wearable items, such as clothing, and utility items, such as place mats and towels, will need frequent washing. On the other hand, if you plan to use your piece for display purposes only, you won't need to wash it nearly as frequently—if at all.

3) Remember that your weft and your warp need not be the same thickness, and playing with textures will result in different styles. A thin warp with a thick weft will produce a finished garment where the weft will be more visible than the warp, and vice versa. If you choose threads of equal thickness for both the weft and the warp, the weave itself will be more apparent.

4) Calculate how much yarn you will need to complete your project and select your color scheme. These two exercises go hand in hand because it is important to purchase all of your same-colored yarns at one time. Nothing is as frustrating as realizing halfway through a project that you are running out of yarn only to find out that the store is out of the same dye lot!

5) Experiment with variety. Thin, cotton yarns will make a lightweight yet sturdy piece of weaving. Textured, handspun yarns will bring color and depth into your project. Mass-produced commercial yarns are both inexpensive and easy to find.

An Easy Beginner Project: Weaving with Recycled Fabrics

For an easy and inexpensive project, use recycled fabric instead of yarn. You can use discarded curtains or colorful bedsheets that no longer suit a new decor. You can even use outgrown dresses or shirts. Your favorite old items can find new lives as place mats.

My all-time nicest place mats are a set I once made of blue toile draperies that didn't suit my new home when I moved. However, they look wonderful under my Blue Willow dishes.

To weave with recycled fabrics, cut the fabric in thin strips and then sew all the strips together, end to end. The next step is to fold the side edges in and steam press and then fold again down the middle and press one last time. This will give you clean strips of fabric that won't unravel along the edges and can be used as weft to weave your place mats.

Happy weaving.

About the Author

Carol Ann Martin is an author and former television personality who divides her time between San Diego and the Canadian west coast. She lives with her husband and an ever-expanding collection of dogs. When she is not writing, Carol Ann enjoys baking and beekeeping.

ALSO AVAILABLE FROM
CAROL ANN MARTIN

LOOMING MURDER
A Weaving Mystery

Della Wright left her career as a business analyst
in Charlotte to open a weaving studio in the
picturesque Blue Ridge Mountains. At her weaving
workshop, she meets many of the town's colorful
characters as they come together to weave
baby blankets for the local hospital.

But Della soon discovers the beautiful town hides a
killer. When suspicion falls on two of her clients,
Della—distrusting of police authority after being
falsely accused of a crime in her past—decides to
use her natural curiosity. Can she weave together the
clues in time to stop the killer from striking again?

"Carol Ann Martin has created a new series
featuring engaging characters, a puzzling mystery,
and the promise of romance."
—Amanda Lee, author of the Embroidery Mysteries

**Available wherever books are sold or
at penguin.com**

Amanda Lee

The Embroidery Mysteries

Cross Stitch Before Dying

Embroidery shop owner Marcy Singer is about to find out that show biz and sew biz don't mix!

Marcy's mom is the costume designer for a lavish film production, and she suggests Tallulah Falls as a great place to shoot. Everyone is thrilled...until the star of the film is found murdered. The police suspect Marcy's mom, who made it no secret she did not care for the diva's attitude regarding her wardrobe.

To keep her mom from accessorizing with handcuffs, Marcy will need to stitch together the clues to catch one crafty killer...

<u>Also available in the series</u>

The Quick and the Thread
Stitch Me Deadly
Thread Reckoning
The Long Stitch Goodnight
Thread on Arrival

Available wherever books are sold or at
penguin.com

facebook.com/TheCrimeSceneBooks

OM0046